JJ MICHAEL

Secrets UNRAVELED

Pathtotruth Press

Printed in the United States of America.

For more information contact Pathtotruth Press, P.O. Box 55804, Washington, DC, 20040, USA or pathtotruth4u@yahoo.com.

Library of Congress Control Number: 2010924228

ISBN: 9780615359014

Cover and Interior Design by The Writer's Assistant

First Edition

Distributed by Ingram Book Group

To Mothers and Daughters

Acknowledgments

I give thanks to the Creator and to my family: my parents, Charles and Gloria Jones; my sister, Charlene Jones; my daughter, Michelle Sweeny and my two beautiful grandchildren, SeDona and Siyah Sweeny; and my cousin, Kim Lewis McKiver. Thanks to Kathleen Wood, Cosmore Marriott, Catherine Lenix-Hooker, Valerie Morris, Mercedes Eugenia, Gary Connell, Mozella Ademiluyi and Ruth Owens for their many years of friendship and support. Thanks to Victoria Christopher Murray for her guidance and support. I would like to express my gratitude to Jessica Tilles of the Xpress Yourself Publishing, LLC for sharing her knowledge and expertise in helping me make this book a reality. To my fans, I'm truly appreciative of your support.

Secrets
UNRAVELED

Prologue

Winter 1982, Washington, DC

Three years ago, I wanted to die when my father died.

My daughter, Lindy, and her satanic worshipers, killed him. There was no reason for me to live except to avenge his death. When I tried to get justice, my husband and many of the church members turned against me. They called me crazy. I became a prisoner in my own home as my husband controlled everything I did or said. The voice of God had deserted me and the voice of the devil became my ally.

Margaret's hand quivered as she wrote in her notebook about the dreadful events that had led to the present moment. Thoughts floated in and out of consciousness, making it difficult for her to write them down. She leaned back into the rocking chair and gently rocked back and forth, letting the swaying of the chair comfort her frail nerves.

Reaching into the pocket of her beige satin robe, she pulled out a lace handkerchief and cried softly into it not wanting to awaken her husband, the great Pastor Alan Pierce, who slept across the hall in the bedroom she no longer shared with him.

Margaret stood up and tightened the belt of the satin robe around her thick body. The twenty pounds she'd gained had made its way to her waistline. She walked a few steps down the darkened hallway to the bathroom, and peeped out of the bathroom window; the street was quiet and dark.

She reached into the pocket of the robe and pulled out the medicine bottle that she kept close. Thorazine, take one a day. It was prescribed to her by Dr. Stan Higgs, Head of the Psychiatry Department of D.C. General Hospital. He'd told her and Alan the medicine would calm her nerves and prevent delusions.

"But I am not delusional," she'd tried telling them.

"But this voice that you hear," Alan said to her, "you talk back to it. And, quite frankly, Margaret, half the time you're not in your right mind. Everyone in the church is talking about your bizarre behavior. Take the medicine or you know what." He'd given her a stern look.

Fear of what Alan might do, she took the pills and kept her therapy appointments with Dr. Higgs. Months passed and she began to feel better. The voice that had been in her life forever, which no one else could hear but her, was gone. She'd begged Dr. Higgs to take her off the medication.

"I don't need it anymore."

"You think you don't but you do."

"I feel fine."

"That's because you're taking the Thorazine. Your time is up for today anyway." He turned his back to her.

Margaret decided that day to take things into her own hands. She purposely missed taking her medication. Then she heard the voice again. At first, it was faint; she had to strain to hear it. But, as the days passed and she continued not taking her pills, the voice became clearer.

Trust me; don't take it. The voice spoke sweetly to her.

"But, if Alan finds out, he's going to commit me to an insane asylum or disgrace me in front of the world."

Listen to me; I'll guide you.

And it had led her to where she now stood in front of the toilet bowl with her medicine in her hand.

Alan wants to destroy you and take away your church legacy. We'll stop him.

"Yes, he wants it for him and his whore."

Do it!

Margaret pulled out a bag of sweet tarts from her pocket. She held it up.

Do it.

She laid the sweet tarts on the counter and unscrewed the medicine bottle. With a big smile, she dropped the pills in the toilet. "I hate them…Alan, Dr. Higgs, the trustees, deacons, and even my…" she mumbled, but stopped before uttering the name of her daughter, Lindy, as she watched the pills flush away.

Hands trembling, she filled the empty medicine bottle with the sweet tarts, several fell on the cold tile. On hands and knees, she picked up everyone not wanting Alan to find them.

Splashing water on her face, she avoided looking into the mirror. The sight of her disheveled graying hair, blotchy face, and sad eyes always terrified her. She was no longer the proud, dignified First Lady of Mt. Olive Baptist Church. Alan had reduced her to a weakling, pill popping zombie.

The hallway seemed long and narrower as she walked back to her room. She stopped in front of Alan's bedroom door.

You could do it now.

"Do what?" she whispered.

Get rid of him and your problems will be over. Go do it, bitch, the voice yelled at her.

Margaret walked closer to the door and grabbed the doorknob when Alan's loud snoring made her jump back. Horrified, she scurried to her room and locked the door.

Sleep eluded her as each minute seemed to drag on forever. Finally the sun made its presence known, but not enough to melt the frost covering the trees and cars. No longer able to remain in her room as the walls seemed to close in on her, Margaret unlocked her door and ran down the stairs.

Within minutes, she stood on the steps of Mt. Olive Baptist Church, dressed only in her bathrobe and slippers, holding on to her notebook. Her fingers, stained with ink from writing all night, ached. She opened the notebook and read aloud the last sentence she had written. "The voice of God has deserted me; and the voice of Satan owns me."

Margaret banged on the double red wooden doors of the church, screaming, "Where are you, God? Why won't you let me in?"

Sobbing, she kneeled on the steps and quietly uttered three words. "Help me Jesus.."

Chapter One

Summer 1933

I heard the shrill voice of my Grandma Hattie calling me. She was standing in the back doorway holding open the screen door with one hand and the other hand held over her eyes to block the sun. I was hiding under Jimmy Taylor's porch across the alley from our house. We were playing house. Sometimes he would lie on top of me and squirm around. He told me he saw his mother and father do that, but they didn't have any clothes on. "Jimmy Taylor," I said, "you're making that up." But I let him stay on top of me anyway. When I heard Grandma Hattie calling me, I pushed Jimmy off of me.

Once she'd gone back into the house, I came from under the porch and straightened my dress. It was covered with dirt stains and brushing it off didn't help. It was no longer white but a dirty brown. Dreading what was to come, I quietly said goodbye to my friend and hurried home.

I couldn't sneak pass Grandma Hattie to go to the bathroom to clean up because she would be in the kitchen cooking, and Lord knows I couldn't use the front door and walk through the spotless living room. The living room and dining room were off limits to me.

I opened the backdoor screen. The smell of fried chicken, collards, mashed potatoes, baked bread, and yams made me dizzy with hunger pains. I'd decided my Grandma Hattie was made of iron because the kitchen was filled with the heat of the oven and the scorching outside heat.

Grandma Hattie was standing over the sink squeezing lemons into a pitcher. I spied a three-layered coconut cake on the kitchen table and wished I'd been there to lick the bowl. Stepping into the kitchen, I braced myself for what was about to happen.

She looked at me and her eyes got very small before she lashed out at me. "You're a disgrace to the Johnson family, child. You have been playing with those poor colored children across the road. How many times do I've to tell you that they are not your kind? You're a Johnson." She stopped squeezing the lemons, wiped her hands on her apron, and walked over to me. "You're filthy and your father and the deacons will be here soon. You know your father likes you to look presentable. Get yourself upstairs and clean yourself up. Then I'll do something with that hair of yours."

Knowing better than to answer her, I ran out of the kitchen to the bathroom upstairs. I took off the dress and put it in the pile of dirty clothes in the basket. Then I washed all the private parts of my body, not forgetting my face. Grandma Hattie had laid out the clothes she wanted me to wear on the bed. I peeped out at the sun again and knew it wasn't long before Papa would be home.

I better hurry, I told myself.

Grandma Hattie had just finished churning the ice cream and putting it in the icebox and surrounding it with ice when I returned to the kitchen. The iceman had come by that morning, selling blocks of clear ice. I watched him use his double-edge pick to chop it down to the size his customers wanted. Grandma Hattie always got the large size for a dollar.

A pan of rolls sat on top of the table. I waited until Grandma Hattie turned her back then I reached over to get one.

Wham!

I felt the switch come down on my hand.

"Ouch," I shouted, as I pulled my hand back and put it behind my back.

Grandma Hattie was not only made of iron but she also had eyes in the back of her head.

"You're a heathen, comes from your mother's side of the family. Lord knows I am trying to put some sense, culture, and dignity in your head. I'm only telling you this for your own good. I'd to step in and help my poor boy when that woman ran off and left him with you, a newborn baby. What woman would leave her husband and baby? I told your grandfather don't let Perlie marry that woman. She came from the woods on the other side of the river. She put a spell on my boy. Come here so I can tidy up your hair. It's so thick; I can hardly get the comb through it."

I sat down on the small stool placed between her legs. Papa had made it for Grandma Hattie to use to step on to reach things in the kitchen cupboards. At eight I was almost as tall as she was. She was short and plump with hair she could almost sit on.

Grandma Hattie took the pins out of my hair and my braids fell down my back. She made me keep them pinned up during the day and then let them out each afternoon before Papa came home because he liked my braids hanging loose down my back. She dipped the brush in a cup of black coffee and then brushed my hair.

I wanted to cry; the brushing hurt because of Grandma Hattie's strong hands.

"You must have gotten this thick wavy hair from your mother's side of the family," she fussed, "because everyone on my side of the family has straight hair like white folks. Your mother had some dark brothers and sisters, darker than you with your kind of hair. Who knows who their father was? One of those dirty Indians or some poor colored fellow. But she was the lightest of all of them. She thought because she'd those blue eyes she could pass, but she wasn't nothing but colored like the rest of us."

I wanted to cry, but I knew better. I thought about what Jimmy had told me about his cousin, Bertha. She'd tried to bleach her baby brother because he was darker than night. Her mother caught her just before she put the baby into the pan of water and bleach. She said, "Momma, I'm trying to get that black off him."

I was glad that I didn't have to be bleached, even if I was darker than Papa and Grandma Hattie.

Grandma Hattie yanked my head toward her, and I remembered where I was. "There's only one thing to do with this mess." She pulled the strings of hair tighter as she braided it. "Thin it out. I should have done it a long time ago."

"How do you thin out hair?" I asked.

"You cut it." She grabbed hold of one of my thick braids and pretended her fingers were scissors. "One day I'm going to do it. Now go sit somewhere and be quiet until dinner."

Cut it off, the voice said to me.

Looking around, I didn't see anyone. But I could still hear the voice. *Cut it, and you'll be pretty like your grandmother.*

I picked up the wooden stool and carried it to the bathroom upstairs. Then I went into Grandmother's room and went through her sewing and knitting basket. It didn't take me long to find what I was looking for.

Back inside the bathroom, I stepped up on the stool to look in the mirror. Placing the scissors over my left braid, I closed my eyes and clamped down on the braid. Nothing happened. The scissors wouldn't work; my braid was too thick.

I undid the braids. I felt something fall on my face and into the sink then the floor. It was like rain falling all over me. And I kept cutting until there was nothing to cut. The braids were gone. Too scared to look into the mirror to see if my hair was now pretty and straight like Grandma Hattie and Papa, I stepped off the stool and began to clean up the bathroom. Grandma Hattie would be angry if she found the bathroom dirty. Now she didn't have to get upset every time she combed my hair. My thick hair was gone. A few minutes later, I heard Papa calling me.

"Margaret, where are you? Dinner is ready."

Standing in front of my bedroom closet door, I thought about the bag of hair I'd just hidden in there. I couldn't bring myself to put it in the trash.

Papa kept calling me then I heard his heavy footsteps coming up the stairs.

Running to meet him, I stopped at the top of the steps. Papa froze when he saw me. Horrified, I watched as his face changed into several colors before settling into a deep dark crimson. Neighbors from blocks away must have heard the terrible scream from him that shook my small frame. I knew then that my hair wasn't thin and pretty. It must've looked a mess—very ugly—if Papa was so upset.

"Perlie," Grandma Hattie yelled from downstairs, "What in the Lord has happened up there?" When Grandma Hattie saw me, she let out a cry.

Papa said, "Who did this to you, child? I'll kill them."

I buried my head in his chest and cried.

"Who did this to you?" He pushed me back and held me by my trembling shoulders.

"The voice told me to do it so I could look like you and Grandma," I told him.

"What voice are you talking about?" His frown only deepened as his eyes stared furiously at me.

"The voice that talks to me all the time."

"Oh Lord, Perlie, she got the devil in her just like her mother. I knew something wasn't right with the child. What are we going to do? You have to beat it out of her." Grandma Hattie handed him her switch.

"No, Ma, we're going to pray it out of her."

After dinner, Papa made Grandma Hattie braid my hair.

"Don't you ever cut your hair again, child. It's your crown and glory. God gave you good hair and don't you forget it. Come to the church when she's finished with your hair," he told me sternly.

I wanted to tell Papa that Grandma Hattie said my hair was thick and ugly, and needed thinning out, but I kept my mouth shut. Daggers shot from her eyes to me and sealed my mouth forever.

Before going downstairs to the church, I ran up stairs and stood on the stool so I could look into the mirror. I had little pickaninny plaits all over my head.

∽ ∽ ∽

The church was in the basement of our house. Several nights a week, the deacons would meet at our house for prayer and meetings. Many of them worked at the post office with Papa. After Papa and the deacons ate, I would sit down with Grandma Hattie and have dinner. Sometimes she would let me have a second piece of cake. Grandma Hattie was the best cook in DC.

I also had to help Grandma Hattie clean up the kitchen then I would sneak downstairs, sit on the basement steps, and listen to Papa pray before he started the meeting. I loved to hear Papa talk about Jesus.

But that evening I was scared. Shivering, I sat facing four of the church deacons. Their shock and frowning faces stared back at me. Papa stood next to me holding the Bible. I closed my eyes. But the loud, unfathomable voice of Papa made me open them.

"Brothers, I called upon you tonight because I've a grave situation right here in the Lord's house. The devil is knocking on the door. He is trying to enter through this innocent child. Take over the soul of this child and make her do his bidding. And we must stop him." Papa paused and looked at the men staring from him to me. "I need you to pray with me tonight to save my child from the very perils of the devil."

Deacon Coleman, Papa's best friend, stood up and walked over to me. I shrunk down into the chair as far as I could go as he put his hand on my shoulder.

"Lord, we call upon You tonight to help our brother Perlie and this child as they walk through the valley of death. We come to You, Lord, to strike down this evilness that has tried to lead this child astray." Deacon Coleman didn't know all that had happened to me, but from the awful pain in my shoulder from his fingers digging into it, he must have thought I'd done something bad. I was glad when he closed his prayer. "We thank You, Lord, for your strength, protection and your glory. We thank You, Lord, for keeping faith and hope in our hearts."

Deacon Thomas had a hard time getting out of his chair. He sat back down and stared at me as his chest heaved up and down.

"Lord, our Redeemer, we rejoice in your name. We know there is nothing that You can't fix." A dirty, crumbled up handkerchief lay in his old brown hand that he kept spitting into after every other word. "We lift up your name in the deliverance of our beloved minister and his family." Coughing, Deacon Thomas wiped his mouth and shook his head that he couldn't continue.

Papa started praying quietly. You could barely hear his voice then he called on God so loud, I almost jumped out of the chair. "Lord, this is your son Perlie. Lord, I need your help. My child and family are being attacked by Satan, himself. Strike him down, Father! Let no weapons form against me and my family. Strike him down, Father! He's knocking on our door; trying to get her to do his bidding. Strike him down, Father, and lead us not into temptation but deliver us from evil."

Papa opened his Bible and read Psalms 91: Verses 7-10: A thousand may fall at your side, ten thousand at your right hand; but it will not come near you. You'll only look with your eyes and see the recompense of the wicked. Since you have made the Lord your refuge, the Most High your habitation, no evil shall befall you, no scourge come near your tent.

"Rise up, I say, child, and take God as your refuge and savior."

I sat there.

"Rise up, I say, child, and let the Holy Spirit deliver you from the evilness that is in your mind and take Jesus as your savior."

Papa pulled me up.

Crying, I didn't know what to say except, "I'm sorry, Papa. I didn't mean to make you angry."

Hot and thirsty, I wanted to run out of the room. The deacons stood around me, closing in on me, even Deacon Thomas; there was no escape. My legs wobbled under me as beads of sweat ran down my flat chest. Then I was on the floor and everything went dark.

Later, Papa told me I'd fainted as the evilness left out of my body. He made me promise that I would never tell anyone about it. I shook my head yes, but I knew the evilness wasn't gone because I could hear the voice laughing in my head.

CR CR CR

When school opened in the fall of '33, Jimmy and his friends would chase me home after school, calling me pickaninny. But the names I hated the most were redbone and high-yellow.

"Get off the swings high-yellow," Dorothy Smith, one of the dark-skin girls, shouted at me on the school playground.

I kept on swinging.

"Just because you're the pastor's daughter and you're high-yellow doesn't mean you get to stay on the swing all day."

I kept on swinging.

"Get off," she screamed, picking up a stone and throwing it at me. It flew by my ear.

The other children had gathered around us and were laughing at me, pointing their finger and making faces. "Hit redbone, Dorothy. Hit her," they yelled out.

I could feel the blood rushing to my head, as I turned red from fear when I heard the voice say, *Darkies love to eat dirt. Feed her dirt.*

Stopping the swing by dragging my feet, I grabbed a hand full of dirt from under the swing. When she came close to me I threw dirt in her face, and then I put some in her mouth.

Stuff her mouth with dirt.

She started coughing and choking, trying to spit it out.

Everyone screamed and ran away as Mrs. Carly, our teacher, rushed over to us. She hit Dorothy on the back several times and then, grabbing us both by the arms, she escorted us back to Mr. Tilly, the principal's office. I waited outside his office while Mrs. Carly took Dorothy to the nurse's office.

Mrs. Carly returned and walked right passed me as if I were invisible and entered Mr. Tilly's office. When she came out she was all flustered, putting her hands on her hips and she stood in front of me.

I wanted to scream out that the voice told me to feed Dorothy the dirt because she was a darkie, but I promised Papa I would never tell anyone about the evilness inside of me.

"Margaret Johnson, why are you associating with people that are not of your status?"

She didn't give me a chance to answer.

"You see what it leads too. You should be inside with the others and not out here acting unladylike and not protecting your skin," she scolded. "What would your father think? Principal Tilly and I've decided to give you a letter to take home about your behavior. Reverend Perlie will know what's best for your punishment. Come with me right now."

She led me into the school library where several other light-skin children were having lemonade and cookies.

ର   ର   ର

"You're a heathen." Grandma Hattie took her switch and swiped my bottom a few times after reading Mrs. Carly's letter. "How many times do I've to tell you not to play with those darkies?"

"I won't, Grandma." I tried to get away from her.

"Go get cleaned up. Your father will be home soon. He has an important meeting tonight with the deacons and don't need to be worried about your heathen ways."

Chapter Two

1933-1937

Grandma Hattie never told Papa about what happened at school and neither did I. Dorothy never returned to school. Later I heard she was expelled for fighting and instigating a riot. No one in the school ever called me by those names again.

After helping Grandma Hattie clean the kitchen and finishing my homework, I sat in my usual place on the basement steps listening to Papa arguing with the other deacons about buying a building for a church.

"We need to get out of this basement and purchase a church building," Papa said.

Deacon Coleman, president of the board, spoke first. "We don't have enough money for one of those fancy buildings."

"We have to do something. This basement is getting too small for the crowd we have now and, thank God, the church family is growing." Papa said, placing his empty cake and ice cream plate on the side of the table.

"How are we going to pay for it?" Deacon Thomas asked, looking around at the other deacons.

"Why don't we buy that old church building over on 16th Street? I checked on the price and we could get it for next to nothing."

"I guess so. If one of the wolves huff and puff and blow on it, the building will not only fall down but blow away." Deacon Coleman and the others laughed.

"That building is made of solid grey stone. It's not going anywhere, just looking bad because the windows are boarded up and the shrubbery has grown wild around it. I went in it the other day with the owner."

"What did you find, Rev?" Deacon Thomas asked, after wiping his mouth.

"I'm not going to lie to you. The inside is a mess. It's been vandalized—broken windows, scratched up pews, the walls covered with non-Christian writing. But I felt in my heart that the building called me."

"What did it say?" Deacon Thomas urged him to tell everything.

"It said, Perlie, love me and I'll serve you and your people all the days of your life."

"Amen." The deacons spoke in unison.

"How much is the owner asking for it?" Deacon Coleman asked before anyone else could say anything.

"$50,000," Papa blurted out.

"We don't have that kind of money," Deacon Franks said. He hardly ever spoke, usually nodding his head to everything anyone said.

"Having bake sales, concerts, yard sales, digging deeper into our pockets, and faith in the Almighty, we'll raise the 10% needed for the deposit!" Papa exclaimed, his voice shrilled with excitement.

"You're going to have to sell that idea to the members," Deacon Thomas said.

"Leave them to me." Papa smiled as he looked around the room at his deacons.

ଔ   ଔ   ଔ

That Sunday Papa let the Holy Ghost tell the people what was right for them. I was glad that the Senior Choir was singing, and I could sit in the audience and enjoy watching Papa preach.

"Jesus was a Master Builder. He knew how to take water and make wine. He took one fish and fed the people, demonstrating what we can do if we believe," Papa shouted out.

"Amen, preach, Rev," one of the deacons called out.

"This is our time beloved ones. Can you feel it? Look around and see yourself sitting in our new home with its stained glass windows, pews, flowers and brother Nate playing the organ. You think I'm having pipe dreams?" Papa stopped and laughed as the congregation hung on to his every word and watched to see what he would do next.

"God said to me, Perlie, tell your people it's time to go to the Promised Land. I promise you that you'll have a building, like Solomon had a temple, to worship me and no other false God. Build it," Papa shrieked at the top of his lungs.

The people jumped up and shouted, "Build it," as the organ began to play. In that tiny over-crowded basement, the Holy Ghost touched so many people that day they sang and danced wherever they could find space.

ଔ   ଔ   ଔ

Two years passed and church services were still being held in the basement of our house. Papa had convinced the owner of the church property to let us pay the down payment of $5,000 in installments.

When the members got discouraged, Papa would preach a sermon on faith and how long it took Moses to get to the Promised Land.

The day finally came when Papa had enough money to make the final down payment and get the keys. He returned home that morning and called out to me.

"Margaret, come with me." He dangled the keys of the church in front of me. I jumped up and down with excitement.

Papa was so proud of the rundown dilapidated building. I thought someone had come to our neighborhood and dropped a bomb on it with its broken out windows, holes in the floor, and dirty black and grey walls. The stench made it impossible to stay in there for a long time. Hobos used it as a resting place between Maryland and DC.

"One day, Margaret, this building is going to be a big fancy church."

"Yes, Papa," I answered.

"I'm telling you this, because I don't want you to think that the building we have now is all that we can achieve. Sometimes you have to start small and work up to something bigger. And once you get it, you never let anyone take it away from you. Do you understand?"

"Yes, Papa, never."

"Good, because I want you always to remember what I told you."

03 03 03

Papa and the other men of the church worked hard to get the building ready for church services. Every evening and weekends, whether there was snow, rain, hail or sun, they worked. The women did their part too—cooking and helping with the cleaning. Papa was relentless in pushing the men to finish by June 19th to celebrate our new church on the day commemorating the ending of slavery.

I begged Grandma Hattie to let me go and help the other families in the church.

"You're a Johnson, child. You're not to get your hands dirty working with people below you. Your father is the minister; he founded the church. They're to wait on you. You don't see Dr. Moore and his family there or any of your teachers. Your father is working hard, child, so you can have a better life. Besides, I keep telling you, you have to stay with our own kind and not with that no good Taylor boy and his friends. Do you understand?"

"Yes." I understood just by looking at Papa's close friends who all had fair skin. The few friends I made in school looked just like me.

"From now on, hold your head up high and act like a Johnson."

ɔ൪   ɔ൪   ɔ൪

I might have been high yellow, but I was Grandma Hattie's slave. She was getting old, and relied on me to help her clean the house and cook. Papa said we could eat off the floor the house was so clean. Do homework, read the Bible, cook and clean was all I ever did.

One Saturday morning, sitting on the back porch, I felt the warm May breeze as it touched my skin, making me dizzy with excitement. I tried to think of a way to get into the new church. Everyone was talking about how good it looked. I was the preacher's daughter and had only been inside a couple of times.

Hammer. I heard the word clearly. I looked over at the green hedges growing along side the yard, hoping that someone would jump out of them. The breeze stood still as time seemed to have stopped as I kept my eyes glued to them. Nothing. Taking a deep breath, I prepared myself for what was about to come. *Hammer, hammer, hammer.* The voice screamed deep down inside of me. Covering my ears with my hands and shaking my head, I tried to make it go away. *What did it want me to do?* I asked myself. Then like a flash of lightening I knew. I hurried down the basement steps and found what I was looking for.

Grandma Hattie was in the kitchen drinking a cup of black coffee. The newspaper was spread out on the table as her thin, pale fingers wrapped around a magnifying glass slowly moving down the printed columns.

"Papa forgot his hammer."

I held it up so she could see it.

She didn't say anything for awhile. I added, "This is his favorite hammer and he might be looking for it."

"Take him his lunch and come right back. I don't want you staying up there with those men folks. Getting in the way. Your place is here, helping me. All you want to do all day is read your father's books and daydream. Crazy, just like your mother used to sit under the tree and said she was talking to it. She just didn't want to do a good day's work. Lazy."

She never looked up at me.

I ran out of the house as her words trailed behind me. Ms. Nellie, whose house was directly in front of ours, was sitting on the porch. She would speak to Papa but not Grandma Hattie. I waved my hand and ran down the block before she could stop me and ask me a thousand questions. Grandma Hattie would be upset if she saw me talking to her—Mrs. Jenkins was not one of our kind.

The new church was several blocks from our house. I had to cross over two major streets to get to it, but I knew where I was going. I passed Jimmy's house, hoping I wouldn't see him. His mother was out back hanging wet, white sheets on the clothesline. She didn't see me, so I kept on walking until I got to 13th Street, full of traffic and stores.

Ahead of me, several men were standing around a beat up old black car. Holding on to Papa's hammer and lunch, I held my chin up and marched right past them, but not before they let me know what they thought about me. As hard as I tried not to show what I was feeling, the whistling and name calling made me blush.

"Hey baby, that's a big hammer you're carrying for such a fine young thing like you." One of them came from around the back of the car and blocked my way.

As I moved to the side of him, trying to get away, he moved with me.

Hit him with the hammer. Hit him!

"Let her alone, man, that's Rev. Perlie's daughter of Mt. Olive Baptist Church. You don't want to mess with him," an elderly gentleman called out from inside the car as he gunned the engine.

The younger man finally moved aside and I ran down the street and ducked into the grocery store almost dropping Papa's food.

Mr. Stein, the owner, stood behind the counter helping a customer. He was adding up the items and adding them to the customer's tab.

"A pound of sugar, coffee, eggs, flour, soap, and molasses. Is that all?"

"Yes," Emily Brown replied, not looking at Mr. Stein. She was a pretty plump woman with big red lips and breasts that, at any moment, might jump out of her dress. She lived not far from us and only came to church when the spirit hit her. Grandma Hattie said she was a hussy, chasing after other women's husbands.

Papa refused to have a tab with Mr. Stein. He said it was a form of economic slavery. On Friday evening, people lined up at the store to pay Mr. Stein for the things they bought during the week on credit. When they couldn't pay, Mr. Stein would take something that belonged to them. Sometimes he took their house.

We paid cash for everything we bought in the store.

Papa had a good job at the post office. He'd attended the School of Religion at Howard University at night. One day he hoped to quit the post office and be a full-time pastor.

Not having much time, I hurried to the aisle where bulks of fabric and sewing patterns covered the table. Grandma Hattie and I were going to make me a new white dress for the church's grand-opening.

The pattern I wanted was one of the newer styles, but she wasn't going to let me have it. Out of defiance, I opened two of my blouse's buttons and tightened the large black belt around my full skirt. She wouldn't let me wear a straight skirt with a split up the back.

"Can I help you with something?" Mrs. Stein's strange voice interrupted my world of dreams.

"No, just looking." I ran my hands over the red satin material, wishing my dress could be straight, red and low cut in the front like the one Emily Brown was wearing.

のら のら のら

As I got closer to the church, I could hear the clanging of the tools and men singing. Making me pick up my pace; I looked up at the sun and it was almost time for lunch.

When I turned the corner leading to the driveway of the church, my heart missed a beat. Jimmy Taylor was sweeping around the steps of the church. Tall and lankly, his dark blue overalls hung off his body. The sun shone on his bare arms and chest, making it difficult for me to know where the black pavement started and he ended.

As I got closer, he stopped sweeping and leaned on the broom.

"What brings you here, Ms. Uppity?"

His hateful words stung my ears. Grandma Hattie was right. He was poor, colored trash.

"None of your business, Jimmy Taylor."

"Oh yeah, I'll tell you what's my business. One day you're going to be mine and I'll knock you up with plenty of babies." His eyes lingered on my body.

I rolled my eyes at him, swung my long braid around to hang over my shoulder, pretending to ignore him.

Jimmy looked around the yard before saying, "You still like to play house?" He twisted his hips and started laughing.

"Don't talk to me like that." I yelled at him, crossing my legs tightly as I felt hot between my legs.

"So what are you here for? You aren't going to do any work."

The buzzing bees swarming around Papa's food made me run right pass Jimmy and into the church without answering him.

"Hey," I heard him call after me, "you can't go in there. Reverend Perlie and the others are in the basement."

Once inside, my eyes adjusted to the sunlight coming in from several stained glassed windows on each side of the church. The church was bare except for the new brown-wooden pews for the congregation and ones on each side of the pulpit. An old, used black piano was placed next to the right choir pew. I ran my hands over the keys, wishing I knew how to play.

Papa had told Grandma Hattie he'd bought the piano from a juke joint in Maryland. She wanted to know what had he been doing in such a place. Laughing, Papa said, "Saving souls." He went on to tell us about the pulpit that Deacon Coleman built in the church.

I walked up to the front of the church and stepped up on it. Standing in front of the lectern, I felt giddy with joy. Suddenly my heart pounded and my ears buzzed with voices calling out to me to preach and heal them. I didn't know where they were coming from. Looking around the church, I didn't see anyone but I could hear them clearly.

One sweet voice stood out above all the others. *Do my will and you shall enter into the Kingdom of Heaven.* It made me delirious with joy.

Papa found me still standing there staring out into the church as if I was preaching to a church full of people.

Before he could say anything, I hollered out elatedly, "Papa, I heard God's voice."

"Come down right now, Margaret," he ordered. "Deacon Coleman hasn't put the second coat of stain on the pulpit," he said, harshly.

I stepped down not looking into his eyes.

"The devil gets into your mind and makes you think and say crazy things. I'm God's reminder. He only speaks to me, never forget that. Do you understand?" Papa raised his voice.

"Yes, sir."

"Show some respect for the men folks and button your blouse. I won't have this behavior from you," Papa said, his face lined with disgust.

"I'm sorry, Papa," I mumbled.

"You're getting older now and it's time for you to speak, look and act as a Christian woman."

I nodded my head.

But that was hard to do, because God kept testing me.

Later that evening in my bed, I thought of what Jimmy wanted to do to me and a funny feeling came over me.

Touch it.

My finger began to creep down to my panties until it found the throbbing between my legs.

Touch it.

Rubbing back and forth hard, I made the old bed creak and then came to my senses. But not before I felt this tingling that made me want to do it again.

Down on my hands and knees, I prayed that God would forgive me for being a slave to the flesh. I vowed never to do it again. I wanted to be a good girl. I climbed back into the bed and the throbbing started all over again.

Chapter Three

Sweat poured down my underarms onto my new white cotton blouse and matching skirt that Grandma Hattie had made. I did all the detail work of making the button holes for the blouse and putting in a zipper on the skirt and hemming it. All the young people choir members had to wear white, except the boys wore black slacks.

My straightened hair was frizzing up under the humidity. Ms. Gladys had told me the day before that it wasn't going to last.

"I don't know what to do with your hair. It's too long for any style. I need to cut it to make it lay down."

"Papa would have a fit if I returned home with short hair."

"Men, all of them, love women with long straight hair like yours."

"My hair isn't straight like my grandmother's."

"No it isn't, but it's got a straight wavy texture to it and I'll try my best to straighten it out, but it's not going to last in this weather."

There was nothing I could do but fan as beads of sweat also danced around the edges of my forehead. Jimmy, sitting next to me, was pressing his leg up against mine making me even hotter. Moving my leg away from him, I gave him a mean look.

"Find a seat for these good people," Papa called out to the ushers.

The ushers had to put folding chairs down the center aisle and along the back wall so everyone could have a seat. But people kept coming and a line had formed outside as they pressed up against the front door.

"I want everyone to squeeze in and let one more person sit next to you. Young people choir, sing, while the ushers seat everyone."

We stood up and sang, *Because We Love Jesus.*

When I heard the voice say, *Do you really love Jesus?*

How dare it question my love for Jesus? The devil was trying to confuse me on the day of the grand opening of the church. I wasn't going to let it spoil my day. I had to fight it like Papa said. I sung even louder to drown out its taunting words.

An hour later, Papa was still preaching as the congregation sat in their seats drenched in sweat. But that didn't stop Papa as he strutted back and forth across the newly stained pulpit.

"Thank you, Jesus; you're so good to us." Papa sang the words, as the people began to stir in their seats.

"Amen," they shouted out.

"Thank you, Jesus," he sang even louder, getting down on one knee. "They said it couldn't be done. But look over yonder and there are new pews and God's children are sitting. They said it couldn't be done. But I'm standing here, Father, in your house."

Papa jumped up and down and I knew that the Holy Ghost was present inside of him. His eyes fixed in deep concentration on the audience as words poured out of his mouth like poetry.

"The Mt. Olive Baptist Church came from dust and tears of hard-working people. We had to take baby steps, making the journey hard and many times slow. Many were filled with doubts, but You carried us on your back. Lasting memories will remain in our hearts of where we came from to get this new building. We bring praise to You today, Father, for You answered our prayers." Papa paused here. He took out his handkerchief and wiped the sweat and tears running down his face. I cried, too. Jimmy turned and looked at me and shook his head.

Emotionally moved by having his dream fulfilled of worshipping in a real church and not the basement of our house, Papa continued. "Mt. Olive is standing today and we're free to pray and serve God. Thank you, Jesus, for this new building. Let everyone stand and praise the Lord and give thanks for this amazing building that He has given us to treasure and keep."

Everyone stood up, clapped their hands and shouted out, "Thank you, Jesus, you're so good to us," as the pianist matched the fervor of the noisy crowd.

"Won't you come and let Jesus be your savior? Come today, this day, not tomorrow, but today to take Jesus in your life." Papa raised his hands to the church.

The pianist played *I Love the Lord* as the choir joined in. The front of the church filled up with people and Papa and the deacons gave them the right hand of fellowship. At the end of the service, I pushed passed Jimmy and went to find the deacons with the money. While everyone was outside or in the basement celebrating, I was counting the money from the collection plates. They were full; it was a glorious day.

CR   CR   CR

Words spread about the church in the neighborhood just like the war raced across Europe. Then the unthinkable happened. Papa was preaching one Sunday when the church doors flew open with such force; everyone turned to see who had come in.

The handy man, Bob, who Papa had hired to keep the church clean, stood in the center of the door with the cold air pouring in.

"The Japs have attacked Pearl Harbor," he shouted out.

"Close those doors and come in and tell us what you're talking about," Papa shouted at him.

I could tell Papa was angry with Bob for interrupting his sermon. He had that scornful look on his face like when I'd cut my braids. I swear I could smell the liquor coming from Bob all the way up to choir pews.

"Sorry to disturb you, Rev," he said, taking off his cap and bowing his head. "But I heard it on the radio in Mr. Stein's store. You can go listen for yourself."

"Are they coming here?" someone in the congregation yelled out.

People began to panic as they tried to get out of the church.

"Calm down, everyone," Papa yelled out. "If anything, we're safe in the House of the Lord."

Everyone froze in place.

"Now I know you want to get home to find out what's going on, but let's not trample over each other. Now sit down while I pray then we'll bring this service to an early closing."

Deacons Coleman and several of the deacons and their wives came home with us. While the men folks sat in the dining room listening to the radio, we served them the dinners we would have had at the church repast.

"Was Bob telling the truth, Papa?" I asked, as he fidgeted with the radio knobs trying to get a clear station to come through from all the static.

"The Japanese have attacked Pearl Harbor," the radio announcer yelled out.

Papa and the deacons moved closer to the radio in shock by what they had just heard.

The announcer continued. "The Japanese navy launched a surprise attack against the United States naval base at Pearl Harbor, Hawaii, this Sunday morning, December 7, 1941."

"We're going to war for sure now," Papa said, taking a seat, his voice full of anguish.

"You don't think we should go? They attacked us and that will be enough reason for war."

Deacon Coleman and Papa debated about everything. I didn't know how they remained friends for so long.

"War is never justification for killing innocent people. And what about our people? I'm worried that, as always, we'll serve and die like the others but without the glory."

Papa was right, we did go to war and President Franklin Delano Roosevelt proclaimed December 7, 1941, a date that will live in infamy.

CB CB CB

The war changed our lives; we became a society of rationing. The country had to feed the soldiers and send food to our allies, creating a food shortage at home. The government issued ration stamps for those foods in short supply like butter, sugar, coffee, and meat. I was careful shopping for food because if I ran out of the stamps, I would have to wait for the next allotment to purchase the ration food. We didn't own a car so we didn't have to worry about the stamps for gasoline or purchasing tires. The one thing I wanted and needed for school was a typewriter. Papa told me to save the stamps for one.

The government also encouraged us to plant victory gardens to aid the war and help with the morale. Grandma Hattie laughed when she read about it in the newspaper.

"Perlie, did you read about these war or Victory Gardens in the papers?"

"They hope to boost citizen morale by making us believe that we're helping out with the war."

"These government folks are dumb; we have been having gardens all our lives. Where have they been?"

"Now, Ma."

"Most of us even have a couple of chickens and a rooster," Grandma Hattie said, laughing.

Every summer I helped to hoe and plow that plot of land behind our house for the garden.

Women worked in factories and wore pants. I wanted some so badly but I knew Papa didn't like them.

"A woman should dress and act like a woman and not like a man. The man of the house wears the pants," Papa would tell me every time we would pass a woman on the street in pants. What even made him angrier was the enlistment of woman into the war as nurses and administrative personnel.

Two years later, a once full church with men and woman was now mostly women. Jimmy enlisted in the army as soon as we graduated from high school. The Sunday before he was to be shipped out, he pulled me into the basement closet of the church and kissed me on the lips. We didn't see Grandma Hattie standing nearby.

She beat my legs with the switch and threatened to tell Papa if I so much as breathed.

Take the switch from her.

I grabbed it, broke it in half and threw it in the trash. I not only scared Grandma Hattie but myself.

"You're not bringing any darkies into this family," she screamed at me.

The next day, I woke up with a violent stomachache and spent the day in the bathroom. She told me that's what I deserved for being disobedient to her and the Lord. Later, I discovered she'd mixed Milk of Magnesium in my nighttime milk. From that day on she never let me out of her sight and I never drank milk again.

Jimmy came home once before being shipped to Europe.

"Wow, look at you. All grown up and pretty. You got a boyfriend?" he asked, as we stood outside of the church.

Boyfriend? I've no one except Grandmother and the voice, I thought. Papa was gone all the time. Before I could answer, he was swamped with two or three giggling girls batting their eyes at him.

Walking away, I looked backed at him and realized Jimmy was a man and not the boy I knew. Our eyes locked for a second and then he was gone.

C3 C3 C3

There is an old wives' tale that death comes in threes. I believe it.

I heard this piercing scream that had everyone in the neighborhood running outside. The scream never stopped; it was coming from Jimmy Taylor's house.

Papa knocked on the door and Mrs. Taylor collapsed in his arms. Jimmy had died in battle. I clutched my stomach and ran back into the house.

Later that day, Grandma Hattie and I fried chicken, cooked a large pot of greens, baked rolls, and two cakes for the family. I took it over to an already packed somber house. The shades were drawn; people huddled in small groups talking or eating, and Mrs. Taylor sitting on the couch holding Jimmy's picture.

I tried to talk to her, but she just looked at me with red cloudy eyes. Jimmy's sister told me that Jimmy had died saving a white solider and would receive the Purple Heart.

I cry at both funerals and weddings. Grandma Hattie admonished me for being so emotional at those services. So, I learned to bite my lip or take my fingernail and stick it in the palm of my hand to suppress my tears. And it worked sometimes. For Jimmy it didn't.

Six months after Jimmy's death, Grandma Hattie died suddenly in her sleep.

Papa had a big service for her and listed it in the newspaper. Grandma Hattie would have been proud of the number of folks who came out for it. I believe it was because of Papa and not for her.

I sat in the front pew, staring at her coffin, remembering how scared I was when I found her body. Papa had gone to work. The house was quiet.

"Grandma Hattie?" I called out to her several times.

And when she didn't answer her door, I pushed it opened. She was still sitting in her rocking chair with the Bible on her lap. At first, I thought she was asleep, but when I touched her shoulder, she was stiff as a board.

I didn't cry at her funeral. The sisters thought that I was in shock over her death. To keep my mind from not thinking about her, I listened to the voice.

You're free. It kept repeating itself.

Wanting to be free of the voice, I wished I could open Grandma Hattie's coffin and stuff the voice in there with her.

One of the deaconesses put all her personal belongings in a suitcase and stored it in the basement.

Within two weeks, I was sitting in the front row pew again listening to Papa praying over Deacon Thomas' body, as I helped the nurse fan his wife.

Chapter Four

1943

I sat in Grandma Hattie's rocking chair and rocked back and forth as if I was on a swing in the park. I was so happy, not because of rocking, but what lay at the bottom of my feet—a box full of pennies, dimes, ration stamps and dollar bills from the church collection plates. Times were hard, but people came every Sunday to the church. They were in need of prayer and faith; giving whatever they had.

We had Bible study and prayer three times a week, and every third Saturday we fed anyone who was hungry. Papa encouraged the church members to give away the things that they didn't want or used to the needy. The church basement looked like a good-will store. Papa's good deeds didn't go unnoticed; he was written up in the local papers several times.

Church activities kept Papa real busy and so did the sisters of the church. Divorced, single, and even the married women were after Papa, but they had to come through me first to get to him. I knew what they wanted. At eighteen, I was First Lady of Mt. Olive Baptist Church.

One afternoon, I heard a soft knock at the back screen door. "Margaret, are you home?"

Looking out, I saw Sister Velma Carter dressed in a tight

black straight skirt that looked as if she was poured into it, a low cut top and red high-heeled shoes and bag.

I smiled, not because I was glad to see her, but because Papa wasn't home. Sister Carter was known for her dancing and shouting in the church aisle some Sundays, causing the married women of the church to poke their husbands to keep their eyes on the choir and not Sister Carter's butt. It jiggled whenever she walked and danced. But I knew that there was only one man she was after—Papa.

"I brought you all some peach cobbler. I know how difficult it is without Grandma Hattie." Sister Carter pushed past me into the kitchen, looking around before she placed the dish on the table.

"Papa gets hives from peaches."

"Oh, poor man, well, tomorrow I'll bring him an apple pie. I'll know that he'll just love that."

"Apples give him gas." Chuckling, I took a sweet potato pie out of the oven and sat it next to the peach cobbler.

"Oh." Sister Carter eyed my pie and marched herself out of my kitchen.

But, it was Sister Julia Palmer that I worried about the most. Papa doted on her and she lasted longer than the other ones. Grandma Hattie would have accepted her. She was one of our kind. Sister Julia had tried everything to win me over. She took me shopping downtown and bought me nice things.

"Margaret this silk blouse is of the finest quality and will look good with your skirt for Sunday. Be sure to wear the stockings I bought you. You're a young lady now and must dress like one."

I never wore any of her gifts, but she taught me how to dress and appreciate good clothes. Then Sister Julia stopped coming around and shortly thereafter, she left the church. I never found out what had happened between Papa and her. I had bigger problems to deal with.

 C8   C8   C8

Since Grandma Hattie's passing, Papa and I often dined out at some of the fine colored restaurants in the city. One Saturday evening, he took me to a fancy restaurant on U Street. Every table was adorned with a white cotton tablecloth, silverware, wine glasses, candles and flowers. The owner came over and talked to Papa.

"Rev, how good to see you, and this is your lovely daughter that you always speak of?"

"Yes, Mr. Towns, meet Margaret." Papa smiled.

"And how is Ms. Julia?"

Papa's happy face turned sad, but he replied, "She's fine."

We ate in silence, except when several people stopped by the table to speak to Papa. It was over desert that the celebration turned into a nightmare. I was enjoying my chocolate layer cake when Papa said, "You'll be the second generation to go to college in this family, Margaret."

"Papa," I blurted out. "I don't want to go to DC Teachers in the fall. I know I've been accepted, but I don't need an education to be a preacher."

Papa's hand shook a little, spilling coffee on the white tablecloth as he placed the china cup on the saucer.

"How many times do I have to tell you? You can't be a preacher; you're a woman. You're going to DC Teachers to be a teacher."

That was the first time Papa ever referred to me as a woman. Had he noticed that my once tall, skinny body now had curves, well-developed breasts, soft creamy skin and nice features? My best attribute, I decided, was my shapely legs. I wasn't the prettiest girl but I wasn't the ugliest one as Grandma Hattie thought I was. I looked a lot like Papa. Having never known my mother or seen a photograph of her, I'd no idea if I resembled her.

"But Papa, I don't want to be a teacher. God wants me to be a preacher. He told me do His will and I'll enter into the Kingdom of Heaven. And His will for me is to preach and heal," I insisted.

"Margaret, God talks to me. I'm the Wayshower of this church family. The devil is upon you again. Didn't I tell you women don't preach? They teach, get married, have babies, and are obedient to their men folks," Papa whispered to me, as he leaned over the table.

"But Papa—"

He held up his hand. "Devil, get behind thee." Papa stared me down. "Being a school teacher is an honorable profession for a woman. No more of this nonsense."

Chapter Five

I didn't hear the chattering of the voice for a long time. When I wasn't studying my school assignments, I read the Bible, preparing to do God's will. Someday, somehow, I would tell myself I would fulfill God's will, despite what Papa said. I had to be prepared.

To my dismay, I was invited to an afternoon social at a classmate's home. The only reason I was invited was because Papa and her father were in the same fraternity—Alpha Phi Alpha. Papa insisted that I go. He thought I spent too much time alone.

"You need to have friends your age, Margaret."

"I'm all right, Papa. I love to read, especially the Bible."

"It's not right for a woman your age to be not thinking about marriage. You're almost finished college—that's old."

I hated going to that party, but it turned out to be the best thing that could have happened to me.

The women were all giggles standing together on one side of the room and the men stood on the other side. I sat in a corner, bored, wishing I was at home in my room reading.

I didn't like small talk, but I listened as the other women talked about one young man.

"Oh God, he's so good-looking."

"I heard he comes from a well-to-do family."

"Did you know he's a resident at Freedmen's Hospital and single?"

"Shh now, he's coming our way." The woman smoothed her hair on the sides and put a big smile on her face.

I dreaded it when the music started. I was left sitting in the corner for every single dance. I decided to leave and reached for my purse that I'd tucked under my chair. It was pushed so far back against the wall; I had to get on my knees to reach it. With my rump in the air, I heard someone clearing his throat. I looked up into the face of the handsome stranger.

"May I have this dance?"

The other women looked shocked as to say, "Why her?" So, I lay my purse on the chair and gave him my hand.

His hands were softer than mine. I promised myself to rub my hands down in Vaseline before going to bed and to put on white gloves.

We danced slowly around the room. I never wanted the song to end. "I don't think we have met," he spoke into my ear. "I'm Benjamin Lee."

"Margaret Johnson."

"I'm from Bowling Green, Virginia, attended medical school at Howard and now doing my residency." He offered the information.

But I already knew everything about him thanks to the ladies that were now staring at us.

"I'm finishing up DC Teacher's and plan, of course, to teach." I really wanted to say, "…and some day be a preacher like my father."

"Are you related to Reverend Perlie Johnson of Mt. Olive Baptist Church?"

"I'm his daughter."

"Of course, you are. Now I can see the resemblance." He held me at arm's length, looking into my eyes. At that moment my heart quivered.

"I've attended there when my schedule permitted. Rev. is one of the best ministers in the city."

"Thank you," I replied politely.

When he escorted me back to my chair, the women looked at me with envy as Ben stood by my side and continued our conversation.

"Have you ever read any of Paul Laurence Dunbar's poems?"

I responded, "Why yes I have."

"This is my favorite," he said and he recited a few lines of *A Negro Love Song* by Dunbar. "Seen my lady home las' night, Jump back, honey, jump back..." Ben jumped back onto the dance floor, almost tripping over another couple.

I laughed until I cried. This stunning man was reciting an old Negro poem and jumping around the room.

"Good, I made you laugh and you have such a beautiful smile."

We stayed another hour at the party; Ben was the life of the party. He was so comfortable with people, reciting more poetry, dancing and telling jokes. I finally enjoyed myself.

Ben escorted me home that night and met Papa who was waiting up for me. "What church do you attend in Bowling Green, Virginia?" he asked Ben.

"Shiloh Baptist, sir."

"And your parents, what do they do for a living?"

"My father's a doctor, and eventually, I plan to work with him. And my mother is a teacher."

"Good, and…"

"Papa that's enough questioning. I'm sure Ben is tired." I smiled at Ben.

I could tell Papa was pleased with Ben. He came from a good family with old money and he was one of our kind.

We dated for several weeks before Ben kissed me. I was getting worried that he didn't think that I was attractive enough or that he had another girlfriend. Returning home from the movies on U Street one evening, we found the house dark. Papa was out.

Ben pulled me into him, penned me against the wall and tenderly kissed me on the lips that turned into a much longer and deeper kiss. I wanted more. Taking his hand, I put it on my breast. Ben stopped and stepped back. Shocked, I looked at him.

"We have to stop here, Maggie."

"But Ben…I."

"If I continue, I won't be able to stop. I want you so badly."

"Then let's do it, Ben; we're adults." My eyes pleaded with him.

"Are you a virgin?"

"Of course. What a ridiculous question, Benjamin Lee."

"We're Christians; it wouldn't be right. I plan to marry a virgin."

Weeks turned into months and my sexual frustration only increased when I was with Ben. He seemed to be perfectly content with our nonsexual relationship. I tried everything possible to break him, but Ben was strong and kept his word. When Ben wasn't on duty at the hospital, he attended church and prayer services.

"You would make a fine minister," Papa told Ben one evening after services. They had finished prayers and ministerial studies that Papa had urged Ben to study under him whenever he had a free moment. I turned red and left the two on the porch, wishing Papa would say those words to me.

ભ   ભ   ભ

Weeks later, Ben asked Papa for my hand in marriage. We sat on the sofa in the living room across from him. I didn't know if I should have been in the room, but Ben told me he wanted me there. Scared to look at either of the two men in my life, I stared at the print floral silk skirt I was wearing, tracing the pattern of the flowers with my eyes.

"Marriage is a very serious step in life. Are you sure you're ready for it?" I heard Papa asked Ben.

"Yes, sir. I am."

"Do you love her?"

"With all my heart."

"Margaret is special and my only child; so do right by her."

Ben nodded his head.

"Then you have my blessings, young man." Papa shook hands with him and quickly kissed me on the cheek. My heart was pounding, and I was bursting inside with joy. I could also see the joy in Papa's face. Ben was the son he never had.

ભ   ભ   ભ

Ben and I wanted a small wedding, but Papa insisted that we have a large one.

"Margaret, you're my only daughter and it is expected that you get married right, in the church with everyone enjoying the celebration," Papa said.

"But Papa," I protested.

"I'm paying for everything." Papa ended the conversation.

I shrugged my shoulders. I was worried that I wouldn't have anyone to sit on my family side. Papa was my only family.

But on the day of the wedding, I stood at the entrance of the church on Papa's arm and looked at my family side of the pews. Every seat was taken with deacons and deaconesses and other church members. Elated, I glided down the aisle full of anticipation of not only the day but the night to come.

Papa played two roles in my wedding. He gave me away and he presided over the ceremony. Ben had one request that we jump over the broom—an old slave tradition. When that part of the ceremony came, I gathered up my handmade beaded satin white gown, showing the white satin shoes and a blue garter around my leg, and jumped that broom. Everyone applauded.

Besides Ben's parents, several of his relatives also attended. They were uppity southern folks. I don't think I was what they wanted in a daughter-in-law. They looked like a group of white folks attending a Negro wedding to see what it was like. Later Ben told me his parents wanted him to marry his childhood girlfriend, who was also a distant cousin. Their families grew up together in Virginia.

I must have spoken all of a hundred words to his parents.

His mother, a short, fair-skinned woman who dyed her hair ash blond; asked me, "Where did you get your gown?"

"I had it made by one of the seamstress' of the church. Each bead was hand sown."

She reached over and touched one of the beads, as if she didn't believe me, never saying it was pretty or even nice.

Papa seemed to get along with Ben's father and uncle. I saw them several times conversing. Ben favored his father; both were tall, with fine features, and broad shoulders.

Ben's family left right after the reception. I was happy when they left and hoped never to see them again. But I did see them one more time and it wasn't under the best circumstances.

೮೮ ೮೮ ೮೮

We caught the train to New York for our honeymoon. It was my first time traveling that far from DC. Ben had made reservations for a hotel in Harlem. We arrived late at night, but the streets were filled with people walking, playing musical instruments, dancing and selling things. Several men stopped us to look at watches that covered their arms and rings on every finger. By midnight, we were sitting in Harlem eating chitterlings, potatoes salad, and collard greens.

"Order me some sweet potato pie," I told Ben, as I looked at my cleaned plate. "This food is good as Grandma Hattie's."

Ben called over the waitress and ordered a slice of pie and ice cream. In no time, I had finished everything.

"We'll come here for breakfast, before going sightseeing. I want you to see the Statue of Liberty, Empire State Building, but I really want you to experience Harlem. So, I've a surprise for you tonight."

"What is it?" I begged him.

"We're going to the Savoy." Ben was smiling from ear to ear.

I'd never seen a dance hall that big. The Savoy Ballroom covered a full city block and people were packed into it.

"Ben," I whispered into his ear. "Whites and blacks are dancing together."

Ben laughed and led me out to the dance floor. My feet ached from wearing heels all day, and I could hardly keep my eyes opened. But the music from the two big bands kept me moving just like everyone else.

"You have to applaud and holler loudly for the band you like the best."

I could barely hear what he was saying. We danced our honeymoon night away until the doors shut. Walking slowly back to the hotel, I was excited and scared of what was to come. But I was too tired to care.

I was the virgin Ben wanted, but I could tell from the way he made love to me, he knew what he was doing. Ben undressed me; kissing me all over my body as he took piece after piece of my clothes off and tossed them aside. He kissed me gently on the neck then between my cleavage, as he moved over to bite and use his tongue to play with my nipples. It wasn't long before we lay naked on the bed. The first penetration brought pain as he broke my hymen. I cried out and he gently and slowly eased his rhythm down to meet mine. I was in utter ecstasy as I felt my husband inside me.

We made love throughout what was left of the night. At the first crack of dawn, Ben finally slept with me cradled in his arms. For once in my life, I felt safe, but most of all loved.

ଔ ଔ ଔ

You would have thought that Ben and I had been married for years. We would sit outside on the back porch of the house listening to the crickets, swatting at mosquitoes, trying to catch lighting bugs, and reading poetry until darkness made it hard to see the words. Ben had a rich baritone voice that people loved to listen to, and sometimes he would play the harmonica or we would lapse into silence and just rock back and forth.

But that night, I shared with Ben something that I'd been holding back. I'd wanted to tell him for a long time. But I was scared he might think I was crazy and would want to leave me.

"I heard voices, but they're gone." I blurted the words out before I could change my mind.

Ben had his arm around my shoulders, and I leaned into his side. He moved his arm and brought his hands together, rubbing them back and forth; my heart skipped a beat. I promised myself if he took the news badly, I would tell him I made it up.

His answer surprised me. "So do I," he laughed, grabbing and hugging me again.

"No, Ben, I really did hear them, since I was a child." I stared into his eyes so he knew I was serious.

"Then tell me more about these voices that have you turning red as a beet, eyes looking like saucers, and your voice changing to a whisper."

I'd never told anyone about the first time I hear the voice.

"It was a woman's voice. I heard her crying and calling out to me, but she called me Maggie, like you do."

"How old were you and do you remember the circumstances when it occurred?"

"I think I was around three or four years old and Grandma Hattie had used the switch on me. I don't remember why, probably for getting dirty. She sent me to my room and I hid in the closet and cried, wishing for my mother."

"Um…children have such wonderful imaginations."

"I never heard that voice again, but another one came."

"Tell me about it."

This was the hardest thing I ever had to do.

"Sometimes the voice is deep, like yours and other times high pitch when it's screaming at me, calling me awful names, or telling me to do awful things." I stopped because Ben stood up, put his hands in his pocket and leaned against the porch's column as he stared at me.

"Is it a man or woman?"

"I always referred to it as the voice. It has no gender. Sometimes it would be quiet for a period of time, but I always sensed its presence.

"I've a friend at the hospital and I can arrange for you to see him discreetly if you want." Ben's face was expressionless; the one I'd seen him use when he'd bad news for a patient.

"A psychiatrist?"

Ben thinks I'm crazy, I thought.

"I'm not going to lie to you, he is a psychiatrist and he has helped me in a number of times to deal with difficult situations in my life. I took several of his classes."

I never thought of Ben as having problems in life. He had good looks, a well-to-do family and great career.

"No psychiatrist, Ben."

"I don't know why the Negro race is scared of seeing a psychiatrist; white folks do it all the time."

"You answered your own question. It's because white folks do it."

"In case you change your mind, his name is Dr. Herbert Walker. One day he's going to be a great man in his field."

"No, Ben." I jumped up to go inside, but he grabbed my arm and pulled me back down to the swing.

"Sometimes when we get frightened or don't know how to handle difficult times in our lives, we listen to all the negative thoughts running through our minds. I block mine out with my music and poetry. Most of the time I'm so tired from working at the hospital, I can't hear anything but my snoring." He laughed.

"I wish it was like that for me."

"I bet you hear a good voice telling you good things, too."

"When I was a teenager, God spoke to me."

"And what did God say to you?" he asked, returning to the swing and sitting down next to me, stretching out his long legs.

"Preach and heal. But Papa won't allow it." I started crying.

"It will be alright, Maggie. There will come a time when you'll be able to do it."

"You're just saying that."

"It's God's will."

Ben picked up his harmonica and began to play. Not long after, Papa joined us and several of the neighbors came by and sat on the steps and grass as Ben played and recited poetry.

 CB CB CB

I secured a job as a third grade teacher. But deep down inside of me I yearned to be a preacher. Telling Ben about what happened to me the day God spoke to me made me grow even closer to him.

Ben enjoyed having some of his colleagues for dinner at our home. Entertaining was new and different for me, if not difficult. But I did my best to please Ben and be accepted by his friends and their spouses.

Eventually, Ben would stir the conversation to talk about racism, equality and the great achievements of the Negro man. He would always read at least one or two excerpts or poems from the books of Langston Hughes, W.E. B. Du Bois and others. Papa would often join us for a short while and he could be just as lively as or livelier than Ben.

My days of being lonely and bored were over. Papa couldn't even keep up with our goings and comings.

"All I ask is that you don't miss church on Sundays, come prepared to pray and for Margaret to keep doing the financial books." He looked at Ben and me. We were on our way to Howard, the Theater of the People.

"Don't worry, Rev, we're just having a little fun. We'll be back early enough to get up to greet the sunrise."

"Good because tomorrow I want to ordain you as an assistant minister. You have done well with your ministerial studies and it's time."

Papa shocked both of us.

"Thank you, sir." Ben shook Papa's hand vigorously.

I hugged Ben tightly, excited, but also disappointed that I wasn't the one. The gleam in Papa's eyes told me how happy he was with Ben.

On the way to the theater to hear Duke Ellington's band and a new singer, Ella Fitzgerald, I was quiet in the car as Ben drove down 7th Street toward the theatre.

"Don't get upset, Maggie. I'll be able to make a way for you," he said gently.

"Really, Ben?" I felt so badly about my reaction to his ordination.

"I love medicine, but I also love ministry. Who knows, one day I may be the senior minister and guess what I'll be able to do?" He glanced at me quickly as the streets were wet from a passing shower earlier that evening.

"Life is going so fast for you."

To this day, I regret saying those words.

൭ ൭ ൭

Three weekends later, Ben was off from the hospital and worried me all day about going out that night. I had ironed his and Papa's shirts, gone grocery shopping, and cleaned the house. I was stretched out on top of the white spread covering the double bed where we had made love earlier.

"I don't want to go," I cried out, even though I'd bathed and put on my black bra and panties.

"Come on, Maggie, it will be fun. Everybody is talking about Billie Holiday, the hottest jazz singer out there and we can dance to her soulful sound." He held his arms up as if he was holding me in his arms and gyrating his hips.

"Papa has been giving me a hard time about us barely making it to church on Sunday and you being an assistant minister."

"We haven't missed a Sunday yet."

"People are talking about us being a party couple."

"Forget what others think. This is our lives. We're too young to be sitting around and turning old before our time." Ben shrugged his shoulders.

"Getting in late disturbs Papa's sleep."

"That's something I want to talk to you about. I appreciate Papa letting us stay here, but we need our own place," Ben said, running his hands through his thick black wavy hair, smoothing it down.

"Leave Papa?" I jumped off the bed and went over to him. "How would Papa make out?" I asked, my voice quivering.

"Relax, Maggie; I just want you to think about it. Come on baby, get dressed." He kissed me quickly on the cheek.

"I'll go this time."

"Wear that pretty red dress I gave you with the one shoulder strap. I also brought you something else. I'll be right back."

As I quickly dressed, I heard him moving about downstairs then rushing up the stairs. With his hands behind his back, he came into the room with a big smile on his face.

He handed me a box with a beautiful white orchid inside it. I stood there holding onto the box.

"Open it. All the women are wearing flowers in their hair, like Lady Day." He came over to the vanity dresser and watched me try to pin it in my straight hair behind my ear. I'd gone to the beauty shop the day before, right after work, and had my hair cut to my shoulders, pressed and curled.

When I finished, Ben turned me around. "You're going to be the prettiest woman there." He whistled.

"I do look good," I said, staring into the vanity mirror.

"I'm going to buy you some of those new slacks I see women wearing."

"Benjamin Lee, have you lost your mind? Didn't you hear Papa's sermon a couple of Sundays ago about women trying to be like men by wearing slacks?"

"I guess it was one of those times I had my eyes opened but my mind was asleep. Let's go baby, the world is waiting for us."

ಣ   ಣ   ಣ

A line had formed in front of the nightclub on U Street in downtown DC. You could hear the music as we approached the club from the parking lot across the street. Ben had a special parking space and the nightclub's doorman ushered us inside as Ben handed off some money to him as he did with the parking attendant.

The club was smoky with the clicking of glasses, people laughing and talking. Ben led me to a table up front near the band and dance floor.

"Make way for his majesty," Dr. Jack Neilmen, one of Ben's friends said, as he grabbed two chairs from another table. The music from the band drowned out the introductions, but we all knew each other.

We had barely sat down when a young woman grabbed Ben by the arm, pulling him onto the dance floor. I was shocked not only by her audacity but also by what she wore—a white strapless dress with a white orchid in her short tightly curled hair. I looked paled in the dress contrasted to her dark brown skin. I saw Ben whisper something in her ear. She quickly glanced at me before taking her arms from around his neck.

Their body movements had a natural flow, flawless. I knew they had danced together before, many times. Rising up to get out my seat, I felt a hand on my shoulder gently holding me down.

"The jitterbug is quite a dance, requires a lot of twisting and turning, I prefer the quieter dances."

I turned and looked into the eyes of Jack.

"Who is she?"

"Just a nurse from the hospital. We all used to come over here whenever we could sneak away from the hospital to release some tension. Seeing and attending to ill people around the clock can be grueling."

See she wants to be you.

Hearing the voice only upset me more. I thought it had disappeared for good.

"May I have a drink?" I asked Jack.

"What might I get you?"

"What are you drinking?"

"Scotch."

"Then make it a scotch."

He hurried off to the bar. I kept my eyes on my husband and the woman pretending to be me.

They all arrived back at the table at the same time. Jack handed me the drink and I saw the look of surprise on Ben's face.

The woman sat in the chair between Jack and me. She picked up the small napkin and patted it between her cleavage. "Damn, it's hot." She looked at me.

Ben, sitting on my left said, "Maggie, meet Ever Carol."

Before I could say anything, the heifer replied in her southern drawl, "Can someone please get a girl a drink before I have to come out of this dress?"

"Here, you can have mine." I poured it down her cleavage.

Grabbing my purse, I ran from the club. Ben caught up with me on the street.

"What in the hell did you do that for?"

"Who is that woman?" I hollered at him. I was walking so fast, I broke the heel off of my new shoes. But that didn't stop me from giving him a piece of my mind. "Touching and grinding with her. It was embarrassing and disgusting."

Hopping along toward the car, Ben followed me shaking his head. We drove home in silence. He pulled up to the curbside, but kept the car running.

Opening the door, I looked back at him. "Aren't you coming in?"

"I'm going back to the club. I want to see Billie Holiday." He glanced at his watch.

I slammed the door and hopped up the walkway to the house.

Letting myself into the house, I leaned against the closed door and wept. Papa heard me and came out from the kitchen.

"What happened?" he asked, dressed in his night clothes and bathrobe. His reading glasses were perched on his nose as he looked over them at me.

"Oh Papa, every weekend that Ben's off from the hospital, he wants to go out to the clubs, someone's house, to the amusement park, lectures, anything but stay home." I sat down at the kitchen table.

Papa was working on his sermon. Papers were all over the table and his favorite Bible was open to the center. I missed listening to Papa reading his sermons the night before church.

"He's young and sowing his wild oats, but he married you. And I believe he loves you a lot. Give him a little room and he will be alright. I was young myself once."

"Tell me about you and Mama when you were young." My eyes pleaded with him.

"It's late and we have a full day tomorrow." Papa picked up his Bible and began to read as if I never asked him the question.

Sighing heavily, I went to my room.

C3 C3 C3

Ben came home drunk and wouldn't get up in the morning in time for church. He slept most of the day. That evening at dinner, with blood shot eyes, he apologized to Papa.

"Sorry I missed church, Papa. It won't happen again. The time slipped by as the night wore on."

Papa just nodded his head and went on to talk about church issues with Ben. Ben looked at me and I rolled my eyes and left the table.

Later that evening, while I was sitting on the back porch, Ben came out with two bowls of vanilla ice cream and offered me one. I ate silently.

"Are you ever going to talk to me again?" He scooped up a large spoon of ice cream.

I couldn't hold back the tears when I thought of Ben with that southern belle.

He came over to me and took the bowl from my hands and put it on the table.

"Talk to me, I can't stand the silent treatment."

"You danced like you..."

"Shh," he put his finger to his lips. "She's an old friend; there's nothing between us. I love you."

Then he led me up to our bedroom and gently washed away all my fears. It was the first and last argument we ever had.

೪ ೪ ೪

We were married less than a year when I got pregnant. Ben was ecstatic and really pushed me to look for a place of our own.

"With the baby we'll need space."

"We can make Grandma Hattie's room the nursery."

"You're stalling. Papa will be fine. He has his life."

"Who will cook and clean for him?"

"Maybe if you step aside and let some of the good women of Mt. Olive get a shot at him, I bet you he would be married before the year is out."

"You're wrong; Papa doesn't fool around with the women of the church."

"At times you're so naive. Just promise me you'll start looking. The war is over and this is a good time to buy. They're building a lot of new homes because the soldiers are coming home."

"Why didn't you go to war, Ben?"

"I didn't enlist because I was in medical school and I might as well tell you, I don't believe in wars. I save lives not take them."

⊰ ⊰ ⊰

My stomach grew and so did my apprehension and joy. Ben would rub my stomach and talk to the baby.

"You're carrying a baby girl," he stated.

"Just because you're a doctor doesn't mean you know the sex of the baby," I teased.

"I just know and we're going to name her Lindy Lee. I like the way that sounds."

Ben assured me that I had nothing to worry about. The baby was fine. He would be there during the delivery. But the feeling that something was terribly wrong persisted. As the months flew by, my uneasiness only grew. I thought it was the baby, but it wasn't.

Ben, my sweet Ben, was killed in a car crash during the worse snowstorm in the city. The day Ben died a part of me died; there was nothing anyone could do to make me feel that alive again.

I was in labor for fourteen hours. Ben was supposed to be there with me; a joyous occasion became a nightmare. I lay in the hospital bed in so much pain, with doctors and nurses who had worked with Ben attending to me. A scream that I'd held deep in my soul since Ben's death came out of me as the baby girl Ben wanted ripped through my legs.

Chapter Six

1945

She was a little pink baby with big violet eyes, mostly bald, but I could see fine sandy hair around the back of her neck. The nurse had put the baby in my arms for nursing. I looked up at her and screamed, "This isn't my baby! Where's my baby?"

"Mrs. Lee, that is your baby and it's feeding time." The nurse looked puzzled. She reached over and checked my wrist band and the one on the baby's tiny wrist. "That's definitely your baby," she said adjusting her white uniform around her wide hips.

"Take her," I said holding up the baby. "This is not my baby."

"I better get your doctor, and, in the meantime, I'll bottle feed her. Why don't you get some rest and in a little while, all of this will be sorted out." The nurse took the baby from me and hurried out of the room.

I lay in my bed wondering where my baby girl was. This baby didn't look like me or Ben.

I was so anxious that I didn't hear the nurse and doctor enter my room. If they had knocked on the door, I never knew it.

"Mrs. Lee, please return to bed. You're in no condition to be standing on this cold floor without a robe or slippers. "Help her," he directed the nurse.

And I don't even remember getting out of the bed and going to stand in front of the window.

She came over and grabbed me by the arm, but I pushed her away. I could see that she was frightened. "What did you do to my baby?" I yelled.

"I'm going to give you a sedative, Mrs. Lee, to calm you down. You had been through a terrible ordeal with the death of your husband."

The mention of Ben only made me feel worse. The nurse reached out for me again and led me back to the bed. She turned me over on my side and pulled up my nightgown. Then I felt a sharp prick and sting in my hip.

C> C> C>

Later that day, Papa took me and the baby home. I was still dazed from the medication and once at home I went right to bed, not caring who was going to take care of the baby. But that didn't stop Papa from bringing her to me to feed.

"No, get her away from me," I shrieked at him, pulling the covers up to my chin.

"What has gotten in you? You're not acting like my daughter, Margaret. You have to get yourself together." Papa looked tired as he left my room rocking her in his arms.

He loves that baby more than you.

"That's not true. Papa loves me. Go away."

But instead, it hurled horrible names at me—bitch, whore, stupid.

Shocked.

Who are you?" I asked, looking around the room as if I could finally see something or someone. I'd lived with hearing voices all my life, but the tone and texture of this voice was new to me. It hissed and made my head ache from its constant rampage of lewd words. Not able to take anymore, I screamed at the top of voice.

"Margaret," Papa yelled over my screaming. He was standing in the doorway, holding the baby, who had started to cry again. "You're frightening the baby. What in God's name has come over you?"

I slid down under the covers and put my fist in my mouth and bit down on my fingers until they hurt. Finally, I slept until I felt someone shaking me.

Throwing the covers off of me, I almost turned over the tray of food that Deaconess Coleman held.

"What are you doing here?"

"You have been sleep for a long time?"

"It's after noon. Rev. called me during the middle of the night. Frantic. The baby was crying and he said you didn't feel well and he needed my help. Let me open the blinds so you can get some light in here."

"Don't touch them."

She stopped at the foot of my bed and turned and faced me. "Then how about getting cleaned up and eating your food?"

"And how about you getting the hell out of my room?" I glared at her.

"Rev. asked me to help you out until you can get back on your feet. I'll have to leave at night, but I'll feed her before I go and you'll just have to do the night feeding."

"I know why you're really here. You always wanted Papa

for yourself. When you couldn't have him, you settled for the closest person to him, Bill Coleman. But you'll never be the First Lady of Mt. Olive Baptist Church."

"Sister Margaret, you're not yourself, and I'm just going to ignore your remarks."

But I could tell she was upset. Her eyes had tears in them.

"Get out of my room," I screamed.

"I'm going to put your food on the nightstand just in case you get hungry."

The smell of the chicken, mash potatoes and gravy, greens, and buttered rolls made me feel nauseated.

"Take it away."

"You need to eat now. We don't want you getting sick." She ignored me as she marched out of the room without taking the tray.

Crying, I felt so bad by what I'd just done. I wanted to call her back to beg her to forgive me when the voice's incessant chatter started up again. I bit my lip and screamed into the pillow to drown out the sound of the voice repeatedly telling me to do the unthinkable.

Get rid of the baby.

In and out of sleep, I would dream of Ben, wishing he were alive. Then the tears would come, and I couldn't stop them. I'd no idea of the time. My room was still dark, and I'd unplugged my clock. Peeking out of my window, the night had crept up on me like a thief, and I had to go the bathroom, but I was scared to walk past the nursery that Ben and I'd decorated together. He'd painted the rocking chair white to match the crib and dresser. Ben was so sure the baby was a girl that he'd trimmed the border of the dresser in pink.

Pacing back and forth in my bedroom didn't do any good.

The pressure in my bladder forced me to go out of my room. Hurrying to the bathroom, I tried not to look into the nursery, but I couldn't help myself. The door was wide opened.

This is your chance, do it.

I stopped in front of the room.

Creeping into the nursery, I stood over the crib and looked down at the sleeping baby.

Get rid of her and everything will be like before; just you and Papa!

Crying again and hopping because of the urge, I didn't know what to do.

Pick her up.

I reached down into the crib to pick her up when I saw a white mist hover over her chest then it went inside her. I recoiled and screamed so loudly until I woke up the baby and Papa. He came rushing into the nursery with a worried look on his face and almost knocked me down getting to the baby.

"What happened?" he asked, patting her on her back.

"Papa," I could hardly get the words out. The voice was still screaming in my head, *Get rid of her.*

How could I tell Papa what the voice was saying to me? I was so terrified as pee ran down my legs, wetting my gown and the floor.

Papa stared at me as if he'd never seen me before.

"Tomorrow you'll go to the doctor's. I can't take this anymore."

慓   慓   慓

Several days passed before I could get an appointment with the doctor. I stayed locked in my room with the horrible voice.

Deaconess Coleman would leave me a tray of food at the door. Sometimes, I could hear the baby crying and I would hide in the closet.

On a cold February day, Papa drove me to the doctor in his new black Cadillac. Even though I had on a dark brown wool coat with a mink collar and hat, I shivered from the cold. Papa turned the heat up for me, but it didn't do any good. It wasn't my body that was cold; it was my heart.

I looked out at the bare trees, the brown leaves on the ground and people huddled together at bus stops. You could see the frost still on some of the parked cars. We barely said two words to each other until we arrived at the doctor's office.

"I'll be back for you in an hour," Papa said, turning the heat down.

"You're not coming in?"

"No, I talked to Dr. Creek early this morning. He's expecting you."

"What did you tell him?" I thought about the incident that had happened in the baby's room.

"You need something to calm your nerves."

"Is that all?"

"You're suffering from the death of your husband." Papa paused. "You're going to be alright, girl. Trust in the Lord. Dr. Creek is a good man, one of my fraternity brothers. I knew you didn't want to go back to Freedmen's."

Papa hadn't called me girl in a long time. I couldn't help myself; the tears flowed as I walked up the driveway to the office.

08 08 08

Dr. George Creek's office was in the basement of his home

on 5th Street, NW. "Your father told me you'd been having some problems since the birth of the baby." Dr. Creek had just finished giving me a physical examination and stood at the bottom of the examination table. I lay there with my legs wide-opened, staring up at the ceiling.

I nodded my head.

"This is not uncommon. The medical term for it is Postpartum Depression. Nothing to worry about."

He was wrong.

I never told the doctor about the voice in my head, because I didn't know how to describe it, and I didn't want him to think I was crazy. As the doctor spoke, I could hear the voice calling me those horrible names. I wanted to tell him so badly, but I thought about Papa. He thought he'd prayed the voice out of me many years ago.

CB CB CB

Doped up on sedatives, I stayed in my room away from everybody, praying that the voice would go away. And eventually it did. I cleaned myself up real nice. Even put on a little makeup to hide the dark circles around my eyes. I knew I was feeling better when I began to think about the latest fashions for the upcoming spring months and the running of the church. *Who was counting the money,* I wondered.

Deaconess Coleman kept trying to get me to feed or hold the baby. Not trusting myself, I refused.

Then I dreamt about Ben.

He was holding the baby. "Look at her, Maggie; she's God's gift to us. So you have to love and protect her. Do that for me."

He handed her to me.

"Ben," I cried out. But he was gone. That same morning as the dream, I went to the baby's nursery and picked her up. Her eyes were opened and she smiled at me and my heart melted.

I sat in the rocking chair and held her to my chest, rocking back and forth. Papa and Deaconess Coleman found us like that. It was the closest I'd ever been to my baby girl—Lindy Lee.

Chapter Seven

1946-1957

I didn't know how to be a mother to Lindy because I never had a mother. My mother abandoned me and Papa, why I don't know. And no one would tell me the circumstances surrounding her disappearance. I asked Grandma Hattie about my mother once and her words stung.

"I don't know why you would want to know anything about her and her people. She left you, heard she ran off with some white man. She thought she was white. I didn't like her or her people. Trash. Be glad that she left you. I'm here."

Papa wouldn't tell me too much of anything about my mother either. He was even more evasive. However, I could see the hurt in his eyes when Grandma Hattie or I mentioned her. She must have been a terrible woman to hurt Papa and leave me.

Only once as an adult did I think about finding out more about my mother, so I asked Papa again. He tried to evade the subject, but I pushed him until he told me my mother, Amanda, came from Caroline County in Virginia.

"Amanda spent a lot of time with the white missionaries, acting as if she was one of them. We found several books in her possession that desecrated the Holy Bible. Papa John, my daddy, warned her about the books and wouldn't let her bring them into the house."

"Did she run off with a white man?" I blurted out the question not thinking how hurtful it might be for Papa.

"It's been rumored. Lots of talk about Mandy during that time because of her strange behavior." Papa looked flustered. "Mandy spent long hours in the woods, picking different plants and using them for cooking and healing. She would tell people what ailed them, if they let her. People in the area were scared of her and started calling her a devil worshiper. Every full moon, they would see her in the woods late at night twirling in circles, with her arms extending to the sky. I watched her myself."

He looked at me somberly and said, "She was not in her right mind. She would talk to the trees and animals and claimed they talked back to her. I buried the past a long time ago and you need to do the same. She left us." He stopped abruptly.

I never asked Papa about her again. He'd told me enough for me to know that madness ran on my mother's side of the family. Praying and reading my Bible daily, I tried to get rid of the despicable voice in my head.

Lindy not only looked like my mother but she was crazy just like my mother, and there was nothing I could do to get it out of her. When she was young, she talked about seeing colors around people's bodies. "Mommy, black is around your head," she would constantly tell me. I ignored her nonsense.

The Robinson family left the church, but not before telling everyone that Lindy had put a curse on their son, Johnny Robinson, a boy in her Sunday school class.

"Your stomach is going to burst open." Lindy pointed to Johnny's right side.

"Shut up. What do you know about anything?"

"Lindy and Johnny be quiet," their Sunday school teacher said to them.

During church, Johnny's stomach was so painful his parents had to rush him to the hospital. On the way there he kept telling them that Lindy said it was going to burst open. He had emergency surgery for appendicitis the same day.

ଔ   ଔ   ଔ

Papa loved her more than me. His eyes would light up whenever she was in his presence. Just as he'd discussed the Bible with me he did with her but with more enthusiasm.

"You must remember this, child, when you go out into the world," Papa said to Lindy. She was only twelve at the time and getting ready to be baptized. "Read 2 Corinthians 11:13, 15: *For such are false apostles, deceitful workers, transforming themselves into the apostles of Christ...whose end shall be according to their work.*

"What does that mean?" she asked him.

"Satanic people are everywhere, preying on godly souls, waiting to destroy their belief and love of Jesus."

"Papa, I don't want them to get me."

"Don't worry, child, as long as I'm the Shepherd of the Lord, you're under my protection. Read your Bible every day and pray."

Chapter Eight

1958

I buried myself in working, raising my daughter, taking care of Papa and running the church. Papa was great at preaching, but never one for seeing to the day-to-day business of the church. He left that up to me.

Deacon Coleman acted in two roles: head of the deacons and president of the Board of Trustees. He was a figure head, relying on me to make all the decisions. We could easily sway the other trustees to go along with whatever I wanted. When he stepped down and a new president of the trustees was elected, everything changed. I had a bad feeling about Jack Porter the first time I met him.

He'd started attending our church and showing off by giving large tithing. He was flashy. Papa introduced us at the repast one Sunday after the service.

"Mr. Porter, this is my daughter, Margaret, and granddaughter, Lindy."

I shook his hand and it was smaller and softer than mine. He held on to mine a little too long for my liking.

"Welcome to Mt. Olive," I replied, nudging Lindy to say something.

Lindy stood there staring at the man, and then said, "Nice meeting you. You shouldn't wear those tight shoes; they're pressing against the corn on your little toe."

"Lindy," Papa hollered out. "Apologize to Mr. Porter." Turning to Mr. Porter he said, "Young people will say anything out of their mouths these days."

Staring at Lindy, Mr. Porter exclaimed, "But she is right! How did you know that?"

Lindy looked at Papa's angry face. "You were standing strange." She ran over to Deaconess Coleman and hugged her.

But Papa and I knew that the devil had gotten into her. Later that night, Papa made her read 2 Corinthians 11:13, 15 until she could recite it from memory.

For such men are false apostles, deceitful workmen, disguising themselves as apostles of Christ. And no wonder, for even Satan disguises himself as an angel of light.

He would make her recite the verse in the morning and before she went to bed as a reminder not to listen to the devil when he tells her things about people that she wouldn't ordinarily know. Papa also prayed over her, but little good it did. As she got older, she was too stubborn and defiant for us to handle.

The years went fast and the work and money that Trustee Porter poured into the church paid off for him. But he didn't fool me. I knew he was after the control of the church. As the president of the board, he questioned my right to be not only a member, but also the treasurer.

Papa answered him vehemently before I could open my mouth. "I appointed her to the board and she has been treasurer for years."

That was the beginning of our battles with Papa acting as referee.

ભ ભ ભ

"The minister needs a home and the one next to the church is now up for sale and would be perfect. The church should buy it," I argued at the March meeting.

"You mean you want a new home don't you, Sister Margaret?" Trustee Porter smiled at me with his tobacco-stained teeth, making me want to cringe.

"This is not a personal matter, Porter," Papa interjected, his voice calm but authoritative.

"No offense, Rev, it's just that the church can't afford to take on the expense of purchasing a new home for you and your family," he replied not looking at Papa.

I wasn't going to let it go. "I'm the treasurer and we have the money. The house would belong to the church and be a good investment."

"There are other projects the church needs to consider like replacing the furnace, and getting the church air-conditioned. And that costs a lot of money." He looked around at the other trustees for support.

"This matter can be settled quite easy. I lived by the principle that the church comes first before my needs. When I first started this church, I didn't take a salary for that very reason. Held the services in the basement of my home, opening it to everyone. We can wait on the house," Papa said, looking around the room at the trustees and me.

I didn't take my eyes off Trustee Porter as he continued with the meeting, playing the big man, throwing his hand around, and flashing the diamond and gold rings on his fingers. His hair was slicker than Nat King Cole's.

Surprised that he followed me out of the meeting, he stopped to talk to me at the front steps of the church, where I was waiting for Papa.

"Sister Margaret, I'm sorry things didn't go your way. But let me make it up to you by giving you a ride home in my new caddy," he said, standing eye level with me.

"You can make it up to me by leaving this church. I know what you're after."

"Your place is in the home, cooking and having babies. I don't know why Rev. has you sitting on the board with the men folks. I'm going to change all of that. I plan to have you butt naked, on your knees, praying in front of me..." He laughed.

Foot.

Moving closer to him, I watched his smile get even wider, but his face soon changed to anguish as I stepped on his foot and mashed down on the corn.

"Yeeeh," he screamed.

Papa and another trustee were coming out of the church when I eased up off it. But I heard him mumble, "Bitch, I'm going to get you."

Later that night, I sat in the rocking chair reading my Bible and praying about what to do about that little man who irritated me.

In a very soft tone, *There's another way to get what you want,* I heard the voice say.

I racked my brain trying to figure out what to do to get the house. Papa's salary and my wages weren't enough to put a down payment on the house, maintain the monthly payments and do repairs on it.

The Sunday following the board meeting, I ran into Trustee Porter after the service was over. I'd returned to the sanctuary to retrieve my Bible that I'd left on the choir pew. After what I'd done to him I didn't know what he might try.

"Good morning, Sister Margaret. Don't you look good this morning." He grinned at me and I wanted to vomit.

"Good morning," I mumbled.

"Now that's no way to treat me because you didn't get what you wanted."

I didn't answer him but moved to get out of his way. He blocked me.

"You're spoiled and need the right man to take care of you and that pretty daughter of yours. I can give both of you everything."

I could feel his hot breath on my neck. "Get out of my way," I said, glaring at him.

Slap him.

"That's what I like about you. You're feisty. I hope you're just as feisty in the bed. I like hot, red-bone broads."

I raised my hand; he grabbed it and sneered at me. "You need a whipping to knock you off that pedestal. Your husband's been dead for years. Who are you saving it for?"

Breaking his grip on my wrist, I hurried out of the sanctuary. I knew he really didn't want me; he wanted to use me to get the church.

γ γ γ

The ushers were waiting for me in Papa's small office with the collection baskets. Sometimes, they stayed and helped me, but today I asked them to leave. I needed to be alone after the encounter with that scum.

As I counted the money, my tears dripped all over it. Porter had touched on a sore spot. I haven't been with a man since Ben. I missed him so much.

An hour later, I was still counting. The hardest part was counting all the coins that took awhile.

Put some aside.

Ignoring the voice, I continued to count, but it wouldn't stop pestering me.

The money belongs to you.

The total for that Sunday came to two thousand dollars; we averaged at least fifteen hundred most Sundays.

Put some aside.

I thought about the house next to the church. I'd gone to see it several times, admiring its large, spacious rooms, hardwood floors, wallpaper on the living and dining room walls, the chrome bathroom fixtures and the room on the first floor for Papa's office. Eventually, we would be able to build a walkway that connected the house to the church. Sitting there daydreaming, I heard the voice say more loudly this time, *Put some aside.*

"Yes," I said, irritated that it wouldn't leave me alone.

Counting out five hundred dollars, I lay it aside. I knew what the voice wanted me to do. Use the money to help purchase the house. There was more than enough. No one would miss it. I stuffed the money into my purse.

I continued to justify to myself about taking the money as I recorded fifteen hundred dollars in the church ledger, bagged the monies and stuffed them in the safe for deposit in the bank on Monday. I made a note of the five hundred dollars I'd borrowed in a new ledger.

Feeling exhilarated for the first time in a long time, I decided I would use a couple hundred dollars to purchase a new suit.

Within six weeks, I'd borrowed enough money from the church to put a down payment on the house. Papa, Lindy and I moved into our new home and we never had to worry about making the monthly payments. I'd promised myself I would put the money back, but I knew I was lying to myself. How can you steal from yourself? The church was founded by Papa and belonged to us. Papa never asked me how I did it, and I never volunteered the information. The house was in his name and separate from the church.

I made sure I was never alone with Trustee Porter again, but when I did see him in board meetings I would give him a big smile.

I wasn't sorry when Papa told me he'd been shot and killed by a jealous husband who had caught him sleeping with his wife.

Chapter Nine

1967

The summer of '67, turned into my worse nightmare. Lindy not only turned into a slut, she also became a member of a satanic group.

We couldn't keep her away from a young man from Alabama, Nick Lewis that she met at Howard University. The day she brought him to the church and home for dinner, I could tell from his clothes and mannerism he was the worst thing that could have happened to us. The thought of his being in our family made me want to scream. His big nappy hair and dark skin should have been enough for Lindy to turn the other way. Papa and I'd tried to teach her to associate with people of her own kind.

Papa had invited Alan Pierce, the new assistant minister, to join us. We sat there eating our desert and drinking coffee when Alan finally spoke out after Papa had drilled Nick. "Stokely Carmichael is the big man on Howard's campus, pushing, 'I'm black and I'm proud.'"

"Thank God my friend, Martin, broke off with him." Papa said, adding a couple more teaspoons of sugar to his already sweetened coffee.

"Yeah, I heard he was removed as head of the Student Nonviolent Coordinating Committee," Alan said, finishing his slice of chocolate cake. I cut another piece and put it on his plate. He smiled at me with a hungry look in his eye. And it was for more than cake.

"He's from one of those islands that began with a "t"—Tob... something." Papa looked at me.

"Trinidad-Tobago." I answered.

"Well, wherever he's from he needs to go back there. Stirring up our young folks with all that nonsense of 'I'm black and I'm proud.'"

The blood seemed to drain from Nick's face as he became ashier than he already was. I seized the opportunity to stir up a little trouble myself.

"Why are you wearing those black, green and red straps around your wrist?" I asked Nick, after ignoring him for most of the dinner.

"The colors of movement."

"What movement?"

He looked at me strangely, before replying, "Black Power Movement."

"Have you been listening to and watching Dr. King? Non-violence is the answer. Are you a member of the Black Panthers?" Papa said, holding his fork with a piece of cake on it in mid-air.

Before Nick could respond, Lindy pushed back her chair and said, " Grandfather, please, no politics today. Nick and I are going to the movies. Let's go, Nick."

They scurried out of the room before anyone could respond.

☙ ☙ ☙

Weeks later after Nick's visit and Lindy's erratic behavior, another one of her friends showed up at the house unexpectedly.

We were fooled by his soft spoken nature and good looks. When he returned for another visit, Papa soon found out, through his questioning of Paul DeVross, that he wasn't a Christian.

"I like to think of myself as universal. I don't adhere to any one formal religion."

"Do you believe that Jesus is the Son of God?"

"I believe that we all are sons and daughters of the God Most High."

"With those types of beliefs, do you go to church at all?"

"I go to the Unity Church of Christianity, Science of Mind and Self-Realization Fellowship most of the time."

"You're one of those people." Papa could barely retain himself from putting him out of the house. I was standing in the hallway outside of Papa's office listening to the conversation.

"What do you mean by one of those people?"

"You're into that New Age fad."

"I wouldn't call the highly evolved souls that I study under a fad. We're about love."

"Yeah, just like those hippies in San Francisco, running around calling themselves flower and love children."

Right after pretty boy left, Papa had one of his burping spells. I ran and got the Magnesium and a tablespoon. "Here." I poured it for him. "You have to stop getting yourself worked up about her friends."

"I'm more concerned about who she is associating with. They're turning her against Jesus. You heard how she challenged me in front of everyone during Bible class about Christian principles. She's getting non-Christian ideas from these new friends of hers.

"These new friends are satanic and probably giving her drugs."

"She not on any drugs." Papa started burping again, and rubbing his chest

"I'm making you an appointment with your doctor. You don't look too good."

Before, I could get him to his doctor's appointment, he had a heart attack the following Sunday while preaching on the horrendous and deceitful ways of the flower children. It was Lindy's fault that Papa had the heart attack. She kept him so upset by staying out late at night and refusing to give up that satanic group and that darkie.

Then she tried to kill him.

She was alone with him in his hospital room when his monitors went off, and the doctors had to rush into his room and save him. I knew she did something to him, but I could never find out what. From that time on, I watched her around Papa.

Chapter Ten

1967-1968

With Papa recuperating from his heart attack, I worked closely with the assistant minister, Alan, to ensure everything in the church was running smoothly. He listened to everything I said and tried real hard to follow my directions. Alan was an educated man, but had no street smarts about him. In a way, that was a good thing for me, because I was positioning him to be the next senior minister if Papa had to step down. Deacon Coleman had resumed his old job as president of the trustees when Porter met his unfortunate demise. Both men came to me before making any decisions regarding the church.

One Saturday evening, Alan and I were in Papa's office preparing for his Sunday sermon. "I was thinking about preaching on Job 19:25: I know that my Redeemer liveth, and that He shall stand at the later day upon the earth," he said.

"There's still a lot of unrest out there among the young people, dressing any kind of way, wearing that awful Afro, and using drugs. I think you should preach on Psalms 140:4; 9:16: Keep me O' Lord from the hands of the wicked; preserve me from the violent man; who has purposed to overthrow my goings... The wicked is snared by the work of his hands." I thought about Lindy as I read from Papa's Bible.

"Well, if you think that would be better," he said, undressing me with his eyes.

"Yes, and Alan add a little flare to your sermon."

"What do you mean?"

"Let the Holy Ghost speak through you."

"You want me to parade back and forth across the pulpit, jump, shout and holler?" he asked, disgustingly.

"You don't have to make it sound like it is something bad. People come to hear the word and be moved."

"I'm not that type of preacher. Your father and some of the others come from that old style of preaching. I'm more of an orator." Alan sighed heavily.

Seeing how desponded he looked, I quickly added, "You'll do just fine tomorrow."

As the weeks passed, Alan and I spent a lot of time together. One evening, we were finishing up some church business when he asked me to have dinner with him.

"Do you like seafood?"

"Yes, especially crabs."

"Ever been to Crisfield on Georgia Avenue? They have the best seafood in the city."

"Crisfield is one of my favorite places. Yes let's go. Since Papa's illness, the Coleman's have practically moved into the house. They will keep an eye on him."

I didn't want to leave him in the house alone with Lindy.

After dinner, Alan invited me to his apartment in Silver Spring, Maryland, not far from the restaurant. I knew what that meant. To my surprise, the apartment was well decorated with a black leather couch and a matching chair. I took my shoes off and dug my feet into the beige shag carpet as I looked around the one-bedroom apartment. Expensive drapes hung from the large sliding glass windows that led to the balcony. The glass end tables, tall brass lamps and the large marble chess set placed in the center of the cocktail table gave the place a touch of class. Not Alan's style. I didn't take Alan for a player, but he was no slouch when it came to his apartment. He walked over to the wall unit lined with albums and books and turned on the stereo. Aretha Franklin's voice filled up the room with her soulful singing.

Sitting on his black leather sofa, I curled my legs up. Alan put his arm around my shoulder and I leaned over closer to him. Alan's lips were on mine before I could say anything.

"Margaret, I've been wanting you for a long time," he said, holding me at arm's length and looking at me.

I gave him my best smile.

"Come into the other room with me?" he asked meekly, standing up and extending his hand to me.

I put my hand in his and he led me to his bedroom. It was neat and just as nicely furnished as the rest of the apartment. A king-sized bed occupied most of the space, and before he could get me in his clutches, I moved toward the bathroom.

"I'll be right back," I told him. Sitting on top of the toilet stool, I had to get myself together. I hadn't been with a man since my husband. Just that quickly, I was getting cold feet.

Future.

The thought of Alan being my future made me want to puke. Instead, I pulled out the lipstick and other makeup I'd confiscated from Lindy and used it. Taking my hair out of the bun, I let it hang down my back. On the back of the bathroom door were two hooks. I hung my dress next to his bathrobe. With only my slip and panties on, I returned to the bedroom.

Alan was under the covers with only his chest exposed as he reclined back on two pillows. When I climbed into the bed, he reached for the lamp and turned off the light.

He pulled at my slip and panties until he got them off. "Oh baby, oh baby, give it to me," he said climbing on top of me as his stomach hung loosely between us. I wanted him to caress my breast and kiss all over me like my Ben used to do. Instead, he slid his tiny manhood inside of me and I let out a little moan not from pleasure but disappointment.

"Did I hurt you, baby? I'll go easy." He moved back and forth slowly.

"Yes, yes," I responded, moving with his rhythm, wishing the fat slob would hurry up and finish. And I did get my wish, he started breathing hard and I tightened my body as if I'd come and hollered out, "Thank you, Jesus." Within seconds he joined me. I gently pushed him off me.

"Damn that was good. I'll be ready for seconds in a little while." He patted my butt as I got up to go to the bathroom.

I wanted to wash up as quickly as possible to get his scent off me.

This is your future. I could hear the voice laughing as it said it.

🚉 🚉 🚉

Alan and I had a regular routine of sex twice a week at his place. He brought some pornographic movies for us to watch one evening with the woman during that nasty thing to men. Ben had never asked me to do that. During the movie, Alan tried to be more romantic, and then he placed his hand on my head and slowly pushed me down.

"No, I'm not doing that ungodly act," I snapped at him, straightening up to stare him in the eye.

Sighing heavily, Alan zipped up his pants. It was the first time I saw him so distraught.

Future.

I got on my knees in front of him and unzipped his pants and closed my eyes as I pretended he was Ben.

ᐸ3   ᐸ3   ᐸ3

My life didn't get any better with Papa recovering slowly and Lindy still under the influence of the devil. Papa and I decided that during the church revival, we would try and save Lindy one more time. He'd asked the beloved and well-regarded Rev. William Jackson to be the guest speaker and cleanse Lindy of the demons. He was going to have Lindy confess her sins of straying away from our Christian beliefs to be a part of a satanic group. Then he would heal her of the demonic force by prayer and laying of the hands.

But Lindy put a spell on Rev. Jackson and the demons attacked him. I never told anyone that I'd seen the demonic creatures with my own eyes; and could even smell them. Two of them circled Lindy. One was very tall with a white hooded robe and the other had a small frame wearing the same attire. Those two demons had given Lindy the power to overcome Rev. Jackson. She'd looked fiercely at Rev. Jackson and the tables were turned. He began to shout and cry out about the awful things he'd done to young girls in his church. No one believed him. We knew Lindy had put a spell on him. Papa banished her from the church before she would hurt others.

"Get thee behind me, Satan," Papa said to her.

Lindy looked at me and I turned away from her as she walked down the center aisle.

Papa continued hurling words at her. "I'll not let the devil or his disciples live in my house or take over my church."

But then the worst happened; the demons had turned to me. I'd looked into their eyes and saw light shooting out from them, a true trait of the devil.

I thought I'd heard them say to me, *Perfect love cast out fear.* Then they were gone, but not before I'd felt my whole body shake as they seemed to pass right through me.

That night, I went to Lindy's room and her clothes and suitcase were gone. I didn't know if to be happy or sad. I told Papa she was gone and it was the first time I saw him cry, but not the last time.

CB CB CB

Papa was back to preaching again and doing all the church activities he'd done before his heart attack. I worried about him.

"Don't fret so much over me," Papa said, as I brought him his medicine and a glass of water. "I could have gotten that."

"Just want to make sure you're taking your pills on time."

"I had a heart attack; I'm not senile."

"Besides, you're doing too much again."

"I know what I'm doing. I'd rather be busy than sitting around growing old and grouchy."

He kept up the hectic pace to my discontentment.

Several days, later while cooking dinner, I heard Papa yell from his office. "They killed him."

"Who?" I screamed back, quickly turning off the burners on the stove before hurrying to his office. Papa was slouched in the chair and Deacon Coleman stood by his side as they watched the evening news on the television.

Dr. Martin Luther King, Head of the Civil Rights Movement, was killed today, April 4, 1968, in Memphis, Tennessee. Crowds of people around the world have gathered in the streets expressing their disbelief and sorrow."

Tears began to run down Papa's face as he shook his head in disbelief. "Why Martin, God?" Papa sobbed.

I'd never heard Papa question God before. He loved Dr. King, often quoting him in his speeches. Papa had participated in the planning of the March on Washington in '63. He also arranged for housing for people and opened the church for weary travelers to refresh themselves and have a meal. I was so tired from cooking, I could hardly make it to the march, but Papa wasn't having it. Papa, Lindy and I, with a large group of the Mt. Olive congregants, stood that hot summer day at the National Mall in DC as King delivered his speech, "I Have a Dream."

The speech electrified the crowd, as we called out, "Preach Reverend, Amen."

Now Papa's idol was gone; shot on a balcony of a hotel. I began to cry as I thought of how Papa and members of the church had gone south to march with Dr. King. The sound of the phone and the smell of chicken frying in the kitchen brought me back to the present moment. I rushed to answer the extension in the kitchen while I tended to the food.

"Hello." I could barely get the word out.

"Did you hear what happened?" Alan asked his voice tense and excited.

"Yes, we're watching the news now. They are showing scenes of the city. People are looting and rioting. Buildings are burning. I'm scared, Alan. You know 14th Street isn't that far from us."

"Don't worry; they'll stick to the inner city where the stores are. I doubt if they'll come into residential areas. I'll come over if you want me to."

"You're right, we'll be okay." I knew he wanted to get me in a corner away from everyone and paw over my body.

Barely hanging up the phone with Alan, several other members of the church called. Then the phones went dead.

The next day, DC looked as if a bomb had been dropped on it with glass along the streets, stores and homes burning, and rioters running through the streets, shouting, "Burn, baby, burn."

Papa's eyes were bloodshot when he came down to breakfast. He'd been up most of the night praying. With tears still in his eyes, he said, "Margaret, call the board. We got work to do to reach out to Coretta and help this city return to peace. What they're doing is against what Martin believed and lived for."

It was impossible to get through to anyone on the telephone. The lines were all tied up. That same morning, President Johnson dispatched Federal troops and declared martial law for DC. We had a curfew; there wasn't going to be a board meeting.

We didn't even have church on Sunday. I was glad because Papa was so distraught over King's death; he was in no condition to deliver the sermon. I worried about him, but like the city he bounced back with time, but not without bruises and pain.

Six years later, the inner city still looked like a war zone, with buildings and houses boarded up. And many communities had turned into drug havens for crack heads. But Mt. Olive was holding steady as Papa, with his charm, good looks, and eloquent services, was still able to pack the people in and the collection plates were full.

Chapter Eleven

1974

Alan and the other assistant minister, Rev. Jesse Garner, preached twice a month; both vying for Papa's position as senior minister. Alan had an upper hand because of our personal relationship. He was at the house most of the time and helped me with Papa's doctors' appointments whenever I needed him to and visited the sick members.

We would wait until Papa was asleep, then Alan would sneak in my room and leave before sunrise. The sneakiness added a little excitement to our sexual liaisons, but not enough for me. Alan was having all the fun and I was his puppet, but not for long I told myself.

One night, he whispered to me, "Promise me you'll get down on your knees and I don't mean to pray."

Much to my dismay, I moved down into the bed when I heard the voice say, *Bite it off.*

I ignored it as I prayed that Alan's loud moans and groans wouldn't wake up Papa.

What are you getting out of this?

Please come soon, I prayed.

Whore.

I stopped just before Alan was going to let loose and said, "Alan let's get married."

"Yes, yes, anything you want, just finish."

And, I thought I wouldn't be doing this anymore once we were married.

We planned a small wedding to take place in the early spring of the year with only a few of Alan's relatives and close church members in attendance. Papa was so elated that I was getting married again to have a man look after me.

I couldn't believe it when a couple of days before my wedding, he asked me, "Don't you think this would be a good occasion to invite Lindy, too?"

"I sent her a handwritten letter, but it was returned unopened." I avoided his eyes. Every year, since Lindy left, Papa worried me about forgiving Lindy and planning a reunion.

"Did you find out anything about her?" he asked me.

"Not yet." I didn't tell him that she'd sent a number of invitations to the house: her graduation from Howard Medical School, her marriage to that heathen Paul DeVross, and a celebration party for the adoption of a baby. She included a photograph of the child. Something was wrong with his head and he was a darkie.

"Are you sure you had the right address?

"Yes. She doesn't want anything to do with us."

"Maybe I should try and contact her."

"She needs to come to you and beg your forgiveness. Have you forgotten her brazen behavior at the revival, denigrating God and you?"

"Why won't she come home? God is a forgiving God and so am I," he said, reaching for his pipe.

"Put that pipe down. You know what the doctor said."

He continued packing the pipe with tobacco as if I never said a word.

"You have high blood pressure and have you forgotten you had a heart attack?" I argued with him constantly about not smoking his pipe and eating right. But it didn't do any good.

"Don't you have something to do for the wedding?" He turned his back to me and walked slowly to his office.

തെ തെ തെ

We were married in the church and had a small dinner reception in the garden. Papa was frail but managed to preside over the ceremony.

When he asked if I would obey this man, the voice in my head said, *Hell no*. I almost laughed. And, "If there is any reason this man and woman shouldn't be joined in holy matrimony." Again, I heard, *she doesn't love him*.

It was then that I wanted to run away or at least cry. Blinking away the tears, I remembered why I was doing this, securing my future. But I did cry at the dinner we had following the wedding, when during our toast, Alan spilled champagne on my baby blue Chanel satin suit.

"Don't cry, sweetheart, I'll buy you another one." Alan tried to clean the liquid off with a napkin.

Pushing his hand away, "Do you know how much a suit like this cost?" I asked, disgusted.

"No, I don't," he said, startled by my response.

Others around the table began to stare at us. I grabbed Alan and kissed him passionately on the lips to stop their wagging tongues.

I didn't tell him that I'd gotten the suit from Cissy the Booster for half price.

Because of Papa's health, I wouldn't go on a honeymoon, no matter how much Papa and Alan tried to get me to go. The thought of being alone with Alan in some romantic place made me sick. Besides, there was an important board meeting coming up next week and I didn't want to miss it because the new president of the board, Daniel Reilly, was worse than Jack Porter.

Alan, like Ben, moved in with us.

Chapter Twelve

1975

"He's the devil." I tried to tell Papa that Trustee Daniel Reilly was up to no good. He'd been on the board with Porter. Once Deacon Coleman stepped down from acting president, Reilly had gotten himself elected president. Like Porter he'd been trying to expel me from the board for years, but with Papa as senior minister, he was unable to do anything. Four new trustees came on board and seemed to be in Reilly's back pocket.

"We need him to help get our people jobs and high positions in the government."

He's for himself.

"Just because he's head of the Federal Department of Personnel doesn't mean he's going to do what you want him to do. All he wants is to control the church."

"Not everyone wants control of the church. You got to let that type of thinking go. It divides the church."

"These new people coming into the church want to change everything and run the show. I won't let them."

"When you can't beat them you join them."

"But Papa, this is your church, your dream. You started this church."

"I started it so it could grow and that's what its doing. Bigger than I could have ever imagined. We have been blessed through the years. I've only one regret, that I'd handled Lindy's desire for independence a little different."

What about me, Papa, and my desire to preach? I wanted to say to him, instead I walked away.

⁊ ⁊ ⁊

Besides his responsibilities as assistant pastor to the church, Alan taught at Howard's School of Divinity. Every day I would lay out one of the new suits, shirts and ties I'd brought him to enhance his image.

"Be sure to talk to Sister Joan today. She's getting up in age and loves attention since her husband died. She'll remember that come voting time for senior minister, when Papa retires."

"Um…okay."

"Try to be the first one at the door after the service to greet everyone and call them by name."

"Umm."

"The election of trustee officers will take place tonight. I wonder what Reilly has up his sleeve?"

"Umm."

"Alan, have you heard a word I've said?"

"Yes. He'll probably be elected president again and Jones vice-president and, of course, you as treasurer," Alan said, as I brushed the dandruff off the back of his suit jacket.

"Well, he did ask me last Sunday to bring the last three years financial ledgers and not just make a report."

"Ah, there's nothing to worry about. You do have everything up to date, right?"

"Yes, they're in perfect order."

"Then, I'll see you later." He kissed me on the lips. I wanted to tell him the honeymoon was over even if we really didn't have one.

After Alan had left and Papa was busy in his office with one of the church members, I locked my door and pulled out both sets of ledgers and put them on the desk next to each other.

Over the years, I'd kept immaculate records, recording every cent ever spent. I reviewed each column: receivable accounts, accounts payable, staff payroll, petty cash and inventory records. Everything looked good. Putting those ledgers aside, I opened my personal one and smiled. I'd a column of all the money I'd taken from the collection plates through the years and what I used it for such as the purchasing the house, the monthly payments, renovation and repairs of the house.

There were several items that I decided might raise eyebrows, but this ledger was for my own personal tracking system. I'd paid hundreds of dollars to Cissy for my clothes and additional funds went for hair appointments, Papa's suits, food, car payments, furniture and petty cash. Papa and I lived well. I was always very careful not to get greedy and take too much. The church always came first then me.

But I was worried about Reilly wanting me to bring the ledgers to the meeting that night.

ᘓ ᘓ ᘓ

I was the only woman present at the meeting that evening, but that didn't intimidate me. I was used to it, but the new board members looked passed me as if I were invisible. The thought of all the injustices to women by men boiled up inside of me. Women deserve to serve in rightful positions in the church. My thoughts and words would fall on deaf ears, even with Papa. Ben was the only one who understood the burning desire in me to do God's will, preach and heal.

I switched my thoughts to the new clothes I'd bought from Cissy for Alan and myself. I knew I looked good. Dressed in a navy blue dress to match Alan's blue suit, I wore a single pair of pearls around my neck and matching earrings. My hair was pulled back in its usual bun, and I'd put on my reading glasses.

Sitting up front with Papa, Alan and Deacon Coleman, I took my time as I reached into my bag and pulled out the ledgers and placed them in front of me on the table. All eyes were on me. I deliberately looked into the faces of all the trustees: Mitchell, Hilliard, Jones, King, Winston, Coleman, Evans, and Miller, saving Reilly for last. We locked eyes and neither one of us wanted to yield, finally I looked away. His horns were showing.

He's out to get you. The voice had been telling me that for sometime.

"Gentlemen and lady," Papa looked over at me," let's give thanks to the Almighty God for bringing us together tonight to do His work. We asked that we may continue to do God's will. Amen." Papa coughed several times. I jumped up and poured him a glass of water as amen's reverberated throughout the room.

"The first order of business will be the election of officers for the Board of Trustees. It has been recommended that we do secret ballots. Is anyone against that?" Papa asked.

No one raised his hand.

I wasn't worried because no one ever ran against me for treasurer. It was an unspoken church law of Mt. Olive that I was treasurer for life. For several years, my position wasn't even included in the voting process.

Then why was I perspiring? I asked myself.

"Then let's began," Papa said.

Trustee Mitchell started handing out a sheet of paper. When I finally received mine, I was shocked. Two other names, including my own, was up for treasurer—Earl Winston and Carl Evans.

I glanced at Alan, who refused to look at me. *Did he know?*

"We try to follow Robert Rules of Order. Are there any names to be added to this ballot?" Papa looked around the room.

Silence.

"Then let's vote."

I was still in shock as I read the ballot. The only office that had one name listed was the president—Daniel Reilly.

My hand shook as I marked the boxes next to each name, omitting a vote for president.

"Everyone finished?"

I looked at Papa for reassurance, but his face was expressionless. *Did he know too?*

My stomach felt queasy.

"I've asked Deaconess Coleman, who has filled in as church secretary and Sister Sarah and Pauline to count the ballots while we continue with the meeting. Trustee Mitchell you can collect the ballots and have the ladies come in to get them," Papa instructed him.

My head pounded and the rest of the meeting was oblivious to me. I read the treasurer's report as quickly as I could. No one asked any questions, and they moved on to the next item on the agenda—committee reports.

The knock on the door finally came, and Deaconess Coleman came into the room and handed Papa the ballot results. Papa glanced at it and laid it on the table. When Trustee King had finished his report on building repairs, Papa picked up the ballot results again and began to read the results aloud.

My name wasn't called as treasurer. I sat there holding back tears. I wouldn't dare cry in front of them. Glancing at Reilly, I could see the smugness on his face.

Holding my head high, I handed over the ledgers to the new treasurer, Trustee Earl Winston.

It was the beginning of my downfall and unfortunately Mt. Olive slid down with me.

Cß Cß Cß

After the board meeting, Papa, Alan and Deacon Coleman and I met in his office. I guess the look on my face said it all.

"Why didn't you tell me they were going to do a secret ballot?" I looked at Papa.

"Because I didn't want Reilly and the others to think we were against the process. And you would have tried to stop it."

"Did you know Alan?" I turned to him.

"Rev. had mentioned it to me, but asked us assistant ministers to not say anything to anyone."

Turning back to Papa, "You have always told me we had to keep track of the money."

"And we'll hold them accountable. But times have changed, Margaret. We haven't been that family church for a long time. New members with new and sometimes better ideas have joined the church. We have to move with the times."

"You just don't understand what you have done," I hollered out.

"What are you talking about?"

My face had turned blood red. I'd never spoke to Papa in such a voice before, but I couldn't hold back. "You think people with money and degrees are the answer to this church's future.

But you're wrong; they'll destroy Mt. Olive because they don't love it. They want the power and prestige that goes along with a church of this magnitude."

Tears streamed down my face as I hurled words at him.

"Get a hold of yourself. I'm still senior minister of this church and everything is under my control," Papa screamed back at me as his face twisted and it looked as if his eyes were bulging out of his head.

"Papa," I cried out.

He fell to the floor and his body curled up into a fetal position, jerking. Deacon Coleman and I reached him at the same time, kneeling next to him. His eyes had turned red and salvia began to come out of the corner of his mouth. We didn't know what to do.

By then Alan had grabbed the phone to call 911.

ભ ભ ભ

An aspirin saved Papa's life. Feeling one of his headaches coming on, he'd taken one before the board meeting. The doctor told Alan and me that Papa's previous heart attack had already damaged his heart and he had an ischemic stroke, his arteries were blocked.

The news spread fast in the church community and the hospital was full of members those first few days. We didn't know if Papa was going to live or die. He was in a coma. I wouldn't leave the hospital. Alan brought me clean clothes and food.

Finally, Papa opened his eyes but he couldn't move or talk. He was paralyzed. All day the deacons came and prayed and when they tired, other church members filled in for them. God answered our prayers and Papa was taken off the respirator and was able to breathe on his own. The doctor recommended a nursing home for him.

"You'll have to rearrange your house and he'll need twenty-four-hour nursing care," he told me.

"I'm taking Papa home."

"He'll mess in his pants."

"I know what they do with them in nursing homes. I won't let that happen to my father."

"Just in case you change your mind, here are the medical forms you'll need."

I left the papers on the tray in Papa's hospital room.

Weeks later, I took Papa home in a wheelchair, with his head touching his chin and saliva drooling drown his chest. He was no longer the senior minister nor was he in control of the church. He couldn't move, talk, feed himself, or piss without my help.

Reilly had already formed a search committee for a new minister. During the time Papa was in the hospital, they had narrowed the search down to the two assistant ministers: Reverend Jesse Garner and Alan.

Chapter Thirteen

"Alan you have to put more passion into your sermons," I yelled at him. It was late Saturday evening and he was still having trouble with touching the spirit of the congregations. They sat there bored and their faces showed it.

"Maybe if I change a few things in the sermon, I could deliver it better. After all, I'm the one who went to divinity school."

"Thanks for reminding me. But I'm the one who knows how to connect with the Holy Ghost. It's in my blood and evidently not in yours."

"I'm not the hollering, stumping, putting the fear of God into men kind of preacher. I'm humble," Alan said, not staring at me.

"We have too much at stake. Last week, Rev. Garner preached a powerful sermon. He had the people on their feet, calling for more. You have to outshine him."

"And if I don't?"

"Then Trustee Reilly will have his way. You know he wants Rev. Garner as minister. Let's practice again."

I grabbed the Bible and ran up to the pulpit. I didn't need the notes Alan was reading from. Reaching deep down into my soul, I preached for about twenty minutes as if the church was filled with people. I could envision them being overcome by the Holy Spirit. The shocked look on Alan's face told me I'd made my point.

"Try it, Alan."

"No." He turned his back to me and walked out of the church.

There was only one thing left for me to do. I went to Papa's office and sat down at his desk, wishing it was mine and that I was the one really preaching tomorrow. Pulling out the church directory from the draw, I started calling the members.

"Good evening, Sister Joyce."

"Yes, Sister Margaret. How is Rev?"

"God is good. He is better, but with your prayers he will make it through this."

"I know he will. What can I do for you?"

"It hurts me to my heart that Papa can't preach anymore and we have to select a new preacher."

"Yeah, so tell."

"Papa is counting on you and the others to put Pastor Pierce in his place. He told me before his stroke, if anything ever happened to him, he wanted his son-in-law to be the senior minister for the church." I left out that Papa had been talking about Ben that's why he'd ordained him as a minister so young.

"Yessum, if that's what Rev. wants. I'll call a few of the other sisters and get things moving, if that's alright with you and Rev?"

"Thank you sister Joyce, I knew I could count on you."

"Why, child, you're like family to me. Your grandmother was my friend and my husband, Deacon Thomas, may he rest in peace, was Rev's right hand man."

I stayed up late into the night calling the members I knew would support Papa. Alan just didn't have what it took to move people.

ଓଃ   ଓଃ   ଓଃ

The next morning, I sat in the choir's pews and watched the expressions on the congregants' faces as Alan delivered his sermon. It wasn't his worst neither was it his best, but it was better than before. The organist played a few notes after Alan said a word or two. Shocked, Alan kept talking and the organist continued to play.

Earlier that morning, I'd arranged with the organist to trail Alan's words to give the sermon an extra boost.

"The devil is always sneaking around, trying to get you to stray away from God's house." Alan raised his voice on the last four words, as I told him to do. Then the organist played a few notes.

Lifting up the Bible, Alan said, "Proverbs 9:1 says: Wisdom hath built her house, she hath hewn out her seven pillars."

The organist played again without looking at Alan, who was perturbed by the encore.

"For those who seek God and live by God's wisdom, this verse can be used as a way for building a Christian life." Alan walked away from the lectern toward the organist.

"Preach," someone hollered from the audience.

The organist played several lines and Sister Joyce and several of the other sisters got up and shouted and danced in the aisles. The choir started singing and Alan, looking around at the congregation standing and praising the Lord, returned to the pulpit where he finished his sermon.

છ   છ   છ

Several Sundays passed with Alan and Rev. Garner rotating the services. As much as Alan detested what he called "circus like behavior" he went along with it because the members were responding to him. I continued to work with him on his sermons, selecting the songs for the choirs and reminding the members about their loyalty to Papa with my calls.

The day of the selection of the senior minister was fast approaching when Trustee Reilly tried to change the rules. After Rev. Garner preached, he announced he recommended that the committee select the minister and not the church body. I knew what that meant...and I wasn't going to let it happen.

Before he could sit down, I was up on the pulpit to everyone's surprise.

"I'm not going to speak long. It's been a long day and I know everyone is ready to go downstairs and have some of the deaconesses' three-layered coconut cake."

People laughed.

"But we have a serious matter to discuss. Appointing the senior minister shouldn't be left up to a handful of men. What about the women's vote?" I paused so that could sink in as I glanced at the deacons and trustees, all sitting in the first two pews. "I remember when Papa wanted to buy this church. He came to the membership and asked for your blessings. Isn't that right?"

"And that's what we're going to do this time, too, Sister Margaret. The church will select the minister," Deaconess Coleman stood up and spoke out.

I smiled and took my seat back in the senior choir.

Rev. Garner came to the lectern and nodded at me. "We were going to ask for a vote?"

"Then let's vote," someone hollered out.

"All those in favorite of letting the committee select the senior minister please stand?"

I held my breath, but only a few stood up. I made a mental note of who they were.

"And those in favorite of continuing with the present process of letting the church body select the minister please stand."

There wasn't a need to count because most of the congregation stood up.

As the weeks turned into months, the Election Day finally arrived.

It rained hard that Sunday morning, but the church was packed. The meeting was conducted before the service. Trustee Reilly conducted the election process. The one thing that I did like about him was his organizational skills. He didn't waste time.

"I've appointed several members from the church along with board and trustee members to count the ballots. You have heard each minister over several Sundays and they have also led Bible study classes. So I don't think there's much to say at this point. The ushers will now pass out the ballots."

Wiping Papa's mouth, I sat next to him in the pulpit. I'd deliberately sat him there as a reminder to people that he'd founded the church.

The balloting process went on for several minutes, before the ushers collected the ballots and handed them over to the committee.

While they were being tallied, the church service was conducted by one of the ministers who didn't make the final cut. He was worse than Alan and I didn't think that was possible.

At the end of his sermon, Deacon Coleman walked down the center aisle. I squeezed Papa's hand so tight it turned red. Coleman walked up to pulpit and whispered into Reilly's ear then he stood in front of the lectern.

"Let me present the new senior minister, Pastor Alan Pierce, to you," Deacon Coleman said, smiling at the congregation.

"Yes," I screamed out.

Trustee Reilly left the pulpit after a quick handshake with Alan. He looked back at me with disdain in his eyes. I smiled.

I hugged Alan, happy that all my hard work to get him selected had paid off. Alan grabbed my hand; we stood together. I knew we were looking good in our black and white outfits. Then I pushed Papa closer to the front to be positioned between Alan and me.

"Praise and Glory to God. I'm a blessed servant of the Lord. Thank you for your support. I plan to continue doing things the way Rev. has. It has served this church well over the years. We don't need to change right now. Let's take our time and stay focused on the Lord."

Alan never acknowledged what I'd done to get him elected. But that was okay, because now the church was back in my hands again. I vowed at that moment to do exactly as Alan had said; keep Mt. Olive the way Papa had run it for years.

Chapter Fourteen

1977

During the years, I hired and fired nurses without a second thought. Most of them sat around doing nothing or spent their time flirting with my husband, who seemed to enjoy the attention.

Punish him.

"Alan I need you to watch Papa for me, I've to run out to the store." I would leave Papa with him for hours. He had to feed him and change his diapers.

Then I just stopped giving excuses, rolled Papa into the office and left.

Sometimes at night I slept with Papa because it was easier for me to check on him and I felt safe from Alan's sexual demands.

One afternoon, while I was in our bedroom searching through the closet for a pair of shoes, Alan admonished me. "You're my wife and suppose to take care of my needs. We haven't been together in weeks."

"That's all you want to do and you don't do it that well. Just like you can't preach worth two cents. We're losing members because of you," I said, striking back at him.

He jumped into my face and his big bulk almost knocked me

down. "Don't put that on me. It's your crazy daughter and her satanic friends of that church of Melchizedek that has the good Christian folks of this city confused."

Moving back and regaining my posture, I yelled, "I told you at the last board meeting to take rigorous steps and expose those heathens at that church. But you said no."

"We're having prayer meetings here and several other churches in the city to combat that circus over there."

"That's not enough. You have to get up in the pulpit and damn them to hell. But you're too scared to use the power of the pulpit to do God's work. Maybe tonight at the prayer meeting you'll at least pray with some passion. But then again, you lack passion in the pulpit and passion in the bed," I taunted him.

Contempt oozed out of his skin as he looked at me. "One day you're going to be sorry you said those words."

Punish him, the voice yelled loudly in my head.

"You're no real man; you're scared of everything," I shouted at him.

"You don't think I'm a man, hum? Come here and I'll show you how much man I am," Alan said, grabbing for the zipper of his pants.

Trick him.

"Come to Mommy, and I'll show you some real passion," I said, thrusting out my lips.

He quickly unzipped his pants, and I could see the look of desire not only in his eyes, but what he held in his hands.

I grabbed my shoes and ran out of the bedroom leaving him with his pants down around his knees.

The voice and I laughed hysterically.

ଓ   ଓ   ଓ

Alan was right about one thing, our church and other churches in the city were losing members because of the Friday night miracle healing sessions at Lindy's church.

The Church had become a force to be reckoned with in the political, social, and economic spheres of DC. Lindy was on the board of the church and it was rumored that she was the Elder Healer, the one performing miracle healing.

The miracle healings were written about in the city newspapers as well as receiving international attention that people had been healed of cancers, blindness, physical deformities, mental illness, rare diseases and birth defects.

I knew it was trickery at hand and we had to run the devil and his worshipers out of the city. They wouldn't be able to stand up and do their evil work when the wrath of the Lord came down on them. There was only one thing to do to save good Christian souls who had fallen for the devil's lies. Clean house.

On the hottest day of the year, with the help of Deacon Coleman, I managed to get Papa to the Melchizedek Church's Friday night healing session.

"Are you sure you want to do this?" Deacon Coleman asked me when I told him I needed his help.

"God has ordained it."

And that was all he had to hear.

I didn't want to tell him it was the voice that told me I was the chosen one to destroy the house of Satan.

The church was packed with people sitting along every wall and extra chairs were placed next to the pews in the center aisle. All eyes turned to us as I made my way through the crowd with my Bible under one arm as I pushed Papa's wheelchair toward the pulpit. The scent of lilies and the oppressive heat from so many people and the humid summer evening made me want to puke. But I refused to let anyone or anything turn me back. I'd come too far to face down the devil and slay his worshipers with the words of the Lord.

But it didn't work out as I'd planned. Just as I was getting ready to steal the attention away from Rev. Betty Goldstein, the unbelievable happened. They murdered Papa in front of hundreds of people using their satanic powers.

I don't know what they did, but somehow Lindy made Papa think that he could walk and he tried to walk down the center aisle.

They even used their powers to paralyze me. I was unable to move to help Papa. There wasn't a sound in the sanctuary as Papa took one laborious step after another. The only one who tried to help him was Deacon Coleman who reached out for him. But I knew then that Lindy had put a spell on Papa, because he pushed his best friend's hand away.

When Papa collapsed on the floor in front of Lindy, I wailed, bringing me out the trance. I knew in my heart he was dead.

ଔ   ଔ   ଔ

I begged the Board of Trustees of Mt. Olive to pursue legal action against Lindy and the board members of her church for killing Papa, but Trustee Reilly and his cronies laughed at me and threw me out of their meeting.

I was determined to go forward with any legal action necessary to bring down the house of Satan. But one thing stopped me. Alan found my personal financial ledgers of the money I'd borrowed from the church over the years and threatened to turn them over to the board president, Daniel Reilly.

"I plan to give the money back," I pleaded with him, grabbing him by the sleeve of his shirt.

"You committed fraud, stealing from poor church members, who dug into their pockets thinking the money was going to support the church," he said, pushing me away.

"And I did! I renovated the church and often gave to those in need."

"Yeah, while you bought a house, car and two and three hundred dollar suits and spent just as much or more on Rev's clothes. And that doesn't include all the other frivolous stuff."

"You're forgetting all those nice suits, shirts and ties I bought you."

"I thought you were taking it out of your teaching salary. But I'm not afraid to stand in front of the church and tell them I had nothing to do with your stealing."

"Are you forgetting that this church belongs to my father and me, so how could we be stealing from ourselves?"

"For an educated woman, you're dumb. Think about what you just said."

Shocked by his remark, I just stared at his warped face. He wouldn't shut up.

"You're also uppity. Thinking you're better than everyone else. You're crazy. I've heard you talking to yourself, sleeping in the bed with your father, and saying anything that comes into your head to others. Well I've had enough."

"What do you mean?"

"You're going to see a psychiatrist of my choice and don't ever again mention taking legal action against anyone or I'll be the one taking action against you. Do I make myself clear?" He stared at me.

I nodded my head and became a prisoner in my own home. The only thing I could do was read my Bible and pray for deliverance.

Chapter Fifteen

Winter of 1982-Present

The black and white notebook with its lined pages worked perfect as a journal for Margaret. When she'd taught elementary school, her students had used the same black and white notebook for their for class assignments. She shoved it as far as she could under the mattress of her bed, where she felt it would be safe from Alan's prying eyes. She couldn't afford for him to get his hands on the notebook; it revealed too much about her.

For the last several days, Margaret had been writing in the notebook steadily reliving the agony and pain of the past. As hurtful as it was to remember the places, people and experiences that had shaped her life, she felt a sense of being connected to something. The present only offered loneliness and despair. She barely left her bedroom, except to eat and attend medical appointments; then she would hurry back to the safety of it. She kept up with the church activities from Deaconess Coleman who would call her at least once a week to check on her.

But, this evening she was going to the church board meeting.

Go to the meeting.

The voice had badgered her for days.

A few days before the church revival meeting, she anxiously asked Alan if she could attend. He continued sipping his coffee before responding to her.

"You can only come as an observer, and be invisible." He said, looking at her sternly. "I don't want any mess from you. Do you understand?"

"No, no mess Alan. I'll be on my best behavior."

And she plan to by sitting not at the table with the deacons, but off to the side in the back of the room, never uttering a word. Nevertheless, her presence she hoped would remind everyone, if it weren't for her father there wouldn't be a Mt. Olive Baptist Church. So, it was important for her to be at the meeting not only for that reason, but also to find out what her enemies were planning against her.

Excited about dressing up, Margaret changed outfits several times before she settled on a beige suit and silk cream blouse. It was old, but she liked the feel of the material even though she could barely fasten the buttons of the jacket or pull up the skirt's zipper. She didn't have the means to buy a new suit of that quality and had to settle for the old ones that hung in her closet. Alan had confiscated several of her credit cards with his name on them. He'd also taken her name off of their joint bank account.

Her hand shook as she patted her face with the powder puff and dabbed her cheeks with a little blush. Not one for wearing heavy makeup, she applied a little more than usual. She wanted to look extra special tonight to quiet down the wagging tongues about her.

Checking on the time, Margaret glanced at the gold watch on her wrist that her first husband, Ben, had given her years ago as a wedding gift. She picked up the Bible off the desk, opened it to Psalms 91 and read Chapter 9, verse 10 aloud:

Because you have made the Lord your refuge, the Most High your habitation, no evil shall befall you, no scourge come near your tent. For he give his angels charge of you to guard you in all your ways. —

Closing the Bible and feeling better that she was now armed with the Word of God, she went to do spiritual warfare.

ෆ ෆ ෆ

Several of the board members greeted Margaret with a quick hug, handshake or nod of the head before she scurried to her seat. Since the death of Rev, they weren't quite sure how to approach her.

Church members were still talking about her dramatic performance at Rev's funeral. Margaret stole Alan's glorifying moment to eulogize his predecessor by giving a very spirited acclamation of her father's life, and ended with her trying to get into his coffin. The local news station and CNN broadcasted that portion of the funeral, bringing a lot of unwanted media cover to the church.

Friends and church members offered their condolences, but Margaret pushed them away. Gossip was she'd had a nervous breakdown and it was best to stay out of her way.

Margaret sat there quietly trying to maintain her composure as she watched Fanny Mae Bishop, the secretary who'd only been with the church a year, and her husband greet the members of the board.

She knew Fanny with her big brown eyes and butt was trouble from the first day she saw her. She was quiet and sneaky like a cat. Not even the sanctified clothes she wore every day could hide her voluptuous body. She had skin that dripped like honey and dark brown hair that she wore short and perfectly styled. Even without lipstick, her lips were her calling card, big and sensuous.

Margaret watched as Fanny moved closer to Alan and brushed the flakes of dandruff off the back of his jacket that was fitting him tightly around the waist. He turned and smiled at Fanny and her whole body lit up. —

She wants to be you. You belong up there!

"She can't be me!" Margaret spoke ardently. "I'm Margaret Johnson Lee Pierce, and I've been First Lady of Mt. Olive Baptist Church since I was a teenager."

"Did you say something, Sister Margaret?" asked Rev. Lawrence Pennybacker, the assistant minister that had taken Alan's old position, as he came over and sat in the chair next to her.

"No, just mumbling to myself. Nothing important." Her voice still filled with anger.

"You look stunning this evening." He attempted to make light conversation with her as his eyes took in every detail of her.

"Thank you," Margaret blushed. "Have I missed any of your sermons?"

"No, you haven't," he said remorsefully. "I've preached once since I've been here."

"That's a shame. I hope you get a chance real soon."

"That's up to Pastor Pierce."

Margaret looked at him. "You have that look."

"What look?"

"The look of a born-preacher and not one of those fabricated from book-learning and giving lectures."

"I'll take that as a compliment."

"That's what it was meant to be," She said, looking at him as he stood up to return to the table where the other men were sitting. He was a big man, more like a football player than a minister. Everything about him was large: his head, neck, hands and feet, and his clothes looked as if they were tailor made for his body. The white shirt he wore made his smooth, dark bronze skin even more noticeable. He had a nice look, except for one thing—he wasn't one of her kind. Nevertheless, there was something about him that she was attracted to. He reminded her of... The thought disappeared as quickly as it had come.

Board meetings were generally boring unless the church had to deal with an important issue. Margaret, lost in her thoughts, reminisced about the old days when her father sat at the head of the table, and she sat to his right. The exquisite room they were meeting in was due to her tenacity to renovate it.

Many of the former board members had protested against the amount of money allocated for the restoration, but Margaret fought hard for it and won.

The walls were paneled with knotty pine wood. The old tile on the floor was pulled out and hardwood floors were installed. The Mahoney buffet was against the wall with a silver water pitcher and crystal glasses on top. The matching large table with its twelve high back chairs dominated the room. She'd found the table and chairs in an antique store in Southeast Washington and had them restored to their natural beauty.

Her father's words floated through her mind—*you never let anyone take away from you what you worked hard for*—as she continued to dream about the past, until she heard the word revival.

Revival.

The word jarred her into the present moment forcing her to focus on the meeting. She'd missed the opening prayer by Alan and the first few issues of the meeting: approval of minutes, budget, corresponding letters, and low church attendance.

And now Rev. Pennybacker was speaking. "I think we need to have a revival. From what I understand, the church hasn't had one in a long time. At my former church, we had them every year. Revivals give the members a chance to connect with each other and bring the church together."

"Huh, I don't know if that would be a good idea right now. The church has so many other problems to attend to," Pastor Pierce responded.

Rev. Pennybacker ignored his concerns and said, "I'd like to know what the others think about it."

He looked to Trustee Lester for support, but Lester lowered his eyes.

To Margaret's surprise, Trustee Thompson spoke up. "Wait a moment Pastor Pierce; I think Rev. Pennybacker might be on to something. A revival could bring us in some much needed revenue for building repairs."

"A revival costs money, too," he replied.

"The revival will pay for itself and generate funds for the building repairs," Rev. Pennybacker added.

Trustee Lester finally spoke up. "Why don't we just vote on it?"

"Yes, let's vote," added Dr. James Henderson, the attorney of the board.

"All in favor of a church revival raise their hand," Pastor Pierce said.

To her dismay, Margaret watched as five hands went up in favor of the revival and only two against it. "No, no revival," Margaret stood up and hollered at the members. "Don't you know what happened the last time we had a revival? Papa promised me we would never have another one."

Pushing his chair back, Pastor Pierce stood up and frowned at his wife. "Margaret, why don't you go on back to the house?" He made a move toward her.

Margaret walked toward the door, but then stopped and looked back at the men. "You'll be sorry. You don't know what you're getting involved in. The devil is at work here." Leaving the room, she slammed the door hard.

CB   CB   CB

Locked in her bedroom, Margaret sat in the rocking chair, mumbling to herself. She knew she couldn't handle another revival. The demons that showed themselves at the 1967 revival might come back to disgrace and harm her like they did Rev. Jackson, making the poor man go crazy right in front of everyone. He was never the same after that, couldn't preach a word.

Just the thought of that night made Margaret want to go and hide somewhere. The rattling of the doorknob startled her.

"Margaret, I need to talk to you," Her husband called out, banging on the door.

"What's it that you want, Alan?" she said, partially opening the door.

Pushing past her and almost knocking her down; he marched into her bedroom and grabbed her by her shoulders. "I should have never let you attend the meeting. I was embarrassed by your behavior." He towered over her.

Hit him! Use the lamp.

Hit him before he hurts you.

Margaret looked at the lamp on her night table. He was bigger than her, but if she moved quickly she could get away from him and reach the lamp with only a few steps, and then pop and it would be all over.

Hit him!

He thinks you're nothing.

She backed away from him. "No, please don't make me do it."

"Do what?" Alan asked, moving toward her. "Crazy, I don't know what you're talking about."

"Leave Alan, please leave my room. I don't know what got into me at the meeting. It won't happen again. Just leave." She screamed.

"Keep your voice down; Fanny is downstairs. And you're right, it won't happen again, because you won't be going to anymore board meetings.

Hit him!

Margaret glanced at the lamp again.

"Why do you keep looking at the nightstand, for your medicine? Did you take it?"

"Not yet. I usually take it before I go to bed." Margaret hurried over to the nightstand and touched the lamp, but quickly picked up the medicine bottle. With trembling hands, she fumbled with the cap.

Alan snatched it from her, opened it and shook out one tablet into her hand. Her heart raced as she quickly put it into her mouth and reached for the glass of water.

Satisfied that she'd swallowed the tablet, he left out mumbling, "She belongs in a nut house."

Trembling, Margaret locked the door and sat on the edge of her bed for a few seconds. She opened the pill bottle and popped several of them into her mouth and thought how sweet and delicious they were.

Chapter Sixteen

The sweet tarts had made her mouth parched, causing her to go downstairs to get a drink of water. The door to her husband's office was not completely closed; light showed through a crack. When Margaret reached the bottom step, she heard moans and groans coming from that direction. She walked quietly to the door and peeped inside the room.

Fanny, sitting on top of her husband's lap, was bobbing up and down with her body arched backward. Her blouse was no longer buttoned to the top of her neck, but wide opened and her bra was pulled up over her breasts, which he was smothering with kisses. They never noticed Margaret watching them as if they were a couple in a movie.

"Baby, I could hardly wait for that stupid meeting to be over with. Seeing you sitting there and all the men wishing you were theirs drove me crazy," Alan said, as he kissed Fanny on her neck and moved toward her ears.

He never did that to me, Margaret thought.

"Big Daddy, I wanted it so badly," Fanny said breathlessly, as she started gyrating faster.

Not wanting to watch them anymore, Margaret stood outside the door with her back against the wall—listening to their lovemaking and whispers of endearments. Just when she couldn't take their being together anymore, she heard them cry out in unison in pure ecstasy.

Her first impulse was to rush in and throw both of them out of her house. But then she heard the voice say, *Let them play now and pay later.* So she eased back upstairs, forgetting what she'd come downstairs for.

Later that night, Margaret lay in her bed and cried. No wonder, she thought, he always wanted to make sure I took the pills at night to knock me out while he screwed his whore.

She thought about how long it had been since she'd felt what Fanny had. If only she could just have it one more time. Beads of sweat ran between her breasts as her temperature began to rise. Her hand moved down her stomach toward her valley of delight. She stopped short of pleasuring herself knowing it was against her Christian beliefs. She called out in the darken room, "Ben, oh Ben, why did you leave me? I'm so alone."

C3 C3 C3

The next morning, the smell of coffee, sausages and southern fried potatoes made Alan come into the kitchen. To his surprise, Margaret was cooking breakfast, something that he had to admit he missed. He never knew when she would be in the frame of mind to be his wife. She hadn't let him touch her in months, but now he didn't care. But he missed her cooking. He'd promised Fanny that he would go on a diet, but that could wait until tomorrow. Pulling up a chair to the kitchen table like old times, he spread the Sunday paper before him and began to read.

"Alan, the food is ready."

He folded the paper and put it next to his already hot black coffee. Sipping it, he found it a bit sweeter than usual, but the two Sunnyside eggs, heap of potatoes, sausages and plate of biscuits made him forget everything.

"Are you coming to church?" He thought he would try and have a normal conversation with her.

"Yes, if that's okay with you."

"Did you take your medication this morning?"

"Yes."

"I don't want any outbursts." He wasn't worried because she would never have been able to be so composed if she'd not taken the medicine.

Church wouldn't be starting for another two hours. Excusing himself, he picked up his mug of coffee and went to his office to review his sermon again.

An hour later, Alan was doubled over with stomach cramps. He broke out with a sweat and barely made it to the bathroom. There he stayed for the next half hour.

Fanny found him in his office lying on the sofa where she'd left him the night before.

"Pastor Pierce what's wrong?" She ran over to him, pretending that the night before had never happened.

"Stomach cramps, diarrhea." He tried to get the words out.

"Do you want to go the hospital?"

"No, just to bed. Call Rev. Pennybacker and tell him he has to deliver the sermon today."

ଔ ଔ ଔ

Margaret stared at herself in the mirror hanging over her dresser. She didn't like the way she looked. The brown dress made her look washed out, but she didn't have enough time to change before church service. At least the choir robe would hide her dress. She brushed her hair and smoothed out the strands that were unruly.

Shaking, she pulled the drapery back and peeped out the window at the dark gray sky. There was a threat of cold rain, but the streets were filled with cars and some were even double parked.

Taking one last look in the mirror, something she didn't like to do too often, Margaret stared at the lines forming around her eyes and mouth and cringed.

I can do this, she told herself. *I can face them.*

It had been months since she'd gone to church or a choir rehearsal. But, it didn't matter, they always sang the same old songs and she knew them all. The choir director couldn't throw her off the choir; she was Margaret Johnson Lee Pierce.

She grabbed her Bible and flipped to Isaiah 45:2, *I will go before me to make the crooked places straight.* Bible tucked in hand, she hurried to join the choir lineup at the entrance of the sanctuary.

"Sister Margaret, it's so good to see you." Several of the choir members surrounded her.

"Welcome back, we have been praying for you."

"We missed you."

"The church hasn't been the same since Rev. been gone," Muriel Hopkins of the Ladies' Aid Society exclaimed.

Margaret flinched with the mentioning of her father's demise. The thought of walking into the sanctuary and all eyes staring at her made her want to run back to her room. Already they were vying for her attention.

Not even noticing Margaret's discomfort, Mrs. Hopkins continued to talk. "I am so glad you're back and especially today. When I saw you, I said thank you Jesus, because the member who was responsible for making the announcements is not here. We need you to do it like you used to." She handed a sheet of paper to Margaret.

"No, I can't do this," Margaret protested, trying to hand the paper back to her.

"Please, Sister Margaret," Mrs. Hopkins pleaded, as she scurried away just as the music started. With her head feeling as if someone had taken a baseball bat and hit her with it, Margaret marched down the center aisle with the choir singing, *Glory Be to Jesus* as the voice said, *Run now.*

When she reached her seat she looked at Rev. Pennybacker, who smiled and nodded his head at her. She could barely smile back, the lights, the music, and the stares and bygone memories only added to her dismay. Turning to run, her gaze fell on Fanny sitting self-righteously in the front pew, dressed in a navy blue suit, white blouse and gloves, and a hat with a veil that covered her eyes. Margaret tightened her hands around the hymn book as Fanny crossed her legs and smiled up at Rev. Pennybacker.

Call the whore out in the house of the Lord.

Her throbbing head and racing heart intensified as she stared at Fanny. In her mind, she began to hurl degrading names at her—whore, bitch, home wrecker, and her favorite, darkie.

Throughout the service, Margaret never took her eyes off Fanny, watching her squirm in her seat. It was Fanny's discomfort that gave Margaret the fortitude to get through the service and give the Ladies Aid announcements.

Fanny raced out of the sanctuary not stopping to shake hands with Rev. Pennybacker or greet anyone. Margaret knew where she was going.

"That was a powerful sermon you gave on being ready when the Lord calls you to do his work," Margaret said, as Rev. Pennybacker held on to her hand, squeezing it ever so often.

"I just let the Lord use me as He will. And I'm praying that Pastor Pierce will be fine."

"Oh, I'm sure it's just a bug or something minor," Margaret remarked, as she thought about the last piece of Ex-lax buried between the makeup and wallet in her purse.

Chapter Seventeen

Dr. Joseph Lopez cleaned his glasses with the corner of his shirt that was hanging out of his pants, and then pulled Margaret Pierce's medical file from the cabinet as he prepared for her visit. He'd read her medical records the night before and disagreed with her former doctor Dr. Stan Higgs' diagnosis of paranoia schizophrenia. His gut told him his superior was wrong, and he always trusted his gut; it was never wrong.

Seeing her only sparked his intuitive interest even more. She marched into his office as if she owned the clinic and he was her patient and not the other way around.

Margaret was taller than he'd thought, immaculately dressed, with a dignified presence about her. She didn't look anything like her daughter, Lindy, with whom he'd attended medical school. Margaret had fair skin, but not as light as Lindy's; her features were broader and hair wavy. She was a beautiful woman, but sadness covered her face like a blanket over a bed. Her eyes were tired; the little makeup she wore could not hide the dark circles, which told him she hadn't been sleeping at night.

Margaret looked uncomfortable in his small cramped office. She'd taken off her coat, and her keys dangled from her hand to be ready for a quick exit.

"How are you?" he asked, taking a seat behind his desk and clearing space for his tape recorder and notebook.

"Don't they come and clean your office?" She nodded at the dirty cup that was on the desk and the trash basket full of McDonald's bags. "Or are you so low on the totem pole you don't count?"

"The cleaners can't get in. I keep missing them. I guess you're right. I am the low man on the totem pole."

"So I get dumped with you," she grumbled.

He already thinks you're a crazy old bat, the voice shrieked in her head.

Margaret grimaced and the knuckles of her hand turned paled as she griped the keys even tighter.

Dr. Lopez looked at her closer. "Are you okay?" he asked again concerned about her distress.

He thinks you're crazy.

"Shut up," Margaret shouted out

Dr. Lopez stared at her, expressionless.

You're crazy, the voice continued to torment her.

"You're putting thoughts into my head," she accused Dr. Lopez. "You think I'm crazy."

"I only met you today. Why would I think that?"

He's trying to trick you. Leave now! You don't need him.

Margaret jumped up.

"Relax, Mrs. Pierce," he said, standing up as he used his hands to motion for her to sit down. "Relax; I'm here to help you. Let me fix you a nice cup of warm Chamomile tea."

He moved swiftly to the file cabinet where on top of it was a hot plate and pan. He connected it to the wall outlet and opened the top drawer of the file cabinet and pulled out two clean cups and a box of tea bags.

"You seem a little anxious today," he said, standing next to the cabinet waiting for the water to boil.

"I don't belong here. I'm not crazy."

"No, you're not," he said with so much conviction that she looked at him for the first time, seeing his large horn rimmed glasses perched on his stubby nose, above thick eyebrows and brown skin the color of a paper bag. His clothes hung off his tall thin body.

She laughed out loud.

"Is something funny?" He hoped that that the tape recorder was working, and he didn't forget to change the batteries.

"She's trying to be first. I'm first."

"Who?"

"The home wrecker, the whore, pretending to be saintly and holier than thou; she's nothing but a bitch."

Dr. Lopez stared at Margaret as her skin darkened and her voice was raspier. He knew instantly what had happened to her. The voice was making its presence known.

Softly he asked, "Tell me whom you're talking about so I can help you or who is talking to you now."

Frazzled, Margaret replied, "I just met you. You may be helping my husband and Shitty Higgy to commit me to some mental institution. But my God is protecting me and will strike all of you down," she said, putting on her coat.

"You're leaving, we haven't finished."

"Yes we have. I don't need you. Alan and his whore are the crazy ones and should be here."

"Are you taking your medication?"

"Yes, I am." Margaret sat back down.

"You're not." He declared.

"If you know so much then why did you ask me?"

Ignoring her, he said, "Since you're not taking the Thorazine, you must be feeling edgy."

"I don't know what you're talking about."

"I'll give you something that's not as strong, but will still take the edge off of your anxieties and agitation." He wrote out a prescription for valium and handed it to her.

Don't take it! Then you won't know what's happening right under your nose.

"Ha, you're in cahoots with Alan. Hook me on drugs and I don't even know what's going in my own home, right under my nose."

"I can assure you I'm here only for you. I've nothing to do with your husband. I've never met your husband. Trust me."

An awkward moment passed between them, as she looked at him closely, trying to decipher if he were telling the truth.

Flipping through her medical record in front of him, he stated. "You lost your father a year or so ago."

Tears sprung up in Margaret's eyes.

Be careful, he's trying to upset you.

"Papa," she said softly, as a floodgate of tears opened up and poured down her face, dropping on her beige sweater like a summer rainstorm showering the grass.

You're letting your guard down and he's going to hurt you just like the rest of them.

Dr. Lopez handed her a box of tissue and waited until the tears subsided. "Your father had a stroke, right?"

Lost in her own thoughts, she replied, "I would never be sitting in this office if Papa were alive."

"Why not?"

"Because there is nothing wrong with me. Papa would have protected me against Alan."

"So, you think that your husband is out to get you?" He looked at her questionably.

"Haven't you heard anything I've said today?"

"Yes, I have."

"They want to steal my legacy, just like the devil worshiper stole my inheritance."

"Okay…I'm trying to keep up with you. You're moving from Alan to the devil worshiper. Who is the devil worshiper?"

"I'm not saying her name. She doesn't exist for me."

"You're referring to your daughter?"

"I don't have a daughter. I'm childless." Margaret looked at him suspiciously.

"Dr. Higgs mentioned your family members in his report." He wasn't ready to tell her about knowing Lindy.

"I don't want to talk about her, she's not my daughter." Her lips had turned into a thin line.

"If you want me to help you, you have to trust me enough to talk about it."

Cuss him out.

"All you need to know is that they killed him."

Dr. Lopez watched as she mumbled under her breath, her face was full of anguish and her skin had darkened again. He gave her a moment to calm down as he fidgeted with the tape recorder and drank his tea. But when he looked up at her, she started ranting again.

"As sure as I am sitting here, they preyed on his mind and turned him against me. Papa always loved and doted on me. They convinced him to change his will. She got all the money."

Because of you, the voice cut into her thoughts. *You paid for everything. He never had to use his retirement money from the post office or his church salary. And look what he did to you.*

"Shut up!" she screamed out.

Lopez looked at her.

"I haven't said anything," he said, calmly.

"I mean the voi—" she stopped speaking and looked at Lopez.

"Say it. You were telling the voice to shut up."

"I don't know what you're talking about."

"Tell me about the voice. So I can help you."

"There is no voice," she screamed at him. "You're trying to make me think I'm crazy, so you can do what Alan wants and put me away."

The tape ran out and Dr. Lopez came around from his desk. "Give me a chance."

"You can't help me, no one can," she said, wearily.

"Your time is up for today. If you need to talk between appointments, call me." He handed her a card with the date and time of her next appointment and his phone number.

She wouldn't take it.

"I don't know if I'll be back. I told you who needs help, aren't you listening to me?" she chided him again.

Looking at her thoughtfully, he replied, "I'm here for you, Mrs. Pierce. Let me help you." Dr. Lopez held up the card again for her.

Taking the card, Margaret quickly read it. "This isn't the hotline number."

"No, it's my personal number, but if you feel it is an emergency crisis then call the hotline number. But I want you to know that you have a lifeline straight to me."

Chapter Eighteen

Dr. Lopez listened to the recording of Margaret's visit as he wrote up his report. He was still very excited about having her as a patient, finding her to be complex and confusing, but nonetheless, very interesting. She would definitely be a challenge because of her strong convictions, her age and she didn't trust anyone. He could understand more thoroughly after meeting her why Dr. Higgs diagnosed her as paranoia schizophrenia. Contemplating on her visit, his gut feeling was even stronger.

Reading Dr. Higgs' report again, he focused on the part that described Margaret's symptom of hearing and getting guidance from different voices throughout her life. This interested him; he'd read about the great seer, Edgar Cayce. He toyed with the thought that Margaret was a clairaudient.

He pulled out his parapsychology text and read the section dealing with clairaudience, the receiving of information from another realm in the form of thought forms or voices. The short definition of clear hearing either internally or externally didn't help him much in understanding how the process worked. He knew he was treading new territory. There wasn't a lot of textbook information on clairaudience. He would have to rely on metaphysical books to learn more about what he was leaning to as Margaret's true diagnosis.

Dr. Lopez began to write down a list of questions he needed to ask her about the voices. Did she actually hear the voice as if she was hearing herself talk or did she hear the voice as if someone was there with her? Has she ever seen spirits and communicated with them? *Perhaps, she could do both,* he thought.

When does she hear the voice? Night or day? Is there a name to go along with the voice? When did the voice start talking to her? Can she speak to the voice at any time she wants to? Dr. Lopez knew he wanted to talk to the voice.

He stayed in his office another half-hour before leaving for his efficiency apartment not far from the hospital. He loved to walk home in the cold crisp air to clear his mind.

As he walked down the corridor to the elevator, he was surprised to see the light on in Dr. Higgs' office again. Higgs had been working late quite a few nights. Lopez decided to stop in and ask a few questions about Margaret that weren't addressed in his report. He knocked on Higgs' inner office door.

"Yes, yes who's there?" Dr. Higgs responded.

"It's Joseph. I've a few questions to ask you."

"Um, um yeah, be right with you."

A few moments passed before Dr. Higgs opened the door and a woman slid between the two men without saying a word.

"Sorry, I didn't know you had a patient this late." Dr. Lopez looked as the woman shut the outer door behind her. Her perfume still lingered in the room.

"We're finished. You'll find out you have to accommodate your patients sometimes. I was just closing up the office. What can I do for you?" Dr. Higgs looked befuddled as they moved to the outer office door.

"How did you get into my office, anyway?" Higgs asked him.

"Your door was unlocked."

"Unlocked? Um, so what do you want to ask me?" Dr. Higgs asked as they walked toward the elevator.

"I met with Margaret Pierce this afternoon and…"

"She's a piece of work. Her poor husband, Pastor Alan Pierce, you know the minister of Mt. Olive Baptist Church, is a good man. I feel sorry for him. He is straddled with her every day. She can really act out."

"How much did she tell you about the voice?"

"It's in the report. Not much. Has she started to quote the Bible to you, yet?"

"Today was my first session with her."

The elevator came and the two men stepped inside with a few other people. They were quiet until they reached the lobby level.

"Joseph, I'm going to give you some advice." Dr. Higgs pulled him aside from the elevator traffic. "You're young and still think you can save or make every one better. Margaret Pierce is a lost cause. The woman will eventually have to be committed or at least her dosage increased. Don't get all caught up in her lies. She'll have you believing that her husband is doing all kinds of bad things to her. When you're ready to have her institutionalized I'll speak to the husband for you." Dr. Higgs patted him on the back and left him alone.

Dr. Lopez stood there for a second to collect his thoughts. *Margaret was right; Shitty Higgy is the perfect name for him. He wants to give her pills or institutionalize her. Where is his empathy or as doctors aren't they allowed to show that side of themselves?*

Walking in a steady rain, Lopez formulated a treatment plan for Margaret in his mind that would definitely get him reprimanded, if not fired by Shitty Higgy.

Chapter Nineteen

Sitting on the edge of her bed, Margaret threw off the flannel nightgown and lay back down on top of the comforter with only her panties on. Beads of sweat had formed on her nose, forehead and between her breasts. It was only 4:44 a.m.

Her notebook and pen lay next to her. She vaguely remembered writing about Grandma Hattie, before dozing off earlier.

Margaret reached for the glass of water on the nightstand and took a few sips, but it didn't calm her nerves. She put the nightgown back on and slipped her feet into the first pair of shoes she found. Grabbing her purse from the chair, she rushed to the door. The walls were closing in on her.

Run,

Get away.

They want to kill you.

The house was dark and quiet as she walked quickly through the kitchen to the back door. Once outside in the yard, Margaret took a deep breath, the air exhilarated her. She hurried along; the full moon providing the light she needed to maneuver the short distance to the church.

Once in the church, Margaret turned on the lights and went to the basement. A few feet away from where the choir practice or meetings were held was a door that led to another level. Just a few steps and she would be in the storage room. The room was full of old furniture and pews, church relics, and the first piano of the church.

Margaret tried the knob; the door was locked. She pulled out her church keys from her purse and tried several of them until she found the right one. Hesitating for a moment, she searched on the wall for the light switch. The light was dim, but she could see well enough to go down the stairs.

At the bottom of the steps, Margaret looked around the cold, smelly room and tried to remember why she was there. The minutes dragged by and her panic only grew. Cold, tired and heart pounding, Margaret began to feel as if everything was closing in on her when she heard a sound in back of her. *Someone is in here*, she thought. *Had Alan followed me?*

Margaret turned around and screamed. Just a few feet away stood a short man with a full beard that was as white as his hair. He reminded her of Santa Clause with his round face and fat cheeks. Holding her purse tightly to her chest, she glanced at the steps. But he was standing between her and them.

"Sorry, if I frightened you, didn't mean too. I'm John, the building custodian. Came in early today to get acquainted with the building, my first time here."

"What happened to Gaines?" She asked about the regular custodian, noticing the grey uniform that John wore with his name on it.

"He had some family business. I'm just filling in. I came down to check on the furnace. It's in the other room; Gaines said it's been acting up lately." He winked at her.

"I didn't know. They don't tell me anything anymore."

"Less for you to worry about, then you can focus on what really counts."

"What do you mean?" Margaret asked. The chills were gone and so was the panicky feeling.

"Life and all the wonderful things that it has to offer. By the way, what are you doing down here?" he asked.

"I'm looking for something?"

"What?"

Margaret felt the uneasiness returning. "I'm not sure." She stared at him.

"Let's see, there're plenty of boxes in here, old furniture, and a suitcase on top of the piano stool."

Margaret walked over to the suitcase and pulled on the name tag. *Hattie Johnson* was written in bold black letters on it.

"Yes, this is what I want." Not sure if it really was what she'd come to the basement for.

John picked up the suitcase. "Here, I'll take this upstairs for you."

Margaret followed behind him. When they got to the top of the steps, John handed her the suitcase. "It's not too heavy, is it?"

"No, she held it with her right hand and her purse swung off her left shoulder." Margaret looked down at her nightgown; it was covered with dirt and dust.

"I have to go back down and check on that furnace." He stopped and looked at her. "You look as if you could really give a good sermon and probably heal, too."

Before she could reply, he shut the basement door although she could hear him whistling as he went down the steps.

Margaret left the church and entered the walkway that led to the house. The kitchen door suddenly opened and Alan stood there taking up the entire doorway.

"Margaret what in God's name are you doing out here this time of morning?" he yelled at her, grabbing her by the arm and pulling her into the house.

The suitcase fell out of her hands lying between them.

"Look what you did?" Margaret snapped back at him as she picked up the suitcase and held it tightly to her chest.

"What's going on here, Margaret? It's not dawn yet and you're out here in the cold. It's only the last of March. Dressed in your nightgown, holding on to a ragged suitcase?" he stated more for his benefit then hers.

She looked at him suspiciously. *Was he just getting home?* she wondered. He was fully dressed.

"I don't know how much more I can take of this. I'm going to secure the church."

"John is there."

"John who?"

"The building custodian filling in for Gaines."

"No one told me about any new custodian. Where is he?"

"In the basement."

Alan started shaking his head in disbelief. "My God, you've been in the basement with a stranger? I'm calling the police."

"No, Alan, no police. He's wearing a work uniform with his name on it. Please just let it go." She walked toward the steps. "I'm going to take my pill and go to bed."

"No, you're coming with me. Grab a coat from the hall closet."

Margaret slipped on her full-length mink coat and the two of them went to the basement. The door was locked and Alan unlocked the door and they went in. There was no trace of John in the furnace room, meeting rooms, or bathrooms. All the doors and windows were locked. Alan stood in the center of the sanctuary and called out John's name and his voice echoed in the empty church.

Silence.

"There is no John! Just like that voice you conjure up, you're seeing things, too."

At the mentioning of the voice, Margaret heard it say, *Screw him.*

She laughed.

"Oh, you think it's funny? Well how about this? The Board of Trustees is thinking about doing a financial and tax audit of the church's finances going back at least seven years. How much do you owe in back taxes?"

Call his buff!

"I've some dirt of my own that the board wouldn't like either. So, if anyone should watch himself it should be you. Maybe you should have a sermon soon on the Commandment-Thou shall not commit adultery. But you can't do that can you?"

"I'd rather preach on the one that says: *You shall not steal.* You know what that means if they get a hold of your financial ledgers. How would it look if they found out that your father, the great Rev. Perlie Johnson, was a big criminal like you?"

"How dare you accuse my father of stealing? You weren't fit to wipe his shoes. "

Margaret grabbed one of the brass candelabras on the table next to the pulpit and threw it at him, missing him by a few inches.

"Get out of my church. This is my church. Do you hear me? My church!" He got up in her face.

"Your church? Ha, we'll see about that!" She backed away from him. Enraged, she hurried back to the house, leaving her husband, standing in the center of the church with his head bowed and arms lifted to God.

Once in her bedroom, Margaret trembled with fear of what had just happened. *I have to find those ledgers and destroy Alan before he destroys Papa's good name and me. It's not his church; it's mine*, she told herself, *and I'm going to get it back from that low-life scoundrel. How could I have ever married him?*

Chapter Twenty

Sleeping most of the day, Margaret woke up with a terrible headache and hunger pains. Stumbling over the suitcase that she'd dropped next to her bed, she went down the hall to the bathroom. She wanted to bathe and eat before she dealt with the contents of the suitcase. She still couldn't figure out what she wanted it for.

While her bath water ran, she peeped out of the window to find everything was covered in white; snow was falling. Was God playing an April fool's joke on them? The wind blew the snow off the roofs of the houses as fast as it fell. Motorists sped up and down 16th Street as if they were oblivious to the falling flakes. Margaret was glad that she was inside the comfort of her own home.

Later, she went to the kitchen and quietly brewed some coffee and quickly fixed a ham and cheese sandwich to carry back up to her room.

When she reached the hallway, Alan's office door swung opened, startling her. Jumping back, with the coffee and sandwich in her hands, she stood there.

"Get a hold of yourself, Fanny!" Alan yelled as Fanny hurried out of the office with swollen and puffy eyes. She attempted to wipe away the tears, but froze when she saw Margaret staring at her.

"Margaret, what are doing? Spying on me?" Alan glared at her as he appeared from behind Fanny.

"I came down to get some lunch," she replied.

"You don't look good and you—" He stopped short of saying the word—deranged. "You need to try and make yourself presentable. You never know who might be visiting me."

Margaret glanced at the large mirror that hung over a table in the hallway. Her hair was hanging loosely around her shoulders and not in the neat bun at the nap of her neck. She was wearing an old house dress.

"What do you care how I look as long as she," Margaret nodded her head toward Fanny, "is hanging on to every word you say and kissing your ass?" She couldn't suppress her feelings any longer.

The voice was screaming in her ear. *He's screwing her in the house your father gave to you. He loves her and not you. Look at the two love birds.*

"Margaret," Alan raised his voice. "I'll not have any of that kind of talk in this house. You apologize to Fanny."

"Apologize to that bitch? I want her out of *my* house Alan. Do you hear me? Get her out. Or," she hissed at Fanny. Fanny moved partially behind Alan as Margaret took a step toward them.

"Margaret, I'm warning you," Alan yelled at her.

Get them.

Margaret threw the sandwich at them, then the coffee, missing both of them by an inch. She ran into the kitchen and grabbed several of the cups that were on the countertop. She threw one at the door and the others on the floor. At the top of her voice she screamed, "Whore, fornicating in the Lord's house. Get out of my house. Do you hear me?" She reached for the saucers and began to throw them on the floor.

Then she went to the refrigerator and pulled out food, tossing it anywhere. She felt incredibly powerful. She started laughing hysterically.

A strong pair of arms grabbed her from behind.

"Let go of me, Alan, you hypocrite," she hollered at him as she tussled trying to pry lose of his strong hold on her. "You're hurting me. You're trying to kill me for her."

"Relax, relax. Calm down now. Nobody is going to hurt you. You're okay. I'm going to let you go now."

Margaret turned to stare into the face of Rev. Pennybacker. She was so distressed; she didn't even notice the physical difference of the two men. Rev. Pennybacker was taller and more muscular.

"What in heaven are you doing here?"

Alan came charging in the room. "I put a call in to her doctor. She's evidently not taking her medicine. I won't have this; I warned you. You don't have your precious father to hide behind now. I won't tolerate this kind of behavior. You need to be hospitalized."

"Shut up. Who are you to warn anybody about anything? You low life charlatan. And by the way, Mt. Olive Baptist is not your church. You can't preach worth two cents. You and your whore better watch yourselves."

Alan mumbled under his breath. "You're crazy. Something's got to be done about her." He looked at Rev. Pennybacker.

Rev. Pennybacker stood between the two of them. He didn't want anyone to get hurt. Both had a wild look in their eyes. But Margaret was holding a stainless steel pot that she'd aimed at Alan's face. He prayed she wouldn't do it. But he was too late. The pot flew past him and grazed Alan's hand that he'd extended to block the flying pot. He hollered out, "I told you she was crazy; she's trying to kill me."

Margaret went charging after him.

Rev. Pennybacker grabbed her again just before she got to her target.

"Pastor Alan why don't you leave for awhile until I can get things under control here?" He nodded his head toward the door.

"She needs to be committed. I'm not staying another night in this house with her. She might kill me in my sleep. The woman is out of her mind," he rambled, on the way out.

"Don't come back. See if I care."

"I'm going to take Fanny home; she doesn't feel good today and she doesn't need this madness."

Trying to get to Alan, Margaret yelled at him, "Why don't you tell him and everybody what's really going on. I'm not crazy. You're the crazy one, parading your whore under my nose in my house. Do you hear me? This is my house and my church."

Go after him!

Get them!

Margaret ran to the kitchen door, but Rev. Pennybacker jumped in front of her.

ℜ ℜ ℜ

Once he was certain that Alan and Fanny had left the house, he let her out of her own kitchen. He watched as she walked from the living room to the dining room cussing and screaming at the top of her lungs. He stood by to make sure she didn't hurt herself. He prayed.

After an hour, she finally began to calm down. He took a chance and led her back into the kitchen that looked as if a tornado had touched down. Rev. Pennybacker rolled up his sleeves and began cleaning.

Margaret looked around at the mess and cried.

Rev. Pennybacker stopped what he was doing and took her into his arms. "Call on Jesus, Sister Margaret. Call on Jesus."

"If you only knew what was going on behind closed doors."

"That is even more reason for you to have faith that God will lift you up and straighten out all crooked roads."

He sounded so much like Ben, she realized. She'd not had a man to hold her so tenderly since Ben. She rested her head on his chest. The beat of his heart was so comforting to her, even if Grandma Hattie disapproved of him.

When he felt her body relax, he held her back from him and wiped a tear away from her cheek.

"Sister Margaret, are you okay now?"

Margaret was embarrassed that he had to see her that way. Again, she looked around the kitchen at the broken dishes on the floor and splattered food. "You don't have to clean this up. This is my mess and I need to deal with it."

"The good Lord sent me here today to help you, Sister Margaret. I was on my way to visit several of our sick members when God spoke to me."

Moving around the kitchen, Margaret began to pick up the few dishes still on the floor. The full impact of what she'd done had hit her. Alan, she realized, would now know she wasn't taking the medicine. *Would he really turn over the ledgers*, she wondered. She had no control over her outburst. She had messed up everything and Rev. Pennybacker probably thought she was crazy. He was just humoring her now.

"What did God say to you?" she asked him.

"God said Sister Margaret needs you. Go now to the house!"

Margaret could feel the tears surfacing again. She wanted to say to him, *Please don't play with my feelings. I can't handle much more,* but she opted for silence.

Trembling she put the broken dish pieces in the trash. She knew he was telling the truth because God spoke to her, too, not all the time, but He spoke to her. She wanted to tell him about God talking to her. But she remembered the last time she told others and they looked at her strangely. It was years ago at a meeting of the Board of Trustees. The trustees asked her from whom did she get her directives. She told them God. She just didn't tell them about the other voice that spoke to her also. They reacted coyly at the time, baiting her into a more in-depth discussion about the voice she heard, only to attack her later.

Rev. Pennybacker's strong baritone voice filled the kitchen as he sang while they worked together to clean up.

His singing was interrupted by the ringing of the telephone.

"Margaret, I received a frantic call from your husband. He said you were hysterical. Do you need to come to the clinic?" Dr. Lopez's calm and reassuring voice helped to relax her even more.

"As I told you, my husband is the one with the problem. Do I sound hysterical to you?" She rebuked him.

"Get the prescription filled and take the medicine. It will help you."

"Yes, I'll do that," she lied.

"Come see me tomorrow at 3:00 p.m. Will you do that?"

"Yes."

"Margaret, if you need me I'm here for you any time, day or night," he said caringly.

Margaret hung up the phone and stared out the window at the late winter snowstorm. The street looked like a winter wonderland, but she knew that was only an illusion. Every time she saw the pure white snow, she also saw Ben's red blood covering it.

 C03   C03   C03

Hours later Margaret pulled out Grandma Hattie's favorite black crocheted shawl from the suitcase. She could still see her sitting in the rocking chair, with the shawl around her shoulders, as she read the Bible.

She tossed the other clothes onto the floor until she came to the bottom of the suitcase and found the Bible. Lifting it out of the suitcase, several photographs fell out.

One was a photo of her father when he was a young man. She stared at it. *He was so handsome,* she thought. She pulled out the next one. Grandma Hattie and she guessed the man standing next to her in the photo had to be her grandfather John. He died when she was a young child and she had no recollection of him.

She looked at the last photograph in astonishment. Turning it over to the back, she read the barely legible name—Amanda. Flipping it back to the front, she stared at her mother—fair-skinned, tall, slim, hair hanging down her back, stopping just below her waist. She looked rebellious and spirited, dressed in a long black skirt and an exquisite white blouse, with her hands placed on her hips and chin held high.

Margaret looked for any resemblance she might have of her. She didn't see any. *Papa was right*, she thought, *Lindy looks like her.*

Curled up on her bed, staring at the photo of her mother, she asked, "Why did you desert me?"

Drifting off to sleep, the photo fell out of her hand and landed in the trashcan next to her bed.

Chapter Twenty-One

Dr. Lopez emptied the trashcan and filed his clients' medical records. Not having enough space for his medical books, he piled several stacks behind his desk. The office was better but still cluttered.

Margaret waltzed into his office as if nothing had happened between her and her husband. Mumbling a greeting, she took off her coat and sat down in the chair in front of his desk.

"Hello, Margaret. Enjoying the snow? Was it difficult getting here?" he asked several questions at once while studying her demeanor.

Margaret was wearing a blouse that buttoned up to the neck, long black skirt, and her hair hung loosely down her back. Not the type of clothes, he thought, someone as dignified as her would wear. This was not the woman who usually dressed as if she was going to church holding onto her Bible. Who was the Margaret sitting in front of him?

"I hate snow and most of it's gone, thank God. The ground is too warm for it to stick around," she hurled back at him.

"I agree, as usual they didn't salt down the side streets." He made small talk, breaking the ice between them and hoping to relax her.

"You're wasting my time and yours with all this talk about the weather."

"Okay. What would you like to talk about today?"

"What did my husband tell you?" She crossed her legs.

"That you were hysterical and needed medical help immediately." He didn't mince his words.

"Medical help or did he say he wanted to have me committed to the loony bin?" She laughed loudly.

"Let's just say he's concerned about your welfare."

"Ha! Alan doesn't give a damn about my welfare. All he has on his mind is that darkie." She realized what she'd said.

The silence between the two of them weighed heavily.

Finally, Dr. Lopez asked her, "Why don't you take the medicine? It will help relax you."

"Because I don't want to be in a stupor and people tell me I'm imagining things."

"What are you talking about?"

"Didn't Alan tell you about my imaginary friend when he called you?"

"You lost me, Margaret. Who is your imaginary friend?"

"Alan tried to pretend that I was hallucinating when I told him about the man I saw in the church basement where I found my grandmother's suitcase. Guess what was in that suitcase? Photos, yeah, a photo of my mother. That witch kept it from me all those years," she rambled.

Dr. Lopez listened attentively to Margaret. She was skipping from one thought to another. Her mind was racing. He came from around his desk, pulled up a chair and sat across from Margaret.

She was trying hard to be tough, but she looked very pitiful and vulnerable. The anger and hurt inside of her was eating her up. If he could get her to release some of the anger, it might divert another eruption like the one last night.

"I need you to face me and relax. I'm not going to hypnotize you, but I do need you to relax. Close your eyes and take some deep breaths. Can you do that for me?" he urged her.

She shifted her weight and after a few seconds, closed her eyes. He could hear her as she inhaled and exhaled. He waited until he thought she was relaxed enough to start the procedure.

"Think back to the first time you became really upset with your grandmother." He waited. "What age were you?"

"I was around seven."

"What happened?

"She hated to comb my hair because it was so thick and long. Every evening before dinner I had to listen to her tirade about my hair or my looks." Margaret stopped for a few moments and sighed.

"What happened? I want you to tell me about it as if you were there again," Dr. Lopez said in his most smoothing voice.

Mimicking her grandmother, Margaret said, "Are you doing what I told you to do?"

"Yes, Grandma Hattie." Margaret changed to herself.

"Good, let me see?"

"Your nose still looks big to me. Child, who is going to want to marry you with your big nose, woolly hair and dark skin? Tomorrow scrub your skin hard and pinch that nose, you hear me?"

"You now know that none of that is true," he said, looking at her apprehensively.

"Knowing and believing is two different things."

"Yes, and we'll get you to the point of accepting yourself just as you are."

"I don't know what you're talking about. Of course, I accept myself. I know who I am, Margaret Johnson, First Lady of Mt.

Olive Baptist Church." She stared at him, daring him to challenge her.

Does he know who he is?

Smiling she asked, "But do you know who you are?"

The voice, he thought, *had told her to ask me that question.* He could tell by the slight shift of her body. Perhaps this would be a good time to approach the voice.

"Who does the voice think I am?"

"You're a homeless little bastard. Just like me, abandoned by your mother. She ran off with some musicians to California to become a movie star, only to end up on drugs and die a horrible death," Margaret spilled the words out without even thinking about them.

She shocked him. He stared at her a few moments before asking, "Let me talk to the voice."

"I don't know what you're talking about. There is no voice. I told you those things about yourself."

"There's no way you would have known those facts about my life. Let me talk to the voice." He raised his voice slightly.

Margaret shook her head. "Why do you persist in asking me about some voice named Natas?" She stopped and looked at Dr. Lopez looking bewildered.

"You call the voice Natas?"

Stumbling, "I don't know where that came from."

He could see how shaken she was and believed that this was the first time the voice had revealed more of itself.

"Let me hypnotize you and we can find out about Natas?"

"No," she screamed. "Papa prayed it out of me. I'm not like my mother or daughter. Papa said the devil was in them. He tried to help them, but they gave their souls to the devil."

"Okay, we'll let that go for now, but I need you to continue going back to the past."

"It's too hurtful."

"Facing it will help you. I want you to go so far in the past before any of that happened with your grandmother. You might have to go back to when you were a baby or in the womb." He waited. She sat there with her eyes closed.

"My mother, she hated me," Margaret finally spoke. "So much so, she left me with someone like my grandmother. She had to know the kind of person my grandmother was."

Margaret felt the tears begin to surface in her eyes. She tried to hold them back, but they ran down her face like a dam that had broken open.

Dr. Lopez handed her the box of tissues that he kept on his desk.

She delicately wiped her eyes. "Why me, why is God punishing me?" she asked looking at him pitifully.

"I'm not a religious man, Margaret, but I don't believe God punishes anyone. Life is full of ups and downs. It's our reactions to these times that determine how we live our lives. You did well today."

She shook her head, trying to shut out the voice that was screaming inside her head. *She left you!*

No matter what Dr. Lopez had said, he was no match for Natas…the voice. It was stronger.

Chapter Twenty-Two

Margaret wandered around downtown in the cold and slush wishing she had her charge cards. Window shopping was no fun, so she decided to break down and buy a few inexpensive items, paying with her checks. Walking through Garfinkel's department store, Margaret remembered the good old days of coming in and buying suits that cost two and three hundred dollars, if she didn't get them from Cissy for half the price.

The house was dark and quiet when Margaret returned home. She went directly to the kitchen, made a salad and warmed up some chicken soup, but couldn't eat it.

The visit with Dr. Lopez had upset her. How could she have known those things about his life? And the voice, it had a name. That bothered her more than talking about her mother and grandmother. Reaching for her Bible in her purse, she pulled it out and opened it randomly to Psalm 102. She read verses one and two: *Hear my prayer O' Lord; let my cry come to thee! Do not hide thy face from me in the day of distress! Incline thy ear to me; answer me speedily in the day when I call!*

Leaving the food on the table, Margaret went up to her room and changed into one of the house dresses, only because she knew it would upset Alan if he saw her in one.

Restless and bored, she opened the suitcase and started going through it. Under the clothes was her grandmother's Bible. She laid it along with the clothes on the bed. Turning the suitcase over, she shook it until the remaining contents fell out of the sides—a brush, comb, glasses and shoes.

She picked up the photos of her parents. That morning she'd found the photo of her mother in trash can. Now Margaret used her finger to trace the outline of her mother's face in the photo then placed it on her heart, hoping she would feel something other than anger and despair.

"Why did you leave me?" She spoke aloud to the photo as if her mother would speak back to her. Instead, it was the voice she heard as she looked at his photo.

Find the ledgers and destroy them.

Yes, she cried out. She would search the entire house this time, not leaving any room undone, hoping that Alan hadn't taken them off the premise.

Margaret put the photos back into the Bible. The ledgers were more important. She had to find and destroy them. Then she would destroy Alan and his whore. Once she was powerful again, she could go after the devil worshipers.

She started with Alan's room, tossing everything out of his drawers and closet. Not forgetting to look under the bed. Margaret didn't bother about tidying up the room. Lindy's old room, the attic and the bathroom became her next places to look, but they yield nothing.

Late into the night, Margaret had searched every room downstairs and the church. She paced back and forth in front of Alan's office. He kept it locked when he or Fanny weren't in there. The ledgers had to be in there, she decided.

Pulling herself together, Margaret knew there was only one thing to do. She felt better and returned to the kitchen to finish her cold soup.

Chapter Twenty-Three

Excited about what she planned to do, Margaret tossed and turned in her bed for hours listening for Alan to come home. Every now and then she would get up and check the hallway. It was after 3:00 a.m. She slipped on her robe and went downstairs. Lights from a car flashed through the living room window from the driveway. He was home.

She grabbed the yellow pages directory from under the credenza to look up locksmiths in the area and scurried back to her room.

Within minutes, she heard Alan's footsteps coming up the stairs. He stopped at her door for a second, and she held her breath. She sighed when she heard him continue to his room, closing the door and turning the lock.

She heard him give out a holler.

Laughing, she turned over and went to sleep.

Margaret dreamt about her father and John. They were together in a beautiful meadow full of all kinds of flowers. They tried to call out to her, but the voice was louder drowning them out as they moved away from her, getting smaller and smaller. She cried out, "No, come back."

Then she saw them giving Dr. Lopez a black and white notebook.

Chapter Twenty-Four

Alan never said anything to Margaret about his room. They avoided each other as much as possible. A week passed before she saw Dr. Lopez again.

"I had this dream last week; I want to discuss it with you. But I want you to know I don't put any stock in them. I don't know why I am dreaming so much. I remember everything about them."

"Our dreams are one of the ways our subconscious mind communicates with our conscious mind. Call it your inner guidance."

"I don't know about all that book knowledge. I think I was sleep walking one night or dreaming, but I can't figure out how I wound up in the basement. I found my grandmother's suitcase that contained her clothes, and photographs of my family that she kept from me."

"There are many different kinds of dreams. Some are precognitive and others are warnings. Some Native American and African tribes believe that a dream is a way to contact the ancestors or spirit guides."

"What's a spirit guide?"

"A spirit guide is an entity who watches over you on this physical journey. They appear in your dreams and some even take on a human form to give you a message."

"Like John?"

"Who's John?

Margaret broke down and told him about meeting John in the basement of the church.

At this point, Lopez was shaking his head. He admitted to himself that he was way over his head. He had to find someone to help him understand and interpret what Margaret was going through.

"I dreamt about my father last night."

"What do you think the message was in the dream?"

"This was very clear." Margaret reached into her bag and took out her notebook.

"Last time you asked me about my grandmother and mother." She handed the black and white notebook to him reluctantly.

Dr. Lopez sat down at his desk and opened it. He decided to scan it because he didn't know if she would change her mind and take it back as quickly as she'd given it to him.

As he read, Margaret read her Bible. But it was difficult if not excruciating for her to sit there and watch him read about her life and thoughts. She fidgeted with her linen handkerchief, touched her hair, and crossed and uncrossed her legs. After twenty minutes she said, "Please finish."

Dr. Lopez finally closed the notebook and carefully laid it on his desk as if it was a priceless jewel. He let the silence between them linger as he contemplated where to start. Taking a deep breath, he carefully chose his words.

"There's one part missing." He looked perplexed.

"What?"

"We must find out about Natas and how he came into your life."

"And how do you suggest we do that?"

"Through hypnosis."

"Where you control my mind? I'm not letting anyone do that." She looked down at the granny boots she was wearing, thinking about how her mother wore a similar pair in the photo.

"Then how about if you just go into a deep state of relaxation by breathing deeply, and once you're relaxed, I'll ask you questions about Natas?"

"How will you know if I'm not making up the answers?"

"Because I'll ask you things you don't know the answer to."

"I'll always be in control of my mind?"

"Yes."

"I'll think about it. I have to make sure it's not part of the devil's work. I think you put that name in my mind."

Shaking his head, Dr. Lopez said, "No that's not possible. The voice is real and its name is Natas."

Margaret grabbed her Bible and held it tightly, mumbling, "I'm not crazy, you are."

"Listen to me. You're dealing with something outside of normal occurrence and scientific knowledge. The umbrella terms for people being able to see, hear, sense, and know things beyond our physical world is called parapsychology. So a person who is psychic has extraordinary mental processes such as hearing voices. This is clairaudience. Seeing things or events that can't be perceived by the senses is called clairvoyance. There is a fine line between being psychic and mental illness."

He paused to let her absorb the information. She sat there clutching her Bible as if it was her lifeline, not responding in any way. Her uneasiness had not abated.

Determined to break ground into this new territory for her and him, he continued. "There are many references in the Bible about paranormal or psychic phenomena. During the Middle Ages, the Catholic Church called psychic occurrences "demonic" unless created by a saint. You have to understand the Church leaders were fearful of people with these special gifts because they couldn't control them. Remember the witch hunts during Puritan times? They burned people at the stakes. If they couldn't control them, they had to destroy them. Margaret, I do believe you were brainwashed by your Grandma Hattie and father to believe that something was wrong with you if you had these special gifts. It was against being Christian. They didn't want you to be ostracized by others. The same way you didn't want your daughter to be outside of the normal."

Margaret put her hands up as if to block what he was saying to her, but he continued.

"There is nothing wrong with being psychic. We all are psychic but have different degrees of the abilities."

"That's not true about me. I'm here because Alan is forcing me to come. He wants to have me committed. Don't think I don't know what he's up to. Get me to agree with you and then strip me of my legacy, Mt. Olive. But you're not going to get away with it."

"I'm here to help you."

"So you say!"

It didn't surprise him when she jumped up, grabbed her coat and hurried to the door. She stopped and held on to the doorknob for a second, before walking out, never looking back at him.

"I guess we're finished for the day," he mumbled to himself.

Had he lost her, he wondered. But, Margaret's life all wrapped up in a cheap black and white notebook laid in front of him on his desk. Had she left it or forgotten it? He picked it up and opened it to the first page.

Later in his report he stated that Margaret was suffering with Body Dysmorphic Disorder. Her journal was full of episodes showing delusions of her physical appearance. She didn't like her body. Now he knew the cause of her poor self-image. Her grandmother instilled the negative belief pattern deep into Margaret's psyche. Margaret grew to hate herself and judged others according to the societal standards of what's considered acceptable beauty. And worse, there was the issue of colorism. Eventually, he would tackle these issues.

He never mentioned Natas.

Chapter Twenty-Five

The next morning Margaret waited until she heard Alan moving about downstairs. She brushed her hair and put on a little makeup to hide the darkness around her eyes.

Margaret knocked softly on Alan's door before entering. Fanny was bending over him at the desk with a low cut yellow sweater on, showing her cleavage; she straightened up when Margaret entered the office. Alan stood up not knowing what to expect.

"Um, um…Margaret?" He showed his uneasiness.

"Alan, may I speak to you for a moment?" she asked in her most docile voice.

"What about?"

"I came to apologize for that unfortunate incident that happened…" She lowered her eyes.

"You showed despicable behavior, embarrassing me in front of Fanny and Rev. Pennybacker. And my room. You really messed that up, but you didn't find what you were looking for."

"I'm sorry. It's not what you're thinking."

"Did Dr. Lopez increase your medication?"

"He gave me a new prescription and I feel much better."

"Good, then I expect you to start acting as if you had some sense," he admonished her. "I think you forgot what I told you about the ledgers. Another outburst and I'll do what I have to do."

"That won't be necessary. I saw Dr. Lopez yesterday and he assured me that this medicine will help me a lot. He thinks I should get more active in the church to take my mind off things. May I come to the revival planning meeting?"

"The first meeting is tonight. I think it's too soon for you to attend; you haven't been on the medicine long enough. Let's wait awhile."

"If you say so, Alan." Margaret smiled at him and Fanny as she left the room.

Fanny locked the door.

ଔ   ଔ   ଔ

"I don't trust her, Alan. She's up to something. Why don't we just leave this place?" Fanny said, taking a seat on the sofa that they often used for lovemaking.

"I told you. We have everything here. She doesn't fool me. Before the end of the year, she'll be in some hospital."

"But what about our other situation? I've made up my mind and I'm going through with it, Alan."

Alan walked over to where she was sitting and pulled her up to him. "Bear with me a little while longer. We'll figure out what's best for us..." When Fanny began to protest, Alan kissed her and fondled her breasts. She pulled back. His touch was too rough for her now.

Chapter Twenty-Six

Margaret returned to her room and called a neighborhood locksmith, Warren & Hoyt, to come to the house at exactly 8:30 p.m., allowing time for the meeting to be well on its way.

By 7:30 that evening, she started getting nervous, thinking that Alan might have lied to her about the meeting. Not able to handle the uncertainty of the meeting being held, Margaret went to find out. She listened outside of the meeting room as Alan was thanking everyone for coming.

Margaret hurried back to the house and called the locksmith to ask him to come earlier. When she didn't get an answer, she stood at the living room window peeking out of it waiting impatiently for him to show. Worried that the Revival Planning meeting might end early, Margaret thanked God when she saw him drive up and park in front of the house. She opened the front door before he could ring the doorbell.

"Evening, Ma'am," he said, wiping his forehead with the back of his sleeve.

"DC weather—snow one week and now hot and humid tonight. You never know what to expect," she hastily said, leading him to Alan's office.

He looked at the lock and pulled out a long tool that looked like a needle. After a few clicks, the door unlocked.

Elated and excited by what she was planning to do, Margaret gave him a big tip.

Margaret entered Alan's office and used a flashlight to get around. Not that she really needed it. She knew the office like the back of her hand. She'd spent many hours in there with her father. And Alan had never changed the furniture around.

She tried the desk drawers; they were locked. *No problem*, she told herself as she pulled out her father's keys from her sweater pocket and found the one to open each drawer. The smug look on her face soon turned to worry as she came up empty-handed. Margaret looked around the room and realized the only new addition to the room was a file cabinet.

Just like the desk drawer, the file cabinet was also locked. Frustrated, she hurried to the kitchen, got a knife and picked the lock without damaging it. There were three drawers to the file cabinet. In the last one, she found a box belonging to her father and the ledgers hidden behind some files. Holding them up in the air as if she'd won a prize, she hugged them to her chest. Leaving everything the way she'd found it, Margaret shut the door behind her not worrying about them finding it unlocked.

Satisfied that the ledgers were all there; she carried them to the living room, sat on the floor in front of the fireplace with a glass of wine that Alan used for special occasions and ripped the pages out of the ledgers and threw them into it. With a smile on her face, she lit the fire and watched until every single page had gone up in flames.

Once in her bedroom, she could still smell the burning paper. The thought of what she'd just done made her giddy with joy. She stretched out on her bed and brushed up against the box she'd brought up from the office. She knew what was inside.

Margaret thought about going to the meeting and exposing the dirty affair between Alan and Fanny. But the revival planning meeting wasn't the right venue for what she planned to do. She needed a large meeting like Sunday church service or the revival to put them on public display. Could she wait that long to see the look of humiliation on their faces? She danced around her room, thinking about how shocked Alan will be when he discovered that the ledgers were gone. No more being bossed and threatened by Alan and no more Dr. Lopez with his satanic talk of being clairaudient.

This evening was one to relish in her freedom. She poured herself another glass of wine and danced around her room. Margaret propped the photo of her father on the nightstand and toasted him. "Thank you, Papa. You'd be so proud of me. I saved our good name and now I'm going to get Alan and his whore out of our house. Like you said, don't let anyone take anything away from you that you worked hard for." She laughed out of joy and the wine had given her a slight buzz.

She went to lie down and the box lay in the center of her bed. "Oh, I know what's in there." She hiccupped.

Get rid of it.

"Shut up, Natas or whoever the hell you are." She screamed at it. "You got me into enough trouble with that crazy doctor. I don't need you anymore, go way."

Bitch! It retorted.

"I'll show you." She opened the box. On top of the old gun was a bundle of letters with a string tied around them. Handling them very carefully, she took them and the gun out of the box.

Get rid of them, the voice goaded her.

"I told you to shut up; go away," she said, taking another sip of the wine.

Margaret looked at the envelope, which had turned yellow and the writing was barely legible. Putting on her reading glasses, she still was only able to decipher her father's first name, Perlie, and the words United Kingdom on the back of the envelope. Trembling, she opened the envelope. Unable to read the small neat handwriting, she reached into the drawer of her nightstand and pulled out Grandma Hattie's magnifying glass.

My dearest husband,

I made it safely to the United Kingdom. I know, in my heart, you followed the will of your father because you were bound by duty and family to ban me from your life and out of the country. But, I forgive you. I pray all is well with you and my precious baby. I've not stopped crying since I left the two of you. How will my darling child ever know who I really am? I miss how she smells and the softness of her skin. Some day I hope to return to reclaim what's mine. I beg of you to intercede for me with your father. I have a hole in my heart because I don't have my Maggie in my arms. Please, Perlie, bring her to me. We can live like a family here. England is much different than the United States. We'll be much freer here. Kiss her tenderly for me. And tell her I love her.

Your loving wife,

Amanda

Margaret let out a wail that was heard by Alan, Fanny and Rev. Pennybacker as they were returning from the revival-planning meeting.

"Margaret, Margaret!" Alan called her from the bottom of the steps.

Pushing past him, Rev. Pennybacker raced up the stairs, taking two at a time. Her screaming and yelling led him to her bedroom. Not bothering to knock, he entered and saw Margaret holding a letter in one hand and a gun in the other hand.

"They lied to me," she said all choked up.

Alan and Fanny caught up with him and stood in the doorway in shock. They looked at the gun. Alan recognized it as the gun belonging to Rev. He'd put the case in the file cabinet for safe keeping. She'd gotten into the cabinet and taken the gun out of its case, which meant she also had the ledgers.

"Margaret, get a hold of yourself!" Alan exclaimed as he stepped around Rev. Pennybacker and tried to grab the gun.

Fanny screamed.

Margaret moved out of his reach. "Don't touch me, you hypocrite." She glared at him, gripping the gun even tighter.

"You promised me you would take your medication," her husband said angrily.

"Who lied to you, Sister Margaret?" Rev. Pennybacker asked calmly. "Talk to me."

Margaret waved the letter she held in her left hand and said, "Lies, all lies, my life is a lie."

"Be careful with the gun, Sister Margaret. We don't want anyone to get hurt. Why don't you give it to me then we can talk about the lies," Rev. Pennybacker said softly, extending his hand to her.

"For God's sake, Margaret, listen to the man and give him the gun!" Alan screamed, as he lunged toward her.

Do it now! Natas yelled.

Margaret pulled the trigger.

Chapter Twenty-Seven

Opening her eyes to a brightly lit room, Margaret blinked several times before pulling at the tight-fitted cuff on her upper left arm. The pressure on Margaret's forearm woke her up from a deep slumber.

"Stop being naughty, Mrs. Pierce, I have to take your blood pressure. Don't give me a hard time now." The nurse tightened the cup around Margaret's arm.

"Where am I?" She managed to get the words out. She felt lifeless as if all the blood had been drained out of her body.

"You're in the hospital. Your doctor admitted you last night. Now be still while I take your vitals."

After a few seconds, the nurse loosened the blood pressure cuff on Margaret's arm. Before she could say another word, the nurse stuck a thermometer in her mouth while she put her fingers on Margaret's left wrist. After removing the cuff, she wrote Margaret's vital signs on the medical chart attached to a metal clipboard.

"Do you need me to help you to the bathroom?"

"What time it is?" Margaret sat up, but feeling unsteady, she lay back down.

"Six a.m. I'll be getting off soon and the doctors will be making their rounds. You might want to clean up a bit. Since you didn't have any toiletries, I got you some."

"Yes, please help me to the bathroom."

Margaret held on tightly to the heavy-set nurse as she steered her to the bathroom. The smell of the chemicals from the nurse's newly done Jheri curl nauseated her. Pulling away as soon as she could grab the rail in the bathroom, Margaret closed the door.

"I'll be right out here if you need me," the nurse hollered to her.

Sitting on the toilet with the cotton gown pulled up around her hips, Margaret tried to push through the sluggishness in her head to remember the reason she was sitting in a bathroom without a mirror or shower curtain. She fixed her eyes on the tooth brush, toothpaste, wash cloth, soap, deodorant, and a comb and brush on the counter. Her thoughts were locked away like money in a bank vault that she couldn't get to without breaking the lock.

"Mrs. Pierce, are you alright in there? You have been in there for several minutes now," the nurse said, opening the door and peeking in.

Margaret was standing at the sink in a daze, as the water ran out of the bowl onto the floor.

The nurse rushed over to the sink and turned off the water. "The doctor gave you a pretty strong sedative last night to calm you down. You could have burned yourself that water was hot. I don't want anything to happen to you on my watch," she said, grabbing Margaret by her arm and leading her back to the bed. "I'll bathe you."

"What ward am I on?" Margaret asked warily.

"Don't worry about that. You have been through a lot." The nurse helped her back into the bed. "Let me get a pan of water and the toiletries. Be right back."

Margaret lay back down in the bed and closed her eyes. *I must be dreaming,* she thought. *This is all a nightmare; I'll wake up in my own bed soon.*

But the nurse returned and took off the gown and began to wash her with a nasty smelling soap and rough wash cloth.

"What kind of place is this? The wash cloth is scratching my skin and the soap smells like detergent. Don't use those things on me and I don't want you touching me anyway."

"Well this isn't the Ritz and you can wash yourself." She handed Margaret the washcloth.

Margaret looked at her. "What's your name?"

"Ever Carol."

*Ever Carol, Ever Carol…*the named echoed through her memories. She looked at the nurse again. *Where had I heard that name before?* It was locked in the safe with all of her other memories. Letting it go, she asked for her purse and a mirror.

"My husband will be coming to get me out of here and I want to be ready. Also bring me my clothes."

"Okay, I'll be right back."

Margaret heard the click of the lock again.

She returned with a hand mirror. Looking into the mirror, Margaret frowned when she saw how tired and tattered she looked. Her hair hung loosely down her back with strands sticking out at the sides. She tried to smooth them down with the hairbrush. "I need a clip for my hair."

"You'll have to leave it loose or braid it."

"Would you bring me some eye drops?"

"Your doctor has to order them."

"Nonsense, my eyes are red and puffy. You must have eye drops somewhere on this floor. Why can't I have a clip for my hair?" Margaret asked, braiding her hair.

"Your doctor should be in shortly and you can ask him for anything that you want," she said. "Hope you feel better. I'm getting off now. Get some rest. You had quite an ordeal," she said, smoothing out the blanket and spread on the bed. "Be good now."

Ordeal? What's she talking about? Margaret wondered.

Margaret heard the door shut then the click. *She didn't bring my clothes,* she thought. *Where are they?*

She looked around the room, ignoring the voice in her head. The room was bare—only a bed occupied the small space. She looked up at the high window. Her mind raced…bars, bare room, and click of a lock.

Margaret rocked back and forth trying to put together what had happened. Everything was a blank. Bits and pieces of the events of the night before trickled in and out of her mind as the effects of the medicine wore off. Then Alan's face flashed before her.

"Oh my God," she cried out. "Alan."

Margaret got out of the bed, gathering up the two pieces of the gown that had opened in the back and hurried to the door.

"Help me," she screamed, banging on the door with both fists. "Let me out, let me out of here. I have to see about my husband," she cried, shaking the knob of the door.

Chapter Twenty-Eight

A big burley male nurse pushed open the door and almost knocked Margaret down. She peeped out into the bright lights of the hallway.

Run

He stood before her and freedom.

"Yes, Mrs. Pierce?" His deep voice terrorized her more than his size.

"I need to speak to my doctor."

"You're doctor will be coming to see you shortly."

"You don't understand, I'm locked in this room and something awful has happened to my husband. I have to find out what's going on. There are no phones or barely anything in this room. You have to let me out!" Margaret tried to go around his huge body.

"You have to wait to talk to your doctor."

"I want to see him now. Do you know who I am?" Margaret asked, looking up into his stern freckled face.

"I'm sure, like everyone else in here, you're a very important person. But for now, why don't you go and lie down on the bed."

"No, I want to get out of here. I'm going home." She took her fists and beat on his chest.

Grabbing both of her wrists, "You don't want to do that! Now go to back to your bed or I'll carry you over there," he ordered.

Margaret hissed at him, lifted her head up and walked toward the bed, not bothering to pull the back of her gown together.

"I'll be right back," he said.

The lock clicked.

Minutes later he was standing over her holding a tray with a small white cup full of water and a pill on it.

"I'm not taking anymore drugs. You people are trying to kill me."

"Your doctor has prescribed this for you to take when you're feeling anxious," he replied, moving the tray closer to her.

Margaret batted the tray out of his hand; spilling the water on the edge of the bed and his pants. The pill fell onto the floor.

Nurse Rick looked down at his pants and laughed; it looked as if he'd wetted on himself. Trained to remain calm in these situations, he picked up the tray, cup and the pill.

"Now get out, get out," she yelled.

He left the room with the tray under his arm, only to return shortly wearing dry pants, accompanied by another nurse holding a needle.

"You have a choice—take the pill or the needle."

Margaret swallowed the pill.

Lying in the bed, she began to fill nauseous and lightheaded as thoughts of the night before flowed in and out of her mind. Her eyelids were getting heavy as if someone had put quarters on them to hold them down. Panicking, she fluttered her eyes and saw a movement at the foot of the bed. Supporting herself on her elbows, she leaned up to get a better look.

John was standing next to her bed wearing a white jacket with a stethoscope around his neck.

"How did you get in here?" She asked, falling back on the bed.

"I walked through the door," he chuckled. "I hope you don't want to play that twenty questions game."

"I don't know what you're talking about. Aren't you the custodian for the church?"

"You could say so."

"Then why are you dressed up like a doctor?"

"I thought about being a doctor once, so whenever I get the chance I become one. Want me to listen to your heart?"

"Don't you come anywhere near me," Margaret snapped.

"Then I'll come back later to check on you. I have other patients in here I must see," he chuckled.

Pulling the covers partially over her face, she took a deep breath before closing her eyes. In and out of consciousness, she thought she heard Dr. Lopez say, "Because she has been through a lot, I wanted to wait to do the initial intake procedures with her. As you can see on her chart, she has been diagnosed with paranoia schizophrenia and had to be admit to the psych ward because she shot her husband."

Margaret threw back the covers and sat straight up in the bed, her eyes glassy and wild. "I'm not crazy. I didn't shoot him. You got to let me go; I'm Rev. Perlie Johnson's daughter of Mt. Olive Baptist Church." She let out a long wailing cry before falling back on the bed.

Tossing fitfully in her bed, she would wake up for a few moments before falling back to sleep. She wasn't sure that Dr. Lopez had actually visited her, and when she tried to get out of the bed she felt too weak.

"It's alright, Margaret," She heard John's voice again.

"You're not real so go away."

"You don't really want me to go away, now do you?" he asked softly.

Before she could respond she heard a familiar daunting voice yell at her.

Bitch, wake up.

"John where are you?" She screamed.

See he left you, too, just like your mother. They know you're crazy.

"John where are you?" she cried out again.

"I'm right here; I'll never leave you."

Don't trust him.

"You can trust me, Margaret."

"You can hear the voice?" she asked looking around the room for John.

"Of course."

"Are you an angel?"

"Is that what you want me to be? Then, yes. Some call me a guide."

He's the devil sent here to tempt you, the voice screamed in her head.

"Get me out of here!" Margaret cried.

John whispered in her ear. "Only you can do that by opening your heart."

The nurse who had entered Margaret's room to check on her left as quietly as she'd entered. Hurrying to the nurses' station, she found Margaret's file and wrote down what she'd observed. *The patient was having a conversation with herself and was still very agitated.*

Chapter Twenty-Nine

The young hospital aide picked up Margaret's lunch tray and was leaving the room when Margaret hollered out

"I'm not finished with that."

The lunch hour was over two hours ago and she had orders to collect all trays from the floor. She didn't want to have to come back. Shrugging her shoulders, she turned around with a smile on her face and sat the tray in front of Margaret.

"I'll wait for it."

She tried not to stare as Margaret swirled the lumpy mashed potatoes on the plate and made a volcano. She picked up a piece of broccoli with her fingers and stuffed it into the center of the potatoes. After filling her volcano with the broccoli pieces, she added in the corn. Pushing the tray away, she stared into space.

"If you're finished now, I'll take the tray away?" The aide wanted to grab the tray and run.

"Lies, you're spying on me. Take this nasty food out of here and bring me some decent food and my Bible. I need to read my Bible," Margaret yelled at her.

"Yes, ma'am." The young girl scooped up the tray and hurried out of the room, vowing to ask for a different floor tomorrow. There were too many crazies on this floor.

ल्ल ल्ल ल्ल

No TV, radio, no other human being to talk to except Nurse Rick who checked her vitals and ignored her, Margaret was glad to hear the door swing open and heard Dr. Lopez's voice. He didn't come right in. Instead, he stood in the doorway. She could hear him talking to Rick, catching only a few words such as basketball and big game coming up.

Margaret yelled out to him. "Get in here!"

Never responding to her command, he continued talking to the nurse.

He doesn't care. The voiced sounded so far away.

Gathering herself up, Margaret slid out of the bed, not letting the unsteady feeling keep her from what she had to do. She held on to the bed railing for a few moments and took a deep breath. *Run.*

Dr.Lopez and Rick were startled when Margaret charged past them as if she was a wide receiver going for a touch down.

Run! The voice came in stronger.

She didn't get past Rick's long arms. He reached out and grabbed the back of her gown, but she managed quickly to get out and it and kept running.

Rick grabbed her arm just before she made it to the locked door of the unit.

"Help me get her back into her room," Dr. Lopez instructed Rick, throwing the gown around Margaret's shoulder only for it to fall to the floor as she struggled to get loose from their tight grip.

Screaming and kicking, they carried her back to the bed.

"I want out of here!" She struggled to break loose from the four strong arms holding onto her.

"You can't leave here," Dr. Lopez said, helping Rick to get the gown back on her and put her into the bed.

"Why am I being held a prisoner?" she screamed at him.

"Because of the events that took place at your home last night."

Margaret put her hands up to her face and thought, *then it's true, I wasn't dreaming.*

"Do you remember what happened?"

"Go away. I don't want to talk about it."

"What else happened?"

"I told you I don't want to talk about it. Are you deaf?" She looked at him defiantly.

"There's a Detective Sullivan that is waiting to talk to you about last night. You can talk to me now or you can talk to him."Dr. Lopez looked into her tear-stained face.

"I shot him," she said softly.

Dr.Lopez sighed heavily. She was in touch with reality after all.

Chapter Thirty

The crystal vase filled with water and a dozen red roses slid across the coffee table. Lindy Lee froze in place, praying that it wouldn't land on the floor. No one was in sight.

"Okay, where are you? Come out wherever you are?" She put her hands on her hips, a signal to her four-year-old twins that she was upset.

Hearing a noise behind her, she turned and looked into their sweet innocent faces. Michael, their older brother, couldn't contain his laughter as the twins broke into giggles. She didn't know whether to cry from frustration or laugh at the absurdity of it all until she saw the vase for a second time slide to the edge of the table. She needed to get control of the situation.

"We thought you might want a rose," Gabby, the oldest twin smiled, as she levitated a rose out of the vase.

"We love you, Mommy," Raphael, her brother, also smiled and levitated a second one.

"You're not going to get away with that sweet talk this time. You could have broken the vase. Daddy Nick bought it for me in Paris."

"Aw Mommy, we're just playing."

"You have to learn to control your gifts."

When they were babies they would throw toys out of their playpen only to levitate them back into their hands. They would also levitate any small objects within their eyesight. It was a game for them and still was.

"I don't think they can control what they do, Mom."

"They have to learn. When we're out in public, they will not be able to levitate objects randomly. There are people in the world that would think they are weird or possessed by the devil. The time is not right yet; but soon my darlings." She looked at all three of them. "We'll be able to take our rightful place in the world and not be persecuted for who we really are," she told them.

Michael nodded his head.

She hated to be so hard on them, but her own childhood experience of being tormented because she was psychic made her want to protect her children even more. Seeing auras, the various colors that surround the body of a person, she was able to diagnose illness and heal them. When she was younger, she'd prayed that the colors she saw around people would go away. She wanted to be normal like everyone else, but the abilities only grew stronger as she grew older.

Now the twins and her adopted son, Michael, were each psychically gifted. They were destined to play a vital role in the evolution of humanity. Exactly what part she didn't know. But since the twins' birth, she'd been watching for a sign and it had begun with their ability to levitate.

Michael had come a long way since birth, fourteen years ago. He was born with hydrocephalus, fluid on the brain, and neurofibromatosis, small tumors. At the age of ten, she'd laid hands on him and with the help of her spirit guide, Mary Magdalene, he'd miraculously walked and talked. Sometimes he'd headaches and his forehead would bulge out. She would lay her hands on his head or pump the little button inside the back side of his skull that was connected to a tube that extended to his stomach. The excess fluid would run out and he would feel better.

"Can we go out and play?" the twins begged her, snapping her out of her daydream.

Lindy looked at the twins who were staring at her with their intense, big blue eyes. "Just for a little while in the backyard. It will be getting dark soon. Michael you go with them. But only for a short time. Bath and bed. And Michael I need to check over your homework."

She could barely finish the sentence before all three were running toward the back door. Shrugging her shoulders, she realized how lucky the twins were to have Michael as a big brother. He was protective of them and spent a lot of time watching over them.

She'd enrolled him in H.E.A.L.S., a private school in Virginia for children with special needs, although he was rapidly outgrowing the school.

After his healing, he'd shared with Lindy unbelievable stories of leaving his body during sleep and going to the planet Sirius where he was schooled about the mysteries of the universe. It was the reason he told her that he had progressed so quickly after his healing.

Later she peeked out the window at the children while she cleaned the kitchen from dinner. Michael was chasing them pretending he was an alien, of all things.

How am I going to protect them from the cruelty and harshness they will encounter from others because they are so different? My own mother and grandfather treated me as if I was a disciple of Satan. Now Nick acts as if something is wrong with them, she thought.

C8   C8   C8

The household quiet for the night, Lindy soaked in the bath, letting all the tension drain from her body. She wished Nick, the love of her life, was there to soothe her nerves. After the birth of the twins, he'd decided to return to Paris on a photography assignment for a week. The week turned into six weeks. Lindy felt as though she was reliving the life she had with her husband, Paul, before they divorced. Paul had worked abroad in India and would only return home a few months out the year. Now, Nick's work required him to spend long periods away from home. He was in Russia working for a fashion magazine. She didn't want him to go.

"I hate not being here with you and the kids, baby. But this offer will set us on easy street for a long time."

"Nick, we have money. The inheritance from my grandfather. I've invested it and it's doing well. And you're already well established."

"I'm making sure that the kids' future is secure. The market could go bad any day. I don't ever plan to be poor again. I know about hard times; you came up on easy street with your grandfather being a rich Baptist minister and your mother a teacher, living on the gold coast."

"But money isn't everything."

"It is for me."

Lindy blew the bubbles and watched the water recede exposing her nipples. She ran more hot water into the tub as she splashed water over her body. She glanced at her stomach and was relieved it was nearly flat again. Breast feeding had tightened the muscles, but her breasts were still large, something that Nick loved. The thought of him playing with her breasts made her quiver as she dried herself.

Dressed in her favorite old flannel pajamas, with several books lying next to her on the bed, she opened the small box she held in the palm of her hand. It had been a couple of weeks since she'd taken her most expensive possession out to marvel at it. The ring sparkled like a thousand brilliant stars of a night sky. She put it on her third finger of the left hand and stared at it. It was beautiful, at least two carats, but it was also too ostentatious for her and, for that reason, she hadn't worn it since Nick left. He had proposed to her just before he left for Russia.

"I love you, Lindy, and want you to marry me. Then we can be a real family. The children need to have the last name of their biological father. We have waited long enough, woman, make an honest man out of me." He grabbed her into his arms.

Her joy turned to panic. How could she tell him that the night the twins were conceived she'd slept with Paul, then her husband, and him? Not wanting Nick to see her anxiety, she smothered him with kisses whispering into his ear, "Yes."

Lindy put the ring back into the box and wrapped her arms around her knees, thinking about the past. Once the twins were born, they looked very much like her. Nick never questioned their paternity, but Paul did. He'd returned home for a short visit to see the twins.

"They're not his children," he told her without any doubt in his voice.

"How do you know that?" she asked.

"My intuition."

"You could be wrong."

"Then let's do a paternity test."

She agreed only if the results weren't part of their divorce proceedings. And she decided not to tell Nick about the test or results.

Paul and her remained friends and he continued to write her. His letters were filled with his adventures in the East or spiritual knowledge he received from his guru. A new letter had come earlier that day and lay on the table in the vestibule next to the daily newspaper that she'd forgotten to toss in the trash.

Hurrying downstairs to get the letter, she hoped that night wouldn't be one of those sleepless nights where her mind dwelled in the past. It was nothing she could do about it, she told herself.

Once in her bed again, she anxiously tore opened the envelope from India. Unfolding the sheet of paper, she began to read Paul's neat handwriting.

Dear Lindy,

I received your last letter regarding the increased awakening of the psychic gifts of our children. I wish I was there to experience this extraordinary event of these highly developed souls coming into the earth's plane. How fortunate we're to be caretakers for them. I feel guilty that I am not there doing my part in their upbringing. I've thought about this for sometime and have decided to come home in the fall. I want to see you and the children.

Love,

Paul

Paul was coming home. They had so much to catch up on. Lindy put the letter back into the envelope and put it into the top drawer of her nightstand where she kept his other letters. She'd inadvertently brought the paper upstairs with her. Usually when Nick wasn't home, she threw them away as fast as they were delivered, an old carryover from Paul. He didn't believe in reading about negative events and neither did she.

Unfolding today's paper she spread the front page out and glanced at the headlines: *The cold war between the U.S. and the*

Soviet Union over nuclear power was heating up. And Saudi Millionaire Osama Bin Laden, 25, raises money to support Afghanistan's mujuahideen guerrillas in their efforts to resist Soviet occupation forces.

As she read Bin Laden's name, she shook with chills. *We haven't heard the last of him,* she thought, *and it won't be good.*

She pulled out the Metro section of the paper and gasped. Her mother's face was in the center of the paper. Stunned, she read the headlines: *Prominent Minister's Wife May be Charged with Assault.*

Her heart raced as she continued to stare at the photo, showing her mother being led out of the house by two men. *It must be some mistake,* she thought.

The photo wasn't a good one and she imagined how upset her mother would be looking at herself in the paper. Her hair was uncombed and she was wearing an old house dress, something the woman she grew up with would never wear. *How horrible, how could it have come to this?* Lindy kept asking herself as she read the article.

Pastor Alan Pierce of the Mt. Olive Baptist Church in Northwest Washington, DC was admitted to Howard University Hospital with a single gunshot wound to the upper left shoulder. He was in stable condition. Pastor Pierce was allegedly assaulted by his wife, Margaret Johnson Pierce, in their home, according to the police report. The couple had been having marriage difficulties ever since the death of her father, Rev. Perlie Johnson, a well-liked and former minister of the church. The report further states that Mrs. Pierce had been suffering from bouts of depression and grief.

Lindy's hand flew to her mouth as she suppressed another cry.

The shooting was witnessed by Pastor Pierce's secretary and the assistant minister, Rev. Lawrence Pennybacker. It is reported that besides the police, Mrs. Pierce's psychiatrist, Dr. Joseph Lopez, was called. He immediately admitted Mrs. Johnson to the psychiatric ward of D.C. General Hospital where she is to remain until she is able to face the court hearing regarding the alleged assault.

The article gave the history of the church, mentioning her grandfather's name several times. Lindy looked at the byline of the article and it was penned by her old nemesis, Grace Perry.

Grace Perry had redeemed herself in the last four years after writing several untrue and detrimental articles about the Church of Melchizedek. The editor published an apology in the newspaper to Rev. Betty Goldstein and the church. Now Grace was back to writing for the paper.

Lindy tore the article out of the newspaper. She didn't know what to do. After being banished from Mt. Olive, she'd lost all contact with her family and church members. The closest she'd come in contact with her mother was at the death of her grandfather.

Painful memories tugged at her heart. She folded the article and laid it on the nightstand. It was times like this that she wished Betty had returned from traveling abroad. She needed a shoulder to cry on.

Betty's last letter had been about meeting her prince on the white horse. She'd met him while lecturing and vacationing in Africa. Betty described him as, "Big, strong, and all night long." Lindy chuckled to herself, remembering the letter.

Betty and her young prince, who really was of royalty, were married in less than six months. They would be returning to the

States to reopen the church by the fall, the same time Paul was due to return. Until then she was alone.

Who could she turn to? What was she supposed to do about her mother? *God I need a sign*, she silently said to herself.

Chapter Thirty-One

Detective Pete Sullivan of the 3rd District Metropolitan Police Department looked at the three people through the two-way mirror sitting in the conference room.

The attractive church secretary kept running to the lady's room, returning to her seat never saying a word. Rev. Pennybacker was calm, too calm for him. And Pastor Pierce acted like a victim of a crime, who might have been molested by a perpetrator, instead of an accidental shooting by his wife. His sources told him that the reverend hadn't been to see his wife, which made him decide to question them one more time.

They were sticking to their stories of the events leading up to the time of the shooting. He'd questioned them the night of the shooting, but now he needed them to sign their official statements. He called Pastor Pierce into his office first.

The detective let his eyes rest on Pastor Pierce whose arm was in a sling.

"I know you just got out of the hospital today and again I thank you for coming to the precinct to sign your statement and to see if there is anything you want to change. We just need to cover all bases before turning the information over to the D.A.'s office. You do understand?"

Pastor Pierce took out a handkerchief from his coat pocket and wiped his forehead. "If we can get through this quickly, the doctors kept me in the hospital overnight because my blood pressure is not good. I don't need it running up."

"I understand. And it doesn't help that you were shot by your wife, no less." The detective frowned.

Pastor Pierce's voice wavered as he wiped his forehead. "What is it you want to know? I've told you everything I remembered. Things happened so fast."

"The gun," he persisted, "why was it in your office?"

"The gun belonged to my father-in-law. It has probably been in that office for decades."

"And your wife knew it was there?"

"I suppose so. We have never discussed it."

"Why did she go to your office and get it?"

"I don't know, Detective Sullivan. You'll have to ask her."

"Why would she have to call a locksmith to open your office door?"

"Hum, um, she probably misplaced her key. She'd not been herself lately."

"Have your wife and you been having martial troubles?"

"No more than the usual ups and downs couples go through. We don't have time for any foolishness at our age." He wiped his forehead again.

"You're sure there's nothing else you want to tell me?"

"Nothing."

"Okay, you can wait in the conference room until your statement is ready. I'll have you sign it. Please send in your secretary."

Pastor Pierce looked terrible as he got out of the chair, and dragged himself out of the office.

Detective Sullivan turned his attention to Fanny. She was a good-looking woman, a little on the pump side, but today he was tired after a long night of crime in the city to care how she looked. Getting right to the point, he asked her. "Do you have a key to the office?

"Yes," Fanny mumbled.

"Who else has a key?"

"Pastor Pierce and I don't know who else." She stiffened.

"And your relationship with him...He's a good boss?"

"Yes."

"Do you spend a lot of time with him?"

"I'm his secretary and work with him during the day and have to attend some meetings at night."

"As Pastor Pierce's secretary, I'm sure you would know if things weren't so good between his wife and him... He would confide in you?"

"I'm relatively new to the church and this position. Mrs. Pierce hasn't been feeling well since the death of her father. They seemed alright to me," she said softly, not looking at him.

"Did he stay out late at night? Drinking?"

"I wouldn't know about that and I've never seen Pastor Pierce take a drink. Are you almost done? I have to go to the bathroom."

She was nervous, sitting on the edge of the chair, wringing her hands in her lap.

"That's all. You may return to the conference room and sign your statement, and then you're free to go. If I have anymore questions, I'll get back in touch with you."

Detective Sullivan followed Fanny out of his office and motioned for Rev. Pennybacker to come to his office.

"I thought you'd completed your interrogation last night," Rev. Pennybacker spoke out before the detective could get started.

"Reverend, you have to understand my position in this matter. Three people come in from a meeting and hear a woman cry out for help. They hear her say, 'They all lied to me.' They run up the stairs and the woman's husband gets shot when he enters her bedroom. No one else was in the bedroom with her. Whom was she talking to or maybe I should rephrase my question? Whom was she referring to that lied to her?"

"We told you everything. Mrs. Pierce has not been well since the death of her father. She has been distraught and under the care of a psychiatrist. The gun went off accidentally."

The detective looked at him. He wasn't going to get anything more from any of them today, but for the record he made them recite their stories again.

"Okay you can return to the conference room."

They were hiding something and he was going to find out what it was. He already had Pastor Pierce on concealing an unregistered, loaded fire arm in a private home. It was against DC law.

"Thank you folks for coming back in and cooperating with us. Once we speak with Mrs. Pierce, I'll get back in touch with you, if there are anymore questions." He gave them his official, *I know that you're bullshitting me smile*, as they left the conference room an hour after their interviews.

ଔ   ଔ   ଔ

Rev. Pennybacker drove them to the home. He could feel the hostility in the car as well as Alan's eyes boring into the back of his head. Fanny sat up front, quiet and distant. She'd turned her head to look out the passenger's side of the window.

"We did the right thing, for the church and everyone here," Rev. Pennybacker cut into the unbearable silence.

"Man, we lied to a District police officer. We committed perjury," Alan mumbled.

"This hasn't gone to court so we haven't done anything wrong. If we stick to our story, then we're okay. And we didn't lie. We told them exactly what happened. We left the meeting and heard Margaret scream out. We ran to her room and she shot you, probably thinking you were a robber."

"Robber? She wanted to kill me and you know it. You were there that day she threw that large pan at me. The woman is crazy and needs to be committed. She broke into my office and got the gun to kill me. I can't let her come back."

"Why would she want to kill you?" Rev. Pennybacker looked into his rear view mirror at the senior minister.

"She's crazy and that's all I have to say about that."

"We agreed it would be best for everyone to play this down. Margaret will get help. You don't want to drag the church through a media circus or yourself and Fanny."

"Fanny? What does Fanny have to do with this?"

Fanny continued to stare out of the window without responding to either man.

"I think you know what I mean" Rev. Pennybacker said, making a sharp turn into the rush hour traffic of 16th Street.

Chapter Thirty-Two

The following day Rev. Pennybacker carried a small suitcase of Margaret's clothes and personal items to her. He'd felt uneasy going through her things, but someone had to do it and Alan and Fanny had refused to help him. Rev. Pennybacker left the suitcase at the nurses' station and one of them unlocked Margaret's door for him.

"Sister Margaret, may I come in?" He hung back at the door, even though the nurse had informed her he'd come to visit her.

"Yes," she responded.

He walked over to her bed and was surprised to see how tired and worn her faced looked. Without makeup and her chic clothes, she still looked beautiful to him, just beaten down.

"Excuse my appearance, I look a mess." She patted the sides of her hair.

"You look fine, Sister Margaret," he said, trying to make her feel better.

"I wasn't planning to be here." She quickly glanced at him. He was casually dressed in a jogging suit that showed off his muscular build.

"We never know what the good Lord has in store for us. What we have to do is trust in God." He had told Fanny the same thing the night of the shooting, when she'd cried on his shoulder. He had to needle out of her what was wrong with her. Now he wished he never found out because it put him in an awkward position. But he promised Fanny he would do everything to help her.

"You always show up when I'm in need of prayer."

"Then let's pray. In John 8 verse 32 Jesus said: If you continue in my word, you're truly my disciples, and you will know the truth, and the truth will make you free."

Don't believe that mess, nothing going to save you from Hell. You're never going to be free again. The voice was faint, but she could hear it.

"I'm going to Hell," Margaret cried out. "I've sinned. What should I do?"

"Ask God for forgiveness and He'll grant you His grace, mercy and peace."

"It's too late for me."

"It's never too late for God. Heavenly Father, we come to You with open hearts and hands to ask that You protect and guide Sister Margaret as she faces the challenges and tribulations of life."

Interrupting his praying, she said, "You don't understand, my whole life has been about suffering. I don't know what happiness is."

"Sometime in your life you experienced happiness."

He could see a little light in her eyes.

Rev. Pennybacker finished praying. "Father, if there is anyone, Sister Margaret has hurt with her actions and words, she asks for forgiveness. Amen."

"Is Alan alright?" she blurted out.

What do you care? You did the right thing. You shot the cheating bastard.

"Yes, he's fine. He has been released from the hospital."

"I didn't kill him," she stated more to herself than to him.

"The bullet grazed his shoulder. It didn't do any damage."

"Thank you, God."

Why are you thanking God? You messed up; next time don't miss.

Nodding her head no, she quickly composed herself and said, "I must be the talk of the town."

"Oh yes, you're quite the star now. You're on the news and in the newspapers."

"What did they say?"

"A shooting had occurred at the home of Pastor Alan Pierce of Mt. Olive Baptist Church. And that you'd shot your husband. They didn't know if it was accidental or intentional." He looked at her for any signs of remorse.

Margaret shrugged. "And the church members?"

"Church members have been trying to see you and one persistent reporter, Grace Perry."

"Definitely not that nosey imposter reporter, Grace Perry. She's after any dirt she can dig up. Keep her away from me. Besides, I'll probably be going home soon."

"You can't go home as of yet. The police would probably arrest you for assault. You're confined here, in the psychiatric ward of the hospital, for observation to make sure you're ready to handle any criminal charges that may be brought against you."

Margaret sat there in silence letting the words sink in. Her worst nightmare had come true. She had to find a way to get out of there.

"There's something I must do."

"Is it something I can help you with?"

"I've to get my mother's letters."

"I have the letters."

"You, have the letters?"

"You had one in your hand and the others were in a bundle on the bed."

"Bring them to me."

"I gave them to your doctor."

"I want them, now. They're mine."

"You'll get them back. The police might want them, too. They might be evidence. Why don't you just let Dr. Lopez keep them safe for you for a while? They are now a part of your medical files and in order for the police to see them they have to have a court order."

Margaret nodded her head and looked at him as if she was seeing him for the first time.

"Alan wouldn't bring charges against me. I'm his wife, the First Lady of Mt. Olive and daughter of Reverend Perlie Johnson."

"A court attorney will be appointed to you unless you have an attorney." He ignored her last remark.

"I don't have an attorney or anyone to help me."

"I think you do have someone."

"Who?"

"God and me. I'll be here every day for you."

Chapter Thirty-Three

Lindy stood in front of the Church of Melchizedek in the quaint Georgetown community. Her eyes scanned every inch of the stone building looking for a sign to tell her she'd made the right decision to come there. The once dynamic church full of life and hope was now lifeless and foreboding. *Did Betty and I do the right thing?* She asked herself. After the death of her grandfather in the very sanctuary of the church, the terminal illness of Betty's husband and the retirement of Ruth and Mark as senior elders of the church, they had decided to close the church down. The membership disbursed and scattered to other New Age churches.

Lindy adjusted her new EK sunglasses that Nick had given her as a Mother's Day present. She wore her usual outfit of jeans, t-shirt and sandals. The hot sun beamed down on her short blond hair and fair skin. This was the last place she wanted to be, but she closed her eyes remembering the distressing dream she had about her mother.

She was standing in a beautiful field of colorful flowers and bright sunshine as she listened to soothing sounds of chanting. Not far from where she'd stopped to pick flowers, she saw a figure dressed in a white robe in the doorway of an octagonal-shaped glass building with gold beams intersecting at each of the eight panels. The hooded figure motioned for her to come to the building. Lindy moved toward the building only to find the figure had vanished. In its place stood the house she grew up in. She found herself inside the house at the bottom of the steps. Fear gripped her as she climbed the steps hearing voices coming from her mother's bedroom. The door partially closed, Lindy pushed it open and looked inside. Her mother was alone, sitting in a rocking chair, holding her hands over her ears, saying, "Go away, and shut up."

A voice boomeranged off the walls and yelled out to her, "You're crazy."

Lindy moved quickly to help her mother. But stopped when the same voice spoke directly to her, "I can make him love only you, child of light. Come closer."

Lindy saw a pin ball of light flickering to the right of her. At the same time her mother extended her hand to her. Bewildered, Lindy hesitated for a moment before reaching out for the light that surrounded her. She found herself at the pulpit of the Melchizedek church.

Shaking off the dream, Lindy walked toward the back door of the church. The sun was getting hotter as it burned her arms and feet. She'd always used the back door to avoid the crowd of people waiting to get inside for the miracle healings performed by the Elder Healer on the First Friday night of each month.

Taking in a deep breath, she turned the key in the lock and opened the door. The beep of the alarm system made her jump; she'd forgotten about it. Betty had it installed before she'd left for Israel because the church had been broken into.

Thinking fast, Lindy tried to remember the alarm code that Betty had given her.

A movement from under the stairwell caught her eye. Lindy looked as a beautiful Egyptian Mau cat ran across the floor to the custodian's office. Was someone in here?

"Hello, hello," she yelled out, taking a few steps toward the lighted office.

A short man with white hair and beard stepped out of the office and looked just as surprised as Lindy that someone else was in the building.

"Who are you?" she asked, backing toward the door that she'd just entered.

"Who are you?" he responded, grinning as he walked over to her.

"Dr. Lindy Lee; I'm one of the founders of the church."

"Oh, I see. I'm John the janitor."

"I didn't know about you."

"I was just recently hired by the real estate agency to take care of the building. It's deserted you know."

"Yes, that's why I was surprised to find anyone here."

"People just up and vanished. Never heard of that happening in a large church before. Have you?"

Why am I standing here conversing with this stranger?

"Things happen for a reason."

"Oh, yeah, why don't you come in? We'll have some coffee and you can tell me about it." John picked up the cat and was gently stroking it.

"Thanks, I don't drink coffee. And I'd better go."

"Iced tea and I've some homemade coconut cake that most people would pay thousands to have a slice." He winked at her and walked back to his office.

She could hear the old pipes crack as the air conditioning came on and the smell of the coffee, and the man seemed harmless enough. He was gentle with the cat and anyone that gentle to an animal wouldn't anyone. Seconds later, she was sitting in his office sipping on ice tea with lemon and enjoying a slice of the cake.

"What brings you to the church today?" he asked, as if they were old friends.

"I," she stuttered, "I'm thinking about turning this basement into classrooms for a healing and metaphysical school," she said, watching for his reaction to what she'd just said. Most people were scared of words like metaphysics, esoteric and the occult.

"What do you plan to teach in this healing and metaphysical school?" He chuckled as he pronounced the word, metaphysical.

"Esoteric subjects."

John raised his left eyebrow and cocked his head to the side. "Sounds very mysterious and profound. Tell me about it, I'm just a janitor."

"Well, I want to share with others who are willing to learn the Twelve Principles of this church, how to heal themselves and others using spiritual mind principles and help them to develop their intuitive abilities using metaphysical techniques such as numerology, astrology, tarot, clairvoyance, and levitation."

"If it isn't too much to ask, and I don't mean to put you on the spot, but please share with me the Twelve Principles of this church." He winked at her.

Lindy thought back to when the founding members of the church—the Awakeners, Ruth and Mark—met with Betty, Paul, her, and several other students weekly to teach them truth principles. Eventually, they framed the list and it hung upstairs in the sanctuary. *It was right in front of this poor man's eyes and he never noticed it*, she thought.

"It's no problem at all. As a truth student, I had to commit them to memory.

We believe in God, the omniscient, omnipresent, and omnipotent.

We believe that we are one with the Mother/Father God.

We believe we are made in the image of the Mother/Father God.

We believe that we co-create with God.

We believe we are spirits with a soul and body.

We believe that the body is a temple that we use for each incarnation.

We believe that the soul/spirit is eternal and indestructible.

We believe in life after death.

We believe in reincarnation.

We believe that love heals.

We believe in God's will.

We believe in God's Plan for humanity."

"This also sounds good, but can you at least explain one of these principles? I'm mainly interested in the last one. What's God's plan for humanity?"

"That oneness and love can be attained through self-realization," she said without any hesitation, but readied herself for a debate.

"Wow, you're deep. But I do have several other questions for you, but I'll limit them to two. What's God's plan for you? And how does what you just told me fit into your present predicament?" John asked, slicing another large piece of cake and putting it on Lindy's paper plate before she could protest.

"I never thought about it that way, but I'm different. I can see things, communicate with spirits and have visited other dimensions of life. So, I'm fully knowledgeable in esoteric wisdom and can teach it. That's God's plan for me," she said, holding her chin up high, daring him to mock her.

"You're a psychic." He chuckled.

"I don't like to be called that."

"Then what?"

"Spiritually gifted."

"I'll buy that. Can you tell me something about me?"

"I've too much on my mind and can't do that now."

John finished his cake and wiped a few crumbles from his mouth. "Sometimes janitors have time on their hands, so we think and read a lot; most of us are like spiritual philosophers, thinking we know everything. I'm not claiming I'm spiritually gifted like you." He chuckled again. "But tell me about some of these things on your mind?"

She looked into his eyes and saw a kind, old soul. "My mother is in awful trouble," she said, pulling the newspaper article out of her purse and handing it to him.

John put on his reading glasses and read the article.

"There's one other thing." She told him about the dream, wiping away tears as she thought about her mother.

"What are you doing to help her?"

"Nothing. She hates me and I haven't seen her in years."

"She doesn't hate you. She doesn't know about having a mother's heart."

Lindy thought about what John said, but she wasn't buying it. "She thinks I'm satanic because I believe and practice occult principles and techniques. It's against her Christian beliefs."

"Now, we are getting into a very interesting area. Remind me of my friend Joan of Arc."

"Your friend?" She laughed. He'd lightened up the moment for her.

"Joan was a French farm girl who had visions and saw lights and heard voices. Come to think about it, like you described yourself. Anyway, because she believed in what she saw and heard, Joan was able to lead the French army to victory over the English."

"And she was sold to the English and burned alive for heresy." Lindy added.

"You're scared to stand up for what you believe. Maybe your mother's troubles are a chance for you to practice your belief of compassion, love and oneness. Isn't that what Jesus' taught?"

Lindy sat there not saying a word.

"I think you're being tested to see if you're ready to be a spiritual warrior for oneness and love." He peeked over his glasses.

"Are you telling me to go and help my mother?"

"Free will, you have free will to do what you desire."

"I wouldn't know where to start. How could I help her?"

"You're not asking a janitor are you?" He gave one of his chuckles. Poured her another glass of tea and wrapped the remaining cake in aluminum foil. John reached up above the table to a small bookcase and took off a book. "I think this is the perfect book for you, Dr. Lee." He read the title aloud. "*Jesus Christ Heals*" by Charles Fillmore and then lay it on the table.

"I'm familiar with Fillmore's work, but I haven't read this one. The minister of this church, Reverend Betty, attended Unity school for ministers."

Getting up and grabbing his hat off his desk, John smiled at her. "Then this one is perfect for you and anyone else you wish to share it with. I have to go out and check on the sprinklers. Stay here as long as you like. The lights are on upstairs. Maybe you'll like to say one farewell to the past and hello to the present." He winked at her.

Making her way down the long corridor of the old basement, she climbed the short flight of stairs leading to another hallway. A right turn led to the area next to the pulpit. She opened the door and walked into a blazing light.

It was difficult to see at first but her vision adjusted to the bright light. Lindy walked to the center of the church right in front of the pulpit. She went to step up on the pulpit when she heard a piercing sound that wouldn't go away. Someone was saying something to her.

"Ms., what are you doing here? Don't you hear the alarm going off?" the police officer asked her.

Startled by his sudden appearance in the church, Lindy shouted back to him over the screeching sound of the alarm. "I'm Dr. Lindy Lee, one of the founders of the church."

"Ma'am, this building has been closed for years. I don't think the utilities are working. We got a call that the alarm had been triggered. Again, what are you doing here?"

Feeling disoriented and confused, Lindy tried to respond to his questioning. "I was checking up on the church. I am one of the owners." *What happened to John and the bright lights?*

"May I see your ID?"

"Yes." Lindy reached into her purse, pulled out her license and a membership card for the church, and then handed them to the officer.

Giving it back to her, the officer said, "I'm sorry, Dr. Lee, but we're always getting strange reports about the church. Neighborhood people report that they see people in here all the time. We always check and the building is locked tight. Do you have the code to the alarm?"

The numbers 11-22-33 floated through her head. "Yes," she smiled.

They returned to the basement. "Before we go, I need to do one more thing. Can you wait one moment?" she asked him.

"Sure, ma'am."

Lindy walked over to John's office and opened the door. It was bare. No hot plate, no coffee pot. Dust covered the table.

The only thing that remained of John was the book, *Jesus Christ Heals,* that she found on the passenger's seat of her car.

Chapter Thirty-Four

Dr. Higgs regretted that he'd turned Margaret Pierce's case over to his young assistant. Because of her last episode, he would have committed her to a permanent mental institution with the blessings of her husband.

The news media was all over the hospital, snooping around to find anything they could about Margaret. He'd promised Grace Perry, his new playmate, the scoop. He'd hinted to her that Margaret's fate didn't look good. Grace was hungry for more.

He'd also said the same exact words to his superior, Dr. Herbert Walker, who had instructed him to get rid of the media and gain control of the situation.

This was the second time that day he had to meet with Dr. Lopez and chastise him about Margaret's case. "We have to talk." Dr. Higgs said to Lopez, using the same nasty tone and inflection that Dr. Walker had used on him earlier that day. To his dismay, it didn't seem to have any affect on Lopez. He continued giving the nurse instructions and then walked along next to him as if they were going to play a game of golf, which only infuriated Dr. Higgs even more.

Once in his office, Dr. Higgs motioned for Dr. Lopez to sit in the chair next to his desk. Another technique he'd learned from Dr. Walker. Don't sit at the conference table with an employee when you want to show whose boss. Sit behind your desk where you're not on equal status.

He was furious when Dr. Lopez told him that Margaret wasn't schizophrenic, but a gifted psychic, influenced by forces she had no control over.

"Is this what you expect me to tell Dr. Walker and the media? Have you lost your mind, man?"

"The media? Is this what this is about?" Dr. Lopez answered with his own question.

"We're running a prestigious hospital and not an experimental lab for your parapsychology hobby."

"What we should be concerned about is the patient and not the media. It is not any of their business about the medical condition of Mrs. Pierce," he replied angrily.

Not liking Dr. Lopez's condescending attitude, Dr. Higgs said, "I've never heard such rhetoric in all my life. We would be the laughing stock of this hospital and the DC courts if we put any such thing in a medical report. I want a report on my desk by this afternoon recommending that Margaret be committed because she is schizophrenic and is a danger to herself and others. Do I make myself clear, doctor?"

"In that case, I request that we go before Dr. Walker. I'll take this even further, if I have to."

Dr. Higgs looked scornfully as Dr. Lopez left his office. He reached into his desk drawer and pulled out a fifth of Scotch. He quickly took a couple of sips and carefully put it back, then he popped a mint into his mouth thinking about how Dr. Lopez had brought into the crazy notion of ESP. Any reputable psychiatrist didn't put any credibility into ESP. There wasn't enough scientific data to prove its validity. Why couldn't Lopez see that Margaret was deranged and should be put away in a mental institution?

The woman had shot her husband and heard voices. Dr. Lopez would write up his report and, if necessary, testify if there was a court hearing.

Instead, this man had challenged his authority as head of the department and disagreed with his medical diagnosis.

Dr. Lopez had a reputation around the hospital as being a maverick and bucking the administration. Well this time he'd gone too far. "I'll break him and send him packing," Dr. Higgs mumbled to himself. "The icing on the cake would be spreading the word throughout the medical field about Lopez being hard to work with." Smiling, he reached for his favorite drawer before picking up the phone to call Dr. Walker.

Chapter Thirty-Five

"I'm old, Lindy. My wife died several years ago and I live in a nursing home in Maryland. I hardly get around, gout and arthritics have me in a wheel chair," Deacon Coleman whispered into the phone.

"I'm so sorry to hear about Sister Coleman. She was like a mother to me." She spoke softly into the phone. Inwardly she wept for him.

He was her grandfather's best friend and practically lived at their house. When she was young, he would pick her up and swing her around until her mother stopped him.

"How did you find me?" Lindy asked.

"DC is a small place. One of my church members worked with you at the hospital and got your number for me."

"I should have stayed in touch with Sister Coleman and you."

"Don't fret about that. She loved you, too. We never had children of our own. She enjoyed caring for you. Always said, you were special."

"Thank you, Deacon."

"Your grandfather keeps coming to me. Can't get him off my mind. I thought I heard him say to me the other night, 'Margaret has gone and got herself in a heap of trouble and you have to help her.' I looked around the room but I didn't see anybody. So,

I ignored it. Getting old, I told myself. Miss Rev. a lot. Then one of the nurses asked me if I had gone to Mt. Olive and I replied yes. She showed me the article about your mother." He paused.

She could hear his laborious breathing, from being in so much pain.

"Rev. came back a second time," he said, rubbing his swollen knees.

"He talked to you?"

"Just as sure as I am talking to you now."

"What did he say?" *Why didn't Papa come to me? I've been waiting years for a sign or something from him.* -

"For you to help your mother."

Silence.

"Don't you remember? My mother disowned me and thinks that I killed my grandfather?"

"Let that go. You have to help her," he replied.

"Help her how?"

"Rev. said you'll know what to do when the times come. But for now go see her. She has no one, but you and your children."

"I don't know." Lindy pondered on his question for a moment. "It always seemed as though I couldn't get through to her. She has a wall up."

"Break down those walls. Like my Minnie said, you're special."

They talked a few minutes more and she promised to come visit him in the nursing home.

೦೩ ೦೩ ೦೩

Later that day, while watching a soap opera, she broke down and cried when the main star's mother died. Her own mother was locked up in a psych ward and she felt helpless. Not believing in coincidences, she felt that reading the newspaper article that night, meeting John in the church and having Deacon Coleman track her down were signs from the Universe to do something. She just didn't know what.

Should she try to heal her mother by laying her hands on her like she did for her grandfather and Michael? But what if her mother refuses her help? Lindy pondered several questions before picking up the phone.

"Hi, Sylvia, this is Lindy. Can you keep the twins a little longer for me? I have an important errand to do?" she asked, not ready to tell her about her mother.

"Sure, no problem. What about Michael?"

"I'll be back in time to meet his school bus."

She was so lucky to have Sylvia for a babysitter, who was a former member of her Church of Melchizedek and knew about the children's psychic gifts. Sylvia was a clairsentient. If you lost something, you called her. Her average of finding things was nearly 100%. She often worked with police departments throughout the country, helping them locate missing children.

Changing into something more presentable than jeans and a T-shirt, Lindy hurried out of the house to face her worst fear—seeing her mother.

Chapter Thirty-Six

Dr. Lopez left out of Dr. Higgs' office and walked the few feet to his own office. There was nothing else he could do or say to Dr. Higgs to get him to see his point of view regarding Margaret. He knew it was wrong for Margaret to have shot her husband, but it was not because she was schizophrenic. The voices Margaret heard were real. She was not delusional. How does one prove the fine line between being delusional and being controlled by forces from the supernatural world?

He hoped what he was looking for he could find at the medical library. He needed a miracle to convince his superior to give him time to work with Margaret. His gut instincts told him he was right about her condition.

When the elevator doors opened, Dr. Lopez looked into the beautiful but sad eyes of Dr. Lindy Lee. His heart skipped a beat. She was in the back of the elevator and never acknowledged him. She probably didn't even remember the dork in the class.

The elevator went up and stopped on Margaret's floor. She didn't get off. When they arrived at the top floor both of them remained on the elevator. He looked back at her and she pushed the button for the first floor.

"I got on the wrong elevator," she quietly stated. "I meant to get on the elevator on the other side of the building."

"I don't think so."

"Pardon me?" She was shocked by his response.

"I think you're hesitating about going to visit your mother."

He turned to look at her as the elevator stopped at the next floor. Several people got onto the elevator and Dr. Lopez moved back closer to Lindy.

"Do I know you?" she whispered to him.

"I'm Dr. Joseph Lopez. We went to medical school together."

"I thought you looked familiar. You're my mother's doctor?"

"Yes," he responded and reached over and pushed his floor. "How is she?"

When the elevator stopped at his floor, he held the door for Lindy to get off. She walked past him and he pointed down the hall. "My office is this way. I think we should talk and not in the elevator or hallways where everyone will know about your mother," he said.

"Hospitals are like Peyton Place." Lindy followed him down the hallway.

Dr. Lopez let her into his small office.

"How long have you been working here?" She looked around, realizing how fortunate she'd been after all when she worked at Howard University Hospital. She had a large office with a window and receptionist.

"It hasn't been that long."

Lindy sat in the chair facing his desk, shedding her silk scarf and light jacket. He pulled his chair from around his desk and sat next to her. She sensed a sudden sense of foreboding as she looked at his grim face.

"Is it that bad?" she asked.

"It's not good, but there is hope." He felt better having run into her on the elevator.

"I read about what happened to Reverend Pierce in the newspaper. How is he?" she asked. It was difficult for her to refer to him as her stepfather, having not really known him in that capacity.

"No major damage. I think he's more in shock than anything else, but he has been discharged."

"Thank God, he's okay."

"The problem is he wants to have your mother committed. He believes she's a danger to herself and others due to the shooting," he said solemnly, handing Lindy the file.

She looked at the name on the file. "It's my mother's medical file. I shouldn't have this." She tried to give it back to him.

Waving his hands in the air, he refused to take it. "It's okay. I need you to review the file and give your opinion about your mother's condition as a gifted psychic healer. I believe you would be straight with me. You'll probably think this is out of the ordinary and you're right. But I'm not an ordinary doctor. You may be able to shed some light on her condition."

"How do you know what I am?" She was shocked by his use of the word psychic healer.

"I read the newspaper articles about you and your church. Let's say I've a hunch and I trust my hunches. Just like I have a hunch now to trust you, knowing you'll put aside any personal differences for a higher good." Dr. Lopez stood up. "I'll go and get us some pastries and drinks." He left out of the room before she could reply.

Lindy opened the file and found Dr. Stan Higgs' report on top. She didn't know he was her mother's doctor. Dr. Higgs had always been very nice to her when she worked at the hospital, a bit flirtatious, but she'd handled him. Whenever his name would come up in a conversation with Betty, she would change the conversation or get quiet. Lindy often wondered if something had happened between the two of them.

Dr. Higgs' report diagnosed her mother as having paranoia schizophrenia. His medical documentation supported the diagnosis. Lindy shuddered at the thought of her mother finally being diagnosed with such a devastating illness.

Dr. Lopez quietly entered the room and set a coke and pastries on the desk in front of Lindy. He left again, promising he would return shortly. Lindy, engrossed in the file, only nodded at him when he returned for the second time. He stood behind his desk, sorting papers. She continued to read. His diagnosis of her mother's condition shocked her. Margaret Pierce was clairaudience and was able to hear a voice from another dimension that transmitted information to her and kept her in a state of confusion and turmoil.

Lindy finished reading her mother's medical record. She sat there for a few moments trying to grasp and sort out in her mind what she'd just read. Dr. Lopez's diagnosis of her mother was a theory without medical documentation to support it. No one would take him serious. His theory would only hurt her mother's case.

She finally looked at him. "Is this a joke?" she asked, holding up his report.

He could hear the indignation in her voice. He didn't expect it from her, knowing that she'd been involved with a church and group of people who were metaphysicians.

"It's the truth. I've worked with your mother long enough to know that she is a gifted psychic with problems. But she is not schizophrenic."

"You may be right about that. But the authorities are not going to accept this presumption. There are people who are psychics but they don't shoot people. You're not helping my mother."

"Don't you understand? She can't control what Natas is telling her to do. He has been with her all her life. She trusts him. The death of your grandfather stressed her out and made it worse. She's grieving, feeling depressed and angry. And I think there are some personal problems between her and Pastor Pierce. Natas took advantage of her fragile emotional and mental condition. She didn't know if she was listening to herself or him."

"Who is Natas?"

"The voice your mother hears. I found out its name."

"What more do you know about this Natas?"

"Just the name."

"How long have you been working with my mother?"

"Not long enough. That's why I need your help?"

Sighing heavily, Lindy looked at him, shaking her head. "I don't know what I can do to help you."

"You're a gifted healer and medical doctor. Your input or review of my documentation will be invaluable."

"I want to see my mother first."

"I don't think that would be a good idea. She's still in shock from what happened."

"I need to see her to connect to her energy field, and then I'll let you know if I'll work with you."

"Follow me, but I warned you."

Chapter Thirty-Seven

Margaret lay in bed with her back facing the door, staring at the walls, plotting her escape. *It must be a way out of here,* she thought. She was figuring out how to bribe Ever Carol when she heard the click of the lock. She refused to turn around.

Lindy stepped into the room and gasped, the stench in the room made her want to vomit. "Why does it smell so bad in here? She whispered to him.

"I don't smell anything. Maybe I'm just used to it."

"No, this is bad. I've smelled it before. In a dream I had about my mother."

He grabbed Lindy by the arm, bringing her closer to her mother's bed.

"I have someone to see you," he said, moving to the other side of the bed to face Margaret.

Margaret turned over and her face contorted. She yelled out, "Get out, Satan," looking at Lindy.

"Margaret please..." Dr. Lopez couldn't finish his sentence.

"Get her out of here. She's a murderer," Margaret continued to yell at him.

She's here to kill you.

"Mother I want to help you." Lindy moved closer to the bed and felt that same energy she'd experienced in her dream. But this time she didn't let it stop her from reaching out to touch Margaret's hand.

Recoiling, Margaret screamed, "Get back, she-devil. Don't kill me!"

"I'm not going to hurt you. Why don't you let me help you?" she said, gently.

Margaret's face still twisted in fear, spitted out her words. "It wasn't enough that you took my Ben from me. He only tried to get home in that snow storm because of you."

"What are you talking about?" Lindy asked, looking bewildered.

She's going to kill you!

Margaret scowled. "You killed Papa and stole my inheritance from me, tricking Papa into giving everything to you. Now you want to kill me."

"No, no, that's not true." Stumbling over her words, Lindy cried out, "I didn't know he was going to give me the money. I'll share it with you, if that would make you happy."

"Share it! Ha! All of it belongs to me. The only thing that would make me happy is if I never see you again. I see how you're staring at me with contempt. You're just like that low down husband of mine; think I'm crazy. I'll show both of you lying, thieving, devil worshipers." Margaret stopped speaking and turned her gaze to the foot of her bed. "You can leave, too," she yelled.

Dr. Lopez looked to where Margaret was staring, but he didn't see anything.

Shocked, Lindy called out, "You can see John?" She nodded toward John, whose eyes were full of sadness.

"You're in this together to get me. I should have known he was a part of your doing." Margaret pulled the covers over her head and hollered, "Get out! Leave me be."

Lindy ran from the room.

The last sound Margaret heard was Dr. Lopez locking the door.

Chapter Thirty-Eight

"I tried to warn you." Dr. Lopez caught up with Lindy at the elevator, glad that it was empty when the doors opened.

Her eyes were a cloudy blue. "I didn't think it would be that bad. She was raging like a mad woman; the demon has a strong grip on her." She said more to herself than him.

"What are you talking about?" He asked.

"The voice or Natas that my mother is hearing is a demon and a bad one at that."

"How do you know that?"

"I saw it in her aura."

"You actually saw the demon."

"Not in a physical form, energetically. Her aura is full of holes and blackness. It's eating away at her energy. That's another reason she looks drained and tired," Lindy responded sadly.

"Are you saying she's not clairaudient?"

"Being demon possessed doesn't mean a person is psychic." Once they were back in his office, she grabbed her blue suit jacket, she'd left on the back of the chair. Lindy added, "I don't know if I can help you with the diagnosis you're pursuing."

"You already have. The information you just gave me. I have to be truthful; I'll think about it. My gut is saying clairaudient."

"Whatever, I can't help you."

"Yes, you can. Just watching that encounter between the two of you gave me a lot of data to work with. Who is John?"

"A spirit guide."

"Where was he?

"He was at the foot of my mother's bed. She saw him!"

"It supports my theory that she is psychic and not some demon of the devil." He scribbled a note about John in Margaret's file.

"There're so many pieces missing. She mentioned my father, Ben. I didn't know what she was talking about."

"I have something else for you to read that might help with that." He uncovered the papers he'd been sorting on his desk earlier that afternoon.

Lindy took the papers from him and glanced at the first page. Her hands trembled as she recognized her mother's handwriting. It was her journal and some letters. "No, I can't take these." She pushed the papers back into his hands.

"Take them." He handed the papers to her again.

"No, this violates patient and doctor confidentiality." The papers were burning in her hands; the energy coming off them was so strong.

"Trust me. I don't usually do this. But my gut is telling me you should read them."

"Your gut? Huh. The answer is still, no." She laid them on the desk and quickly moved toward the door. "Thank you for your trust. But you don't need me to be your guinea pig for my mother's malady. You need real medical documentation regarding psychic phenomenal."

"I was on my way to the medical library when I just happened to run into you. And I do need you." He handed her his card.

"Happened to run into me or was this a synchronicity event?" she smiled, closing the door leaving him wondering if he would ever see her again.

Chapter Thirty-Nine

Dr. Herbert Walker, administrator of the hospital, clasped his hands together in front of him and let his elbows rest on the cherry maple conference table. Before speaking, he looked at the two men sitting on each side of him. The head of the psychiatry department, Dr. Higgs, had requested a meeting regarding the patient, Margaret Johnson Pierce. He felt it was a delicate matter considering the circumstances surrounding her admittance to the hospital and who she was.

For once, Higgs was right about something, he thought. Dr. Walker thought he'd finished with unorthodox healing treatments with the resignation of Dr. Lindy Lee, when they were both employees at Howard. She was an outstanding physician but he was glad to see her go. As far as he was concerned she was a liability. Every time he picked up the *Afro* or *Washington Post* newspapers there were articles about her and the church she attended. And of course, the articles always mentioned she was a physician at the hospital. Here it was smack in his face again--now the mother.

Dr. Walker made a few notes on his notepad to himself. Lately, he was always forgetting things. He peeked over his glasses at Dr. Higgs and the man looked like shit to him. Higgs had a reputation for being a playboy. He'd cautioned him about his over friendliness with the nurses and female patients. All he needed was one solid complaint and Higgs was out of there as far as he was concerned. One thing he couldn't tolerate was an uppity doctor, especially one who had an eye on his job. He was the only god of the hospital. He'd left Howard University Hospital a few years back and came to DC General to help change the poor reputation of the hospital and make it as outstanding as Howard. Many of his old staff followed him.

"Dr. Higgs since you called this meeting; I'll let you present your case first."

Dr. Higgs looked squeamishly at his superior as he read from his report. "The patient, Margaret Johnson Pierce, was under my care for a total of four years. She has a severe mental disorder associated with brain abnormalities and typically evidenced by disorganized speech and behavior delusions and hallucinations. The diagnosis for such illness is paranoia schizophrenia. I had her on Thorazine, which I believe she either stopped taking or was taken off." He looked at Dr. Lopez. "The most recent episode was the shooting of her husband. I recommend that she be committed to a mental institution immediately until she is able to stand trial. It would be too much of a burden on the hospital to keep her here for any length of time. We have to think of any negative repercussions the hospital might incur." He slid his recommendation to both men.

"One question, Dr. Higgs. Why did you stop seeing Mrs. Pierce?"

"Um, humph, heavy administrative duties and case loads. I thought Dr. Lopez could handle her. When I turned her over to him she was very docile. The medication was working."

"Dr. Lopez, I understand that you disagree with Dr. Higgs' recommendation; why?"

"Sir, with all due respect to my superior, there were areas of Margaret…Mrs. Pierce's life that weren't being addressed and were vital to her recovery—grief, low self-esteem and Body Dysmorphic Disorder. She hated her physical appearance.

"But what about the voices?" Dr. Walker pulled his shoulders back, a habit he'd acquired early on in life to make him look grander and taller than his short statue.

"These are articles from well-known medical journals citing many case histories of patients who were thought to be mentally ill, but who were gifted psychics." He passed them to the two doctors.

"This is ridiculous. If we proceed along these lines, we'll be the laughing stock of the medical profession. We can save a lot of time and problems by getting this woman out of our hair," Dr. Higgs interjected.

"The woman is our patient, Dr. Higgs, and as doctors, we're here discussing the best treatment for her. What else, Dr. Lopez?"

"There is one major psychic ability that I'd like to discuss that I believe influences Mrs. Pierce's behavior—clairaudience. The word clairaudience means clear hearing. It is the psychic ability to hear voices and other auditory phenomena not present to ordinary hearing. Such voices may be pitched on such an auditory scale or vibration as to be inaudible to most people. Included with the articles is a report with a more in-depth study of psychic abilities."

Dr. Walker picked up the report. He looked up at Dr. Higgs who was sitting there glaring at Dr. Lopez. He nodded his head as if to say read the report.

Dr. Lopez sipped on his glass of water as both men scanned the article.

"How do you know she really has ESP, Dr. Lopez?" Dr. Walker asked a few moments later.

Dr. Lopez wished he could tell them that he trusted his own intuitive ability of claircognizance. But instead, he said, "I need time to do a medical workup, psychological and Extrasensory Perception test on her. Many parapsychologists have done extensive research to support the hypothesis that humans, as well as animals, have the capacity for ESP. This is a talent they believe we're born with. Some of us are born more talented than others based on our past lives. And most of us have had at least one or more ESP experiences."

"This is absurd!" Dr. Higgs yelled out. He looked at his boss for support.

Dr. Walker flipped over a few pages of the psychic report before asking his next question. "How much time?"

"I can't believe you're considering this?" Dr. Higgs shook his head in disbelief.

Dr. Walker ignored Higgs' charade and remembered when he was eager and excited about the medical practice. That was a long time ago. Now, all he did was sit behind a desk and make administrative decisions. The fire was gone out of him. Sometimes he wished he was back working the floors.

"The night she was admitted, the police didn't want to arrest her?" he asked.

"The assistant minister of her church, Rev. Pennybacker, called me immediately. When I arrived, she was hysterical, and in no condition to go to a police precinct. We called for two ambulances—one for her husband and the other for her. I admitted her."

"And the police, what did they say?"

"Rev. Pennybacker told them it was an accidental shooting. Detective Pete Sullivan has been calling my office. He wants to interrogate her." Dr. Lopez took a long drink of his water. His throat was dry from talking.

"Prepare a letter to go out under Dr. Higgs' signature to the courts that we're holding her for further observation due to her unstable medical condition that has been diagnosed as paranoia schizophrenia. A complete psychiatric examination of Mrs. Pierce is warranted at this time. And Dr. Lopez, you only have a small amount of time." *I can do that for my old college friend, Rev, her father. We both were outsiders in this town and had worked our way into the DC elite. And his son-in-law, Ben Lee, had been one of my favorite students.*

Dr. Higgs gasped. He stood up and started gathering up his papers.

"Sit down, Dr. Higgs; there are other things I need to discuss with you." Dr. Walker walked over to the window and looked out at the street. With his hands behind his back, he sighed. "And Dr. Lopez, we're exploring unchartered territory. There is to be no publicity associated with this case. That goes for the both of you. What we have discussed in this room stays here. I hope I made myself clear!"

Chapter Forty

Margaret counted the days. She'd been in the loony bin for three weeks. Days of loneliness and the lack of sunshine had forced her to go to the Day Room. The windows were larger and the sound of people moving about gave her a sense of comfort.

She looked around the room. Patients sat together at tables playing games, others watched TV and several stood staring out into space.

They're loonies, like you.

"No, I'm not like that."

Then why are you here and not at home?

"Did you say something, Ms. Margaret," Nurse Ever Carol appeared out of nowhere and asked her.

"No." She sighed, "It's time for my spring cleaning and who's going to tell the gardener what flowers to plant or check to make sure he pulls all the weeds? I have to get out of here."

Crazy, you're never leaving this place.

"Get away."

"I know you're not talking to me, Ms. Margaret, but I'm going over there to check on Mr. Bill, but if you need me, just holler out." She walked away.

Don't trust her. She's jealous of you.

Margaret looked around and Nurse Ever Carol was staring at her.

She's after Alan, just like she was after Ben.

"No," she cried as a flood of memories came back to her.

Nurse Ever Carol walked over to Margaret. "Did you take your meds today?"

"You're the one who danced with Ben that night."

"And you're the one who poured liquor down my cleavage and ruined my dress?" She laughed

"You were carrying on with my husband."

"You got it all wrong."

"He stayed out all night with you."

"Calm down, Ms. Margaret, that was a long time ago."

She's after Alan.

"You whore. You're just like the rest of them. You're after my husband," Margaret said out loudly. Stay away from me and my husband. You can't be me. I'm the First Lady of Mt. Olive," Margaret mumbled to herself, as she hurried to her room.

"Ben loved you. Jack and he took me home after the dance." She called after Margaret, as the others in the room stopped what they were doing and looked at the two women.

ᑲ   ᑲ   ᑲ

Dr. Lopez found Margaret in her room curled up on her bed, clutching her Bible and reciting the 94th Psalm.

"He will send his angel to protect you," she kept repeating.

"Margaret."

She wouldn't look at him or respond.

"Margaret, what happened?" He walked around her bed to face her. He'd been working with her every day since she'd been admitted. Time wasn't on their side. They would meet in the morning and evenings. The hospital staff called her his special patient and treated her as such.

What happened? He asked himself, as he bent over her.

Margaret looked up at him. "You lied."

"Lied about what?"

"You promised not to lock me up and now I'm in this crazy place with these crazy people. Why does everybody always lie to me?"

He was surprised at her regression. They had gone over several times why she was there. Instead of succumbing to her whining he asked, "Tell me who lied to you the night you shot your husband?"

"I don't know what you're talking about. I don't remember."

"You screamed out they lied to you. Who are they?"

Don't listen to him.

"Go away. I don't want to talk about it."

Don't trust him. He put you here.

Dr. Lopez opened the folder he had under his arm and pulled out a sheet of paper.

Margaret, recognizing the worn paper, tried to grab it out of his hands. "Don't read it. I don't want to know."

He stepped back and read.

Dear Perlie,

It's cold in London.

"They lied," she cried. "My father and grandmother told me my mother had abandoned me. All my life, I hated her for it."

"And now it's time to hear the truth."

I miss the warm days and nights of our beloved country, the woods and streams where I spent many hours gathering herbs and flowers. But most of all I miss my baby sucking at my breast, her little feet and hands. Has her hair grown in now? She was so beautiful. Please write and tell me if she is sitting up and that she's a happy baby. Tell her I love her. I beg of you Perlie bring her to me. My heart is broken. I promise not to question or go against the religious teachings of your father. I'll become a faithful steward of the church and give up my disobedient ways just to be with you and my baby.

Your loving wife,

Amanda

Margaret buried her face into the pillow, but he continued reading letter after letter. When he finished he put them back into the folder as the silence between the two of them made the room seem even smaller than it was.

Then her tears came like a dam breaking open.

Chapter Forty-One

Lindy heard his voice before she saw him and her heart fluttered. Joseph Lopez stood in her front doorway smiling at Michael. He had called her every day since they first met asking about different events that happened while she was growing up, the philosophies of Mt. Olive Baptist Church and how Margaret and her grandfather addressed her psychic gifts. As painful as it was to recall those incidents, Lindy found some solace in discussing those hurtful times. They were fast becoming friends, talking long into the night about her mother, medicine and metaphysics.

She wanted to laugh when she saw him. He looked like a young college boy, instead of an accomplished doctor, with his preppy clothes hanging off his tall, thin body. Perfect large white teeth seemed to take up most of his face when he smiled. His thick black eyebrows and wavy hair gave him a bit of an exotic look. She had not noticed any of those qualities when they first met.

"Joseph." She gleamed, not meaning to put so much exhilaration in her voice.

"Hope you don't mind that I came a little earlier. I was in the neighborhood," he replied. Then he added, "Forget the 'in the neighborhood' part. If this isn't a good time, I can wait in the car." He smiled, melting her heart.

"Please, come in." She motioned for him to follow her into the living room.

Michael stood there looking at the two.

"You met my oldest son, Michael?"

"Yeah, that's a great photo of you over the fireplace," he said, to him.

"My dad is a famous photographer."

"Nick Lewis is your dad?"

"Yes."

"I love his work. One of the few black photographers of today. Do you know who the other one is?"

"Gordon Parks," he answered.

"I'm impressed, young man."

"Dad got me his autograph. Do you want to see it?" "Maybe later, Michael," Lindy interrupted. "Why don't you check on the twins for me?"

"Okay, Mom."

"I didn't know you were married to Nick Lewis." He said to her after Michael had left the room.

"I'm not. Michael is my adopted son and Nick's biological son."

"But you're married?" He asked reluctantly, scared to hear the answer.

"I was married to my best friend, but we divorced shortly after the twins were born. He's in India pursuing his life's dream to be a guru of an ashram. And you?"

"Never been married."

They sat on the sofa looking awkwardly at each other, lost for words.

Finally, Lindy asked, "How's my mother today?"

"She's still confused and rebellious, vomiting up her meds or hiding them under her tongue."

"Are you going to use force to get her to take them?"

"Never, she'll come around."

"Give her time."

"Time is what I don't have. My superiors and the detectives are breathing down my neck."

"What are you going to do?"

"Pray for a miracle."

"Can I see her again?"

"I don't think that would be wise."

"This time I'll listen to you."

"Here are the articles from the medical journals about psychics and mental illness I wanted you to read." He pulled a pile of papers out of his briefcase.

Lindy reached for the several Xeroxed copies and glanced at the title of the first one: *Hallucinations or Supernormal Hearing? You Decide* By Bruce Patterson, Ph.D.

"That one is fascinating. A psychologist followed a young woman for several years. She met every criterion for schizophrenia. She had hallucinations, bizarre behavior, disorganized thinking and speech. She also heard voices that instructed her to do things. But there was one voice that would come through and told her things about people. The more she listened to that voice she began to get better. Was it an angel, I wonder?" he eagerly explained, as if he was giving a lecture.

"I can't wait to read these," she responded, thinking he doesn't understand that this is about more than her mother being clairaudient; a demon was using her as a host.

"You don't have to read them now. Good bedtime reading." Dr.Lopez pulled his ear, a nervous habit from childhood.

"Mom, we're hungry," Michael yelled from the kitchen, interrupting their conversation.

Dr. Lopez sighed in relief.

She put the letters back into the envelope and laid it on the coffee table. Turning to Dr.Lopez, "Please, join us for dinner?" she asked.

"I haven't had a home cooked meal in a long time."

After dinner, while Lindy cleaned the kitchen and Michael did his homework, Joseph kept the twins entertained with magic tricks. But he was in for a surprise when they showed him their special magic.

Joseph made a quarter disappear and reappear. Once he dropped it on the floor and when he went to retrieve it, the twins psychically moved the coin from his reach. He thought that his foot had accidentally kicked the coin a few inches away. When he walked over to retrieve it, the twins lifted the coin and then let it fall. Joseph stared at the twins.

Lindy watched the encounter from a distance.

Joseph turned and looked at her. "Whoopee!" he exclaimed. "Oh my, God, they can levitate. Do it again," he pleaded with them.

She didn't scold or stop them. They gauged her reaction to him and knew he was safe. The twins, delighted with the attention, lifted the coin from the floor and dangled it in front of Joseph.

"Occult magic, this is pure levitation. They used their aura body or bio-electric field by interacting with the energy field of the coin," Joseph exclaimed, not taking his eyes off them.

Joseph told her about his claircognizance abilities, he had a high acute sense of knowing things. "When I was a young boy, my teachers thought I was smart, but I never studied; the answers to quizzes would pop into my head as long as I didn't analyze or doubt them."

He also shared his dreams to unravel the mysteries of the universe and help others to explore their psychic gifts. At 1: 00 a.m., he stood at her front door apologizing for keeping her up.

"Promise me you'll let me come back."

"Of course, Joseph."

"You were right that our meeting wasn't a coincidence but synchronicity. I looked it up."

"You looked up our meeting?" She looked at him quizzically.

"No, the word synchronicity. As a psychiatrist, I should have known that it was coined by Dr. Carl Jung and means the occurrence of two or more events which are causally unrelated happening together in a meaningful way."

"My meeting you on the elevator was not a coincidence?"

"I'm treating the mother of a woman who I went to medical school with, who happened to visit the hospital and be on the same elevator with me. You tell me."

"Time will tell. Goodnight, Joseph."

Chapter Forty-Two

"They're dirty devil cards and I won't have anything to do with them," Margaret said, sitting across from Dr. Lopez with her arms crossed over her chest and her mouth so tight it looked like a straight line.

He's out to get you.

Dr. Lopez shook his head as he shuffled the cards and laid them face down on the table. "These are called Amieler or ESP cards that were created by Dr. J. B. Rhine and Karl Amieler of Duke University in North Carolina in 1930. They test for telepathy, clairvoyance and precognition."

False gods.

Her eyes narrowed as she pointed to the cards. "I know your kind, trying to trick me into worshipping a false god."

Turning the cards over, "Look at them," he said, ignoring her response. "The deck consists of twenty-five cards with five symbols imprinted on them: a square, a circle, a cross, and a set of three wavy lines."

Get away from him or he's going to put a spell on you.

"Oh Lord, don't put a spell on me. And I won't have anything to do with those symbols of the devil. Get them away from me. You're supposed to be my therapist not a charlatan. I want out of here."

"Calm down, Margaret, no one is going to do anything to you." Dr. Lopez quickly gathered up the cards and put them back into the box. He had tried three times to get her to take the test, but she'd refused. It was a standoff. "You're one of those rare people who are able to hear from the spirit world or outside the range of normal perception."

Margaret stared at him with a blank look on her face.

"What I'm trying to tell you is that it's okay to be a clairaudient. It doesn't make you a devil worshiper." He paused so she could absorb what he was saying.

"And you need to read your Bible—Matthew—and join the church. That's your problem, you're not saved."

"I'm your doctor not your minister. You can start by taking your medication like you're supposed to. I don't want to use extreme methods."

Don't listen to him; he's trying to threaten you.

"So you can drug me and have your way with me like the other in here. I know what they do in places like this," Margaret spat.

Horrified by her statement and the look of contempt on her face, Dr. Lopez stood up. "We're done for today."

Margaret burst out laughing just like the voice in her head.

ଓ   ଓ   ଓ

Later in his office, Dr. Lopez spoke into his recorder about his session with Margaret earlier that day, omitting any references to the ESP Cards. There were no records of his sessions with her on parapsychology or his unorthodox treatments of trying to read minds or seeing into the future. Instead his notes reflected the emotional work he did with her regarding her dysfunctional childhood. He made inroads into that area of her life. He used her notebook and her mother's letters for her to see and accept the truth of her childhood, starting with her earliest memories, working to the present.

Margaret had come a long way since that early spring day when she'd been admitted, but today was a setback. Still shocked from his last session with her, he tried to figure out what had triggered her negative reaction. Was it all the talk about her clairaudience? He'd touched on a sensitive area and she was fighting back. She didn't want the voice to go away or the voice didn't want to go away. But time was running out.

They were in the middle of summer and he'd received several short, long and nasty calls from Detective Sullivan inquiring about Margaret's mental stability to handle questioning. Dr. Higgs was also pressuring him for a report. But he was determined that he wouldn't release her until she was fit enough to give a statement and face the consequences of the shooting.

Chapter Forty-Three

Lindy's eyes popped open and she adjusted her sight to the partial darkness of her room, bits of light filtered in from the street. She glanced at the time on her new digital clock—2:30 a.m. Lying there, she remembered the events of the previous weeks. She admitted that Joseph had captured her attention with his unorthodox ways of doing things. Her mother's uncanny behavior toward her didn't upset her as much as the photo in the July issue of *Jet* magazine.

Nick had his arm around a young beautiful Italian model in one of the photos. The caption stated they were vacationing together off the Greece islands. Lindy stared at the photo, feeling the old pain griping her heart. He'd called her. "Don't pay any attention to those photos."

"I thought you were in Russia."

"We flew to Greece to do a short shoot. They're publicity stunts."

"I don't know what to believe."

"Believe me, baby. I love you and will be home soon."

His words didn't console her as much as she would have liked. There had been so many of these incidents in the last four years.

As quickly as she'd awakened, sleep snuck up on her and within seconds she snored slightly from being rest broken.

Deep in REM sleep, Lindy heard the sounds of chirping birds and running water. She looked around at the tall trees, the waterfall and a pinto horse, grazing not far away. Startled more by her dark brown arms, long black braids, buckskin clothes, and moccasins than her surroundings, she ran over to the lake and looked into the water.

"Who am I?" she asked.

"Two Feet."

Swirling around, Lindy saw an old man; his reddish brown skin was dry and wrinkled; hair the color of fresh fallen snow as well as the buckskin clothing he wore and the horse he sat on. He held a white spear with feathers on the top of it.

The name White Dove floated into her consciousness as the lifetime of Two Feet flashed before her.

She saw White Dove teaching Two Feet how to perform sacred Sioux tribal dances and use the various ceremonial pipes for rituals and healings. Every so often the scene would switch, but White Dove was always the teacher and Two Feet the student.

White Dove stood at the head of a dying woman lying on a mat. His hands covered her eyes as he sang one of the Sioux sacred songs, cleansing the space and raising the vibration of him and the woman. After several moments, White Dove opened his arms wide and called on the Great Spirit to send great beings to rid the woman of the demon that had possessed her body, making her ill with fever and not able to sleep. Puffing on his pipe, White Dove let the smoke float above them, creating circles. Three beings came into sight and hovered over the woman's body. They began to tug at the center of her body; she began to jerk and scream. A dark creature ejected from her body. The beings formed a triangle entrapping it; they floated upward and disappeared. White Dove chanted as he moved along the woman's body, using his hands to make circular motions; sealing her body with the white light of protection. Lifting her head off the mat, he gave her several sips of a liquid from the pouch he carried across his chest. She lay back down and then dozed off to sleep.

White Dove took a sip out of the same pouch, and offered it to Two Feet. Lindy felt her own eyes become heavy with sleep.

Cଃ   Cଃ   Cଃ

Later that day, Lindy thought about the dream and wrote it down. With the children in summer camp at Sylvia's house, she went to the patio to finish reading the medical articles Joseph had given her weeks ago. He was driving her crazy with his insistence that she read them.

She dumped the contents of the envelope on the table and several photos fell out of it. *How did they get in there?* She wondered. Looking through the stack of papers, she found the Xerox copy of her mother's journal and letters.

He wanted me to find these photos of my family and my mother's things in the envelope, she surmised. Her face turned red, as she thought about the position Joseph had put her in. Lindy picked up the photo of her grandfather's smiling face, bringing back memories of him holding her as a child and teaching her the Bible.

She looked closely at the photo of her great-grandparents, and wondered what they were like.

Just like her mother, the photo of her grandmother Amanda held her attention. She put it on the table and stared at it. Untying her hair and shaking it loose, Lindy carried the photograph to the bathroom and held the photo next to her face and stared into the mirror. *I look like her.* Lindy wished she could have seen the color of her grandmother's eyes, but she already knew from what her grandfather had told her, they were the same as hers—blue/violet.

Lindy returned to the sun room and put the photographs back into the envelope. She dreaded what she was about to do. Promising herself she would read the papers from a professional perspective, but just holding the pages she felt chills run through her body.

He must feel very strongly about me reading it to risk our friendship and his professional career. She remembered Joseph's words. "The journal will also help you."

The first words of the journal hooked her when she read, *Three years ago, I wanted to die when my father died.* Lindy felt that way herself not only when her grandfather had died but also when Nick and she'd broken up the first time and didn't see each other again for ten years.

Half-way through, she stopped and wiped away the tears. As she continued to read, she traveled back into time and relived everything through her mother's eyes. Consumed with pain and anguish, she couldn't read anymore.

She called Joseph. "You tricked me," she blurted out, not even saying hello.

"You found the photos and papers?"

"I could have your license for this."

"You won't."

"Why did you do it?"

"I don't have a good answer to give you. Just call it my gut; the answers you're looking for are there. And, as I told you, I always follow my gut even if it gets me in trouble; eventually it works out fine.

"So, now you're my psychiatrist?"

"No, but I'm here for you as a friend."

CЗ CЗ CЗ

Lindy replaced the receiver, but it was still hot when it rang again.

"Hello, Kiddo. Are you having trouble with your phone line to heaven?" John chuckled.

I know that voice, she thought.

"John, the custodian or I should say, spirit guide," she said hesitantly.

"Both." He chuckled again.

"You're calling me by phone?"

"Why not? Wish they had them when I inhabited a human body."

"You were once alive?"

"Consciousness never dies. I've always been alive, just in and out of physical forms. Lived a good thousand or more lives. My favorite lifetime was one of a Holy man of the Sioux Indians."

"White Dove!" She exclaimed excitedly.

"Yours truly. Thought I'd brush you up on your healing skills. Sometimes we forget our gifts and skills when we reincarnate into a new life. But they're in your DNA; you just have to become aware of them and they will pop out like Jack in the Box."

Static cut into the phone line.

"I can't hear you."

The static was getting bad.

"The woman healed was possessed with demons."

"Like my mother." She could hardly hear him.

"Kiddo, you're learning fast. But one last thing, guess who's spirit inhabited this woman?"

Lindy remained silent for a moment. "No, not my mother?"

"When we don't learn the spiritual lesson the first time, it just follows us from lifetime to another until we get it."

"What should I do?" she yelled into the receiver.

"Deliverance."

The phone went dead.

Chapter Forty-Four

Dr. Lopez sat in his office contemplating the next steps for Margaret's treatment. Things weren't going as he'd hoped. She still resisted taking her medication and refused to participate in any treatment dealing with the paranormal. He felt they had come to a standoff. He read through her medical file again, hoping that he would find something to give him a clue on how to proceed. An hour later, he leaned back into his chair and put his feet on top of his cluttered desk. He knew what to do. Margaret's evening appointment was within the hour. Hurrying to get dinner, he felt excited again about her treatment.

ଔ   ଔ   ଔ

Margaret entered the new meeting room escorted by Rick, who remained standing by the door. Dr. Lopez was waiting for her, sitting in a chair next to a bed.

"Come in, Margaret, and lay here please." He pointed to the bed in a very forceful voice.

Complying with his orders, she lay down holding on to her Bible.

He looked at her sternly and said, "We are going to do something we did when you were coming to me as an outpatient."

Not saying a word, she never took her eyes off of him. Her hands began to tremble a little.

"Rick, you can wait for Margaret outside." Dr. Lopez waited until Rick left the room before continuing. "I'm going to relax you using the relaxation method I used in my office to talk to Natas."

"No, I'm not going…"

He quickly interrupted her. "Then you leave me no recourse, but to recommend for you to be institutionalized as Dr. Higgs recommends. I'll get Rick. " He stood up and walked toward the door; he grimaced.

"No, wait. I'll do it."

Composing his face, he turned around and walked back and sat in the chair. "Let's get started. You can lay your Bible next to you on the bed." He continued to give her commands.

Dimming the lights and making sure Margaret was comfortable, he started the relaxation technique.

"I want you to focus on a spot on the ceiling as I count down from ten to one. And whenever you're ready you may close your eyes. Breathe in and out," he said in a very soft tone.

He repeated several breathing exercises until he sensed that she was relaxed enough for the next step.

"Margaret, how do you call upon Natas?"

"I don't. He's always with me."

"Good. Then I'd like to speak to him."

There was a long pause and Dr. Lopez noticed that Margaret flinched. Was she resisting to responding or was it Natas?

"Hello, Natas."

The pause was even longer this time. Dr. Lopez sat there watching Margaret's body reactions, when he heard in a voice that was definitely not Margaret's. "What do you want, Sissy?"

Dr. Lopez almost dropped Margaret's file and his pen on the floor. Sissy was the name the older boys in his childhood neighborhood called him because he was physically small for his age and preferred to read than play ball.

"Who are you?" He tried to remain calm.

"You didn't fight Tony, because you were scared and a coward. You ran home to your auntie like a little girl, Sissy."

He hated that name. He was starting to feel agitated over an incident that happened when he was in junior high school when a group of boys had ganged up on him after school. The leader of the gang that put up his little brother to fight him; the boy was smaller than he and had his hands up ready to fight. He'd always wished that he'd stood up to the boy. From then on he was scared to go to school. His aunt and uncle had to talk to the principal to get the boys to stop harassing him. He was embarrassed.

"Who are you?" he asked again, raising his voice. The room had a foul smell, something he hadn't noticed before. He untied his tie and unbuttoned the top button of his shirt as sweat poured down his sides.

"You're always running away. Scared to live. You ran away from your mother, didn't you? She came to take you with her to California, but you hid behind your aunt's dress. Sissy."

"You don't know what you're talking about. I didn't know who she was." He found himself arguing with the voice.

"You ran away from the whore your uncle got you for your sixteenth birthday. You're not a man. Sissy."

The word sissy continued to vibrate through his head. *Oh no*, he thought, grabbing his head, feeling nauseated and sick.

Margaret laid there with her hands collapsed tightly over her stomach. I have to bring her out of this now if not for her shake then for me. Taking deep breaths, he willed himself to block the mocking voice out of his head.. He grabbed the bottle of water on the table behind him and gulped down most of it before pouring the remaining amount onto a paper towel; he put on his forehead.

Slowly he brought her out of the trance.

"You don't look so good," she said to him, swinging her leg across the bed to sit up.

"Do you know what the voice said?"

"The only thing I remember is the word sissy." She smiled at him.

Chapter Forty-Five

Lindy received an urgent phone call from Dr. Lopez. He was coming to see her within an hour. She had a bad feeling in her stomach from the way he sounded and the urgency of his visit.

"Joseph, come in," she said, shocked by his unshaven face, red eyes and wrinkled suit, which only heightened her concern. *Does he think I'm still angry about him putting the journal in the envelope? I told him several times by phone I'd forgiven him.*

"I need to talk and a cup of hot, black coffee would do me good."

"What happened?" she asked, not waiting for him to settle down as she prepared not only a fresh pot of coffee, but also breakfast.

While the coffee brewed and the smell of bacon teased his taste buds, he described the relaxation session with Margaret, not leaving out anything.

"The demon is getting stronger." Lindy frowned wearily.

"What do you mean?"

"It's taking over her mind. We'll lose her if something isn't done soon." She spoke with urgency in her voice.

"I have to get her back to where she was before this change in behavior and that means making sure the medication is getting into her system."

"That's only a temporary solution. When she's off the meds, the demon will re-emerge."

"She may never be off the meds. I wish you'd stop calling the voice a demon. This is about psychiatry and parapsychology and not about demons and Satan."

"It's all of those things."

"The next thing you're going to tell me is that she needs an exorcism and we need to find a priest." He looked drained.

Seeing his discomfort and tiredness, Lindy went over and stood behind him and began to massage his shoulders.

"That feels so good."

"You know our consciousness, or if you want to call it our soul, doesn't die when we are separated from our physical body."

"I've read a little about the afterlife."

"There are discarnate spirits that don't accept physical death, so they prey on incarnates to do their bidding or fulfill their addictions."

"How do these discarnates do this?"

"If a discarnate spirit was addicted to smoking, he or she will carry that addictive feeling into the afterlife with them. Constantly craving for something that he can no longer feel, he seeks out smokers. Let's say you're a smoker. The discarnate spirit will attach itself to your energy field, hoping and looking for a way to get inside of your field. Any physical, emotional, mental and spiritual weakness gives him that opportunity." She stopped rubbing his shoulders and poured herself a glass of orange juice.

"But your mother was a child when this discarnate spirit attached itself to her."

"Children are easy prey. Their energy fields are underdeveloped, especially children that are sickly and mentally, physically and emotionally abused. We wonder why our children have so many health and mental problems. This could be the reason. The discarnate is like a python snake wrapping around its victim, slowly squeezing the life out of him or her.

"Based on what you told me then why did Natas select her?"

"I don't know. Maybe the answer is in her notebook."

"Have you finished it?"

"No."

"Why don't we read them together and see if we can discover the root cause?"

"Okay, just one more thing."

"What?"

"I don't think Natas is his real name."

"Why not?"

"Because it is an anagram for Satan. The demon has been playing you."

He followed her to the patio, happy just to be in her presence. Lindy pulled the envelope out of a drawer of a small white wicker desk standing in the corner of the room. They sat down next to each other on the rattan sofa and put their feet up on the ottoman.

Her voice sounded sweet and innocent to him although she tried to keep it sterile and emotionless as she read aloud from the pages of the notebook. He practically knew the notebook by heart. He'd read and scrutinized it several times with and without Margaret. At various parts, Lindy's voice quivered but she kept reading.

Joseph braced himself; he knew the next section was going to be very difficult, if not impossible for her to read. She started again as he sipped on his cold coffee.

She was a little pink thing with big violet eyes, mostly bald but I could see fine sandy hair around the back of her neck. The nurse had put the baby in my arms for nursing. I looked up at the nurse and said, "This isn't my baby! Where's my baby?"

Not able to read anymore as streams of tears flowed down her face, he took the papers out of her hands and began to read. He'd watched her mother cry over the same words.

Lindy's tears became unbearable as he read the last section… *The voice kept telling me to get rid of her. The doctor gave me some tranquilizers. Ben came to me in the dream. He was dressed in his white coat that he wore at the hospital. Ben was holding the baby. He said to me, "Look at her, Maggie, his nickname for me, she's God's gift to us. So you have to love and protect her. Do that for me." Ben handed me the baby and smiled.*

Later I went to the baby's nursery and picked her up. Her eyes were opened. She smiled at me and my heart melted. I sat down in the rocking chair, and put her on my chest and just rocked back and forth. Papa and Deaconess Coleman found us like that. It was the closest I'd ever been to her.

Lindy curled up next to him, he stopped reading and took her into his arms. She sobbed quietly against his chest, as he rocked her back and forth. He kissed her gently on the forehead, then the cheek until he found her lips. She responded to him fervently. He untied her hair and ran his hands through it as it fell to her shoulders. Not stopping there, he let his hand fall on her breasts that he'd imagined touching so many times. He lifted her up and laid her on the sofa. "I don't want to rush anything, if you're not ready."

She kissed him again passionately.

Her body was exquisite—soft and smooth, and smelled of lilies and roses. He took his time to savor every inch of her as her moans of pleasure only excited him more. All the worries, thoughts and problems of yesterday vacated his mind as he could think of nothing but her.

She felt his hardness against her as he slowly, with tantalizing movements, slid into her. Hot sensations hurtled through her like bolts of lightning. She clung to him tightly as he buried his face in her neck, kissing her until they both forgot the demon and her mother as they got caught up in a rapture of paradise.

Later, when she was alone, she cried. *What have I done? I don't want to hurt Joseph.*

Chapter Forty-Six

She's coming.

Escape now.

They're going to kill you.

Margaret, restless from the voice repeating chatter all night, decided to take her medication. An hour later, the voice was still going strong with the same theme.

Escape now.

Or you'll die tonight.

Get up!

Escape. The voice hollered at her with such force that Margaret climbed out of her bed. She had to get away. Drowsy from the pill, she reached down to find her slippers and tumbled over, hitting her chin on the metal rail of the bed then the floor.

Ever Carol found her on the floor, with blood on her face asnd nightgown. She was unconscious.

Dr. Lopez was summoned.

Chapter Forty-Seven

Hot and humid, Lindy had the air conditioner on high, as she sped across town toward the hospital. The streets were deserted, but the closer she got to hospital the ladies of the night were on several street corners.

The nurse had called her as Margaret's next of kin to let her know her mother had fallen out of the bed and was under the care of the emergency physician on duty. Lindy knew she had to act now. She called Sylvia to come stay with the children.

The visitors' section of the hospital parking lot was empty. Pulling into the first available space, Lindy parked, grabbed her tote bag and ran to the entrance. She prayed she wasn't too late for what needed to be done. Dr. Lopez was waiting for her at the nurses' unit and, when he saw her, he pulled her into an embrace. He didn't care who knew how he felt about her.

"She's fine, sleeping," he said, looking into her strained face.

"How did she fall?" She backed away from him.

"Drowsy from the medication, she was probably trying to go to the bathroom, fell, hit her chin and had to have several stitches." He looked disheveled, having only left her hours ago.

"I want to see her."

"Follow me," He said as he led her to Margaret's room, apologizing that she had to come out that time of morning.

A few moments later, Lindy stood at the side of her mother's bed. Margaret looked thin and pale. Her chin was bandaged, but Lindy could see where blood had seeped through. A small ringlet of gray hair had fallen on her forehead. Lindy carefully moved the strand of hair off her mother's face.

Child of light she's mine.

"I need to be alone with my mother," she said to Dr. Lopez, looking at him gravely.

"What's wrong?"

Touching his hand, sending a current through it, Lindy whispered to him, "I don't have time to explain, except to say— deliverance is called for." Her eyes pleaded with him.

"I'm staying."

"Okay." She took a small leather notebook out of her large bag and stood there for a few seconds reading.

"What do you want me to do?"

"Move her bed out from the wall and put the rails down. And I can't be disturbed," she ordered him.

Dr. Lopez left the room and returned quickly. He told the night staff that he was going to do an all night stay with Margaret and didn't want to be disturbed. He had everything under control.

When he returned to the room, Margaret only had a thin sheet over her. Several quartz crystals were placed down the center of her body in a row, starting at her forehead and ending at her genital area.

"Don't just stand there, move the chair to the head of the bed."

She took out a small brass jar and lit the contents.

"What's that smell?" he asked.

"White sage. I used it to cleanse the room."

"Smells like grass. They're going to think we have been smoking a joint in here."

"Can't help that. I have to do this," she said, moving around the room with the sage and then holding it over Margaret.

Dr. Lopez coughed.

"You have to leave. I can't have any distractions and interference, besides it might be too dangerous for you to be here. You're not prepared to handle this kind of energy. He will go after you to divide and conquer us. Sit outside the door. Trust me." She folded her hands in prayer.

"Won't he come after you too?"

"Oh yeah, but I've powerful beings working with me," she said, thinking of Jesus, White Dove, the Elder Healer, and Mary Magdalene.

He left, wondering what in hell had he gotten himself into.

ಚ   ಚ   ಚ

Working quickly, Lindy sat at the head of the bed. She didn't know how long Margaret would be under the influence of the medication. And the second problem was the deliverance. Because of Margaret's religious beliefs, Lindy knew that a metaphysical exorcism wouldn't work for her. She needed to be delivered, something that her healing training by White Dove hadn't prepared her for. But her last conversation with John had put the idea in her mind to do it. She read over the dream again she'd recorded earlier in her notebook. Changes would have to be made, but she prayed that John or White Dove would be with her.

Lindy closed her eyes and cleared her mind of all outside distractions. It took a while, but she finally focused on the divinity of Margaret's spirit, mind, and body, seeing it pure and full of light as the demon hurled insults and names at her. Sighing heavily, Lindy recited the Lord's Prayer and at the end of it, using her right hand, she said, "Thou are…" and touched her forehead, "…the Kingdom," she touched her breast bone, "…the power," the right shoulder and "…the glory," the left shoulder.

The loud screaming of the demon tried to wear her down and scatter her energy.

You really don't believe all that garbage, now do you?

Murderer. You killed your grandfather with that voodoo mess.

Whore, sleeping around on Nick. You're worse than him.

She ignored its ranting and read several passages from the Bible provoking the demon.

She put the Bible on the bed next to her mother and took the jar of burning sage and blew the smoke above Margaret's heart. The smoke formed circles and floated up.

Lindy opened her arms and called in the great beings. Reciting from Psalms 24, verse 9, 10:

Lift up your heads. O' gates!
That the King of glory may come in.
Who is this King of glory?
The Lord of Hosts,
He is the King of glory.

Would they come? She asked herself.

They're not coming.

The smoke from the sage seemed to form the words, *Perfect love cast out fear.*

They're not coming, the voice continued to shout as Lindy repeated the words *Perfect love cast out fear.*

She bowed her head in prayer as she waited.

You wait for nothing.

You should be home with your children.

Aren't you worried about them?

I can check on them for you. It laughed hysterically.

Singing a few verses of *Amazing Grace*, she blocked it out. She focused on the healing White Dove had performed on the woman. He had no doubt. She blew more smoke over her mother's body, circling her several times before whispering, "I love you."

Lindy saw the tip of the wing first. It fluttered then a feather fell on the bed. She picked it up.

"Thank you Jesus," she called out as the Archangel of the white light of protection, Michael, descended over Margaret's bed and aimed the point of his sword at Margaret's chest. He swiftly carved into the air above her heart a flaming blue five point star that vanished inside of her.

Then he pointed the sword at Lindy's third eye and just as quickly carved the star over it. She felt a sting on her forehead as it entered her. Everything went dark.

Mysterious white and gold letters floated before her eyes as she read the soul history of the demon.

The soul came to the planet earth from Nibiru, called by the Sumerians, the Planet of the Crossing, before the great Deluge. He was a god of his planet, who succumbed to the materialistic trappings of earth by mating with the daughters of man thereby losing his royal status and powers. To regain his powers he made a pact with Satan to do his bidding—turning souls from the light. His name Anunnaki (those who came from Heaven to Earth) was changed by his new father to Natas.

She opened her eyes and watched as Margaret's body heaved up and then sank into the bed as a slimy, murky green foul form ejected from her body and landed on the tip of the angel's sword. Then he enfolded the screeching demon into its wings and disappeared as quickly as he'd come.

Overwhelmed by what had taken placed, Lindy barely heard Margaret moaning and tossing in the bed. The crystals fell off her onto the bed and floor.

Lindy quickly ended by using the same motion as White Dove by using her hand to make circular motions around her mother sealing her with a prayer of gratitude.

She picked up the crystals, made sure the sage was no longer burning before she put the container in her bag, and lastly she put the white feather inside her bag.

Kissing her mother on the forehead, she left out of the room feeling as if she was the one who'd been delivered.

Chapter Forty-Eight

Margaret was awakened by Nurse Ever Carol gently calling her name and shaking her shoulder.

"Are you alright, Ms. Margaret?"

Head aching and a dry mouth, Margaret sat up touching her chin.

"Why do I've a bandage on my chin?" She looked at the nurse, feeling disoriented.

"You fell last night. But the doctor checked you out and you're okay, just a little cut under the chin. Let me take your vitals," she said pumping up the bed to its usual height at her waistline.

Margaret lay there looking around the room as if she was seeing it for the first time. It smelled.

"What's that terrible smell?"

"It's awful whatever it is. I'll get housekeeping up here right away. Your vitals are fine."

"My head aches." Margaret swung her legs around to the side of the bed.

"Dr. Lopez ordered you a pain killer."

"Dr. Lopez was here last night?" She looked surprised.

"Oh yeah, he sat outside of your door all night," Nurse Ever Carol said, recording the vitals on Margaret's medical chart.

"If I wasn't that hurt, why was he sitting out there?" she asked casually.

"Hmm…" She smiled uncertainly at Margaret. "Maybe you should discuss that with him. Don't try to get out of the bed by yourself. I'll go and get your medication and notify housekeeping to come and clean this room. If I didn't know better, I would think you and that lady had a party in here."

She scurried out the room before Margaret could question her about her last remark.

Margaret picked up her Bible that lay next to her on the bed and not on the nightstand where she usually put it before retiring for the night. She waited for Ever Carol to return but Rick brought her medication and helped her to the lady's room. She dressed and sat up in the chair with every intention of praying and reading her Bible. But feeling joyful but bone-tired within seconds, she was asleep again until she heard her name being called a second time.

"Mrs. Pierce, wake up."

Margaret looked into the face of Dr. Higgs. This was the first time that he'd come to see her. She smiled nervously, waiting for the voice to tell her what to do. But it never came.

"How are you?" he asked, motioning for the other doctor to step forward.

Barely audible, she answered, "Good."

"This is Dr. Flowers, a new resident of the hospital. We're making rounds of the patients under our care. I was telling Dr. Flowers about why you are here—for shooting your husband and having hysteria fits. Am I right, Mrs. Pierce?"

Margaret felt all the joy from earlier ooze out of her body. She struggled to pick the right words to say to him. Her voice a little slurred, she gazed at him then said, "The devil."

Dr. Higgs looked at her and shook his head. "Mrs. Pierce, do you understand that you shot your husband and not some devil?"

"Don't answer that." Dr. Lopez came rushing into the room looking fiercely at Dr. Higgs and the resident.

"Dr. Lopez are you forgetting who I am? Would you please answer my question, Mrs. Pierce?"

Slowly Margaret lifted up her head, feeling a surge of energy flowing through her mind and body.

"God told me there would be those who would test me but He would be by my side if I just have faith, and not give into the devil's temptation. The devil will appear, wearing sheep's clothing, but don't be fooled by it. So, get thee behind me Satan." She pointed her finger at Dr. Higgs.

"We have seen and heard enough," he stated, walking over to Dr. Lopez and whispering in his ear. "Change your clothes man, you reek of grass."

Too dumbfounded to respond, Dr. Lopez stood there until they left.

"That was quite a sermon you just gave," he said gently.

"He's a poor excuse for a doctor."

"And I think you let him know that."

She laughed, feeling the joy coming back into her body.

Dr. Lopez pulled up a chair next to her bed, tired from staying up all night. He'd never gone home, because he wanted to be there when she awakened. It seemed as though he was a little too late.

"I had one of those strange dreams."

"Tell me about it."

"An angel came and got me last night. He took me to a city paved in gold. But before I could go in, I had to face my fears in the house of darkness that stood on the edge of the city. I went into the house and it was full of screams and cries for help. It was so dark and smelly in there, I couldn't see anyone, but I felt their hands grabbing for me, trying to pull me down into the crevices of hell. Then a mirror appeared before me and I saw every judgmental and critical thing I'd done and said against myself and others. My Grandmother Hattie was sitting in her rocking chair in front of me, and I felt hate for her. She crumbled up in pieces right before my eyes. I screamed and fell to my knees, the dark beings were all over me and I sank deeper into their world. Then I heard singing, "I was lost, now I'm found." And a sweet voice said I forgive you and I love you. Hearing those words, I got up and forgave everyone in my life that had trespassed against me and asked their forgiveness in return. Then the angel appeared again and took me into the City of Gold."

"Is that all?" he asked, wishing he had his tape recorder.

"With my eyes wide opened, I walked down the gold paved streets as the sun shone brightly above. There were houses on either side of the street; each one had a name on it such as joy, peace, happiness, brotherhood. I stopped at the one that had the word joy carved in gold over the doorway. I walked through that door into a world of bliss. My mother and father and Ben, were waiting for me. I felt this tremendous amount of love coming from them. My grandmother..." Margaret choked up and looked at Dr. Lopez, who looked spellbound. "She thanked me for forgiving her. And then I felt the presence of an angel singing the song *Amazing Grace* to me. The dream began to fade and God said, 'Do my will, heal and teach wherever two or more gather.'"

"Anything else?"

"Yes, one other thing." She pulled a white feather out of her Bible. I found this under the cover, next to my heart.

ඥ   ඥ   ඥ

Not ready to go home, Dr. Lopez stayed at the hospital then in his office working late into the night. He leaned back in his chair and muddled over what Margaret had told him earlier that day. Had Lindy really summoned an angel to drive the demon out of Margaret?

He called Lindy and told her about her mother's dream and Dr. Higgs' visit and that he feared for the worst. "Tell me what you did to her?"

Lindy described the healing process she used for entity possession even including how she found out about her ability to do spiritual warfare and healing through a past-life vision.

"Anunnaki is the real name of the demon."

"How did you find out?"

"Archangel Michael opened my third eye and I was able to read the Akashic records, the recordings of all soul's life stories written in the ethers."

She told him the life story of Anunnaki and that he attached himself to her mother because Margaret was an easy target; she didn't love herself, except he underestimated her. Margaret loved Jesus and God. She became a challenge to him; he began to wear her down, always trying to get her to hurt others.

"This is unbelievable."

"Why is it so hard for you to believe that the battle between good and evil is real?"

"Because I can't see God or Satan. I'm a scientist." He sighed heavily, his voice sounding tired.

"Neither could you see the voice, but you believed in it," she retorted.

"One last question. Do you believe your mother intentionally meant to shoot Pastor Pierce?"

"I have no doubt in my mind she was being controlled by Natas and was upset by finding out my grandmother didn't abandon her. And what do you believe?"

"That the gun went off accidentally."

"Joseph, go and get some sleep. You can process all of this later."

Instead, he put a sheet of paper in the Remington typewriter and began to type Margaret's medical report he had to prepare for the court. After finishing, he found several small typo errors that he corrected with white out liquid before stuffing the report into his drawer.

Locking up the office, he walked toward the elevator, with his shoulders slumped, head hung down toward the floor as he shuffled along still thinking about Margaret's transformation. He wanted to work with Margaret a few more weeks to make sure she was ready for the outside world, not quite trusting mother and daughter's faith in an unseen God.

But time wasn't on his side.

Chapter Forty-Nine

Dr. Walker hoped that he wouldn't have to have a second meeting with Dr. Higgs and Dr. Lopez. But, Dr. Higgs had called him early Friday morning, practically shouting in the phone of his disturbing visit with Margaret Pierce.

"There is something terribly wrong with Dr. Lopez."

"What do you mean?"

"He's too involved with the Pierce's case. Personalizing it. He embarrassed me and questioned my authority to examine Mrs. Pierce. He's stepped over the line."

Now Dr. Higgs and Dr. Lopez were waiting for him in the conference room. He took his time as he finished his coffee and talked to his secretary about her elderly parents.

Entering the conference room, he acknowledged both men and sat in his usual place at the head of the table. Opening his leather bound notebook, he put the date at the top of the paper and then looked at Dr. Higgs.

"What's going on, Dr Higgs?"

"Humm, I had a chance to observe and talk to Mrs. Pierce yesterday and she isn't doing any better. I stand by my first diagnosis of paranoia schizophrenia."

"You set her up. And further more…" Dr. Lopez yelled out.

"Dr. Lopez, get a hold of yourself. There will be no yelling in here. We're here to determine what's best for our patient, Mrs. Pierce. Now, why do you come to that conclusion, Dr. Higgs?"

"She couldn't answer the basic questions I asked her. She is delusional; instead of answering why she's here she sermonized, and I thought that she was going to leap out of the bed and do me bodily harm."

"She wasn't unruly. You tried to bate her. It was the way you asked her the question."

"Dr. Lopez, I'm warning you, no more outbursts. You'll get your chance."

"What are you recommending, Dr. Higgs?"

"That she be institutionalized immediately," Dr. Higgs said, looking directly at Dr. Lopez, who looked contemptuously at him.

"How far have you gotten with her treatment, Dr. Lopez?"

"She has done remarkably well considering all the things that she has gone through. Mrs. Pierce always wanted to be a preacher..."

"We aren't here to hear about what she wanted to do in life. Is she ready to meet with the detectives?" Dr. Walker interrupted him.

"Yes," he said, with as much conviction as he could.

"And you still stand by your diagnosis that she is clairaudient... that is the right word?"

"Yes," he answered, thinking about Lindy's exorcism of the demon out of Margaret.

"Is she cured of the voice or voices?"

Dare he answer what he didn't know? "I believe she is not being haunted anymore.."

"You believe, but do you know, doctor?" Dr. Walker wrote a few notes on his pad.

"Do we know anything definite in medicine until we try various ways to cure a patient?"

"You don't know."

Dr. Higgs poured himself a glass of ice water and took a long drink; he was pleased that Dr. Walker had finally come to his senses and seeing things his way.

Leaning back in his chair, Dr. Walker paused for a moment before proceeding with the meeting. Both men sat there staring into space, each lost in their own thoughts of what should happen.

"Dr.Lopez, you have one week to get her ready to see the detectives or arrange for her to be institutionalized. I'll be leaving for vacation at the end of next week and I want this matter resolved before I leave."

Chapter Fifty

Dr. Lopez cleared his calendar for the week to work only with Margaret. The adrenaline was running high in his body. He knew his career depended on Margaret's outcome. Dr. Higgs wasn't going to let this go.

He found Margaret sitting in the Day Room with Rev. Pennybacker, who had faithfully come every day to see her, reading the Bible with several other patients around them. Knowing this wasn't a good time to pull her away; he sat down nearby to listen to what they were saying.

"If I've said or hurt anyone here, I ask for your forgiveness." Margaret paused for a second and looked around the group.

He thought she'd looked directly at Nurse Ever Carol and Rick who were both working the day shift.

The loud clapping of the staff and patients made him wish that the two doctors he'd met with earlier that week could be present.

Maybe the coming week of working with her won't be as bad, he thought. It was the beginning of the weekend and he was going to see Lindy later that evening. Yawning, he decided to go home and take a nap. *God seemed to have everything there under His control,* he thought, laughing to himself.

Chapter Fifty-One

Lindy was going out on a date with Joseph Lopez, after telling herself not to encourage his advances. She couldn't resist his tender eyes and sexy smile.

Shelving guilt in one of the many compartments of her brain, Lindy focused on pleasure. Her last conversation with Nick didn't go well. He was back in Russia, complaining about the cold and wishing he was at home with her and the children. When she told him about the children's latest levitation feat, his reaction was cool.

The medium-sized quartz crystal that was normally placed on the mantel of the fireplace shattered in several pieces. One piece floated up and dangled in front of her, she told him, then fell to the floor. The twins had levitated together. They were very strong as a team.

"How can they lift things into the air and make them fly about?" Nick asked his voice full of skepticism.

"I told you it's called PK or psychokinesis. They are able to move things with their minds and not by physical means."

"Most normal children just reach for things."

"Normal children? Are you inferring that something is wrong with them?" she asked, feeling herself getting upset.

"You know what I mean."

"No, I don't, please explain."

"I'm sorry, baby. It's just that this is a lot for me to handle. Have you forgotten I'm in Russia? We'll figure this out when I get home."

All of a sudden she didn't look forward to that day.

Lindy dabbed a drop or two of perfume on her neck, between her cleavage and wrist. *I'm not having sex with Joseph tonight. We're just going to dinner,* she told herself several times.

Slipping the green sun back dress on over her black strapless bra and panties, she reached behind her to zip it up. The dress fit perfectly; she'd returned to pre-birth weight through doing yoga.

He arrived on time with flowers and a bottle of red wine. Quickly placing the flowers in a vase and the wine in the refrigerator, she made small talk. "I don't know anything about you. Where are you from?"

"DC."

"The name Lopez, it's Latino."

"You're wondering how a black boy could have a Latino name," he teased her.

"I know there are Afro-Latinos."

"My mom is Panamanian and my father, one of those soldiers who were stationed in Panama. She got pregnant and he was shipped back to the states."

"You don't know him?"

"I've no idea who he is. And I was raised by my aunt and uncle."

"And your mom?"

"She went off to Hollywood to become a star but instead died under the stars."

"Oh, Joseph, I'm so sorry."

"I was very young and don't remember her at all."

"We both have been abandoned by our mothers."

"You were emotionally abandoned, but not physically. I promised myself I wouldn't talk about work tonight."

"I'll allow you ten minutes to talk shop."

Walking to the car, he told her about Dr. Higgs' accosting her mother, the meeting with him, and then observing Margaret in the Day Room.

He took her to Blues Alley, a jazz club, in Georgetown, where they dined on shrimp, lobster and champagne, and listened to the soulful music of a jazz quartet.

As hard as they tried not to talk about Margaret, she kept surfacing in their conversation.

"She actually asked people to forgive her?" Lindy couldn't get over what he'd shared with her about her mother.

"Yes, she said if God can forgive so can she."

"Do you think she is ready to see me?"

"That I can't answer until I work with her next week."

Later, they walked around Georgetown, window stopping, watching the street musicians and dancers, and ending with an ice cream sundae. Walking back to the car in the balmy weather, he grabbed her hand and held it tight.

He drove slowly back to the house, with Barry White singing softly in the background. When they arrived at the house, he didn't pull into the driveway; instead he parked the car at the curb and kept it running.

"This has been one of the best times of my life." He turned to her.

She reached over and turned off the car and got out.

He followed her into the dark house and reached for her, kissing her gently on the lips then with more passion.

His hands were everywhere. She didn't even know when he'd unzipped her dress. Pulling off her dress and bra, he held her back from him for a second before he took one breast at a time into his mouth. Lindy closed her eyes and let him tantalize every nerve in her body.

"Joseph," she tried to tell him not to fall in love with her, but couldn't complete her sentence as he pulled her closer to him. Joseph knew where to touch her with his tongue and hands to bring her pleasure. Somehow they managed to get to her bedroom and she didn't want him to stop as she muffled her cries of pleasure.

Chapter Fifty-Two

"Tell me what's going on with my husband and the church?" Margaret asked Rev. Pennybacker, as she nibbled on the fried chicken he'd brought from the church's repast. They were sitting in their usual space in the Day Room. He had just finished praying with her and the others that wanted to join in that Sunday afternoon.

"Pastor Pierce is fine. He's back to preaching."

"Still boring?"

He laughed.

"Has he asked about me?"

Rev. Pennybacker decided it was best to be honest with her. She had to find out sooner or later that he didn't want her to come home. "No."

She cringed.

"What are people saying in the church?"

"The usual gossip; because they don't know anything," he said, not telling her about all the negative gossip surrounding Fanny. She didn't need to know that now. He was worried that the detectives might find out and use this as motive.

"Papa would be so disappointed in me, winding up in this place and having people talk about me."

"Don't you worry about that. I'm sure your father would be very proud of you."

"And the board?"

"They're grumbling, wanting to bring closure to the media circus that keeps popping in and out of the church."

"You mean Grace Perry?"

"Right. She is a member of the church, but the woman doesn't have any scruples when it comes to a story."

"She's not going away until she gets what she want, the scoop."

"The board is also worried about the declining membership."

"Do they think it is because of me?"

"No." He reached over and patted her hand. "The church, like any organization, is going through a downward cycle. It needs to be revitalized. But don't you concern yourself with that now. Let's read about Abraham, Sarah and Hagar. I'm thinking about preaching about their story. I'd like to hear what you think about that?"

"I wish I could be there," she blushed. The thought, he's not our kind, surfaced in her consciousness and left as quickly as a train passing through a small town.

Chapter Fifty-Three

On Monday morning, Margaret waited for Dr. Lopez in her room. The nurse had informed her he planned to meet with her at 9:00 a.m. sharp. It was now a quarter past nine, and he was late, reminding her of her first appointment with him, so long ago, she mumbled to herself.

He came rushing into the room, looking quite fresh and rested.

"Good morning, Margaret," he greeted her exuberantly.

"Got a piece this weekend, uh?"

Shocked by her statement; he didn't know how to respond. Pulling up a chair next to hers, he asked how she was feeling.

"Calm, peaceful and apprehensive."

"Why apprehensive?"

"I don't know what the future has in store for me. You believe in that crystal ball stuff. What does your ball tell you?"

"It tells me we have one week left. Then a decision has to be made whether you'll be institutionalized or face the courts."

"You don't give me much of a choice? Mental institution or jail?"

"Where should we start?" he mumbled to himself.

"How about the night you sat outside my door."

He wondered how much he should tell her. He didn't want her to get hysterical once she found out about Lindy, nor did he want to lie to her.

"This is a very delicate matter."

"This delicate matter you're speaking about is my life. I know something happened and I want to know what?" she pressed him.

"A good friend of mine, who wishes to remain anonymous, worked on you."

"Worked on me how?"

"She removed anything that was in your system that shouldn't have been there."

"Don't play games with me, Dr. Lopez. You're talking about Lindy and that evil Natas."

"Yes."

"How did she get rid of him?"

He told her everything, watching closely for any signs of distress. When he finished, he braced himself for the worse. He could see Dr. Higgs gloating, "I told you, she'd to be institutionalized."

"Natas or Anunnaki, whatever his name is was trying to get me to turn to the darkness. All these years I've been running away from the devil, and the more I ran the more he came after me."

"Indulge me and tell me the story of Satan."

"Where have you been all your life? Probably had your head in those medical books and playing with those devil cards. The devil is pure evilness."

"You believe that the devil is real?"

"I can't believe you asked me that after what I've gone through."

He was agnostic, his knowledge about religion was limited and he didn't believe in God and Satan, until maybe now. He'd refused to attend the Catholic Church of his uncle and aunt's.

"Don't you know the story of Satan? He wanted to be God and have God's powers. You can read this for yourself in Isaiah 14:12-15 and Ezekiel 28: 12-19 of the Bible." She spoke rapidly with authority in her voice.

"I enjoy hearing this from you. What happened to God's right hand man?"

"God cast Satan out of Heaven and he became the leader of all the fallen angels." She leaned in closer to him. "They live in the world beyond, yet always tempting us to rebel against God."

"Lindy said Natas was trying to turn you dark. Could he have been one of those fallen angels and not a soul from the planet Nibriu?"

Margaret thought before saying, "Quite possibly. Maybe the fallen angels are from Nibriu."

"Do you believe there are people who have the knowledge and skills to do spiritual warfare or heal?"

"My father was one of them. He would preach all day and night to keep the devil from entering..."

"But he couldn't stop the voice in your head that told you to do bad deeds?" He cut her off.

She started to cry. "No one has been able to do that..."

"Until now. Do you still hear the voice?" He stared at her intently.

"No, no," she said softly. "I haven't heard it since the night I fell."

"And you feel better?"

"My heart is opened."

He was elated about her healing at last. "I need you to do one favor for me and it's a big one."

She looked at him apprehensively. "What it is?"

Read a book this afternoon, called *Jesus Christ Heals.* Then we'll discuss it at our evening session. Will you do that for me, Margaret?"

"Why do you want me to read it?"

"It's the type of book that needs to be passed on to others. And I want to use it as a focus point as part of our discussion about the devil trying to control our minds. I believe that the book, along with your Bible, will strengthen your mind even more."

He left out that Lindy had given it to him to help him understand metaphysical healing principles.

C3   C3   C3

Margaret pulled up a comfortable chair in the Day Room and sat next to a window where the sunlight streamed in. She missed the smell of the flowers, the sun, and plain old fresh air. It was time to go home. The thought that she might be institutionalized or incarcerated made her flinch. She didn't want to think about that.

I'll do anything to get out of here, she thought. She wanted to go home so badly, she opened the book he wanted her to read, *Jesus Christ Heals* by Charles Fillmore.

Hours later, he found her in the same spot, deeply engrossed in the book with an open Bible lying on her lap.

"It's time." He tapped on his watch.

She bookmarked her page and followed him to the small conference room on the floor where they often met.

"So, what do you think?"

"I've never read a book except the Bible about the healing methods used by Jesus."

"Does he contradict what the Bible says?"

"No, but he says some outlandish things."

"Like what?"

"We can use our mind to transform the body, such as healing the cells and tissues of the body." Her voice no longer was weak and apprehensive, but full of enthusiasm and marvel.

He'd finally touched upon something that didn't turn her off about metaphysical teachings. Before he could say anything she continued speaking, "He talks about prayer and finding God in our minds."

"What does that mean to you?"

"Years ago when I told my first husband about hearing that negative voice, he told me I also heard a good voice and to focus on that. This man is saying the same thing as my Ben."

"I think you'll be able to hear the voice of God very clear now that you don't have all that static or negative chatter."

"I thought you didn't believe in God."

"I didn't until now." He smiled at her.

"May I keep the book tonight?"

"Yes. And Margaret, this is the healing method your daughter used on you."

He could still hear the doubt in her voice when she replied, "We have to be careful of the devil masquerading as an angel of light."

"At some point in time, we also have to trust others."

CB   CB   CB

The week sped by quickly for them. He continued to meet with her twice a day, letting her discuss anything that she wanted to. She always came back to the healing methods of Jesus. On Friday, she asked him, "What other books do you have on healing?"

"Hum, just that one. I can get you more."

"Yes, please do. Today, if you can."

He called Lindy and explained what he needed. "She wants books dealing with healing, like the Fillmore book you gave me. Nothing too difficult that would turn her off." He was still very sensitive about Margaret's healing. Trusting his intuition that she was healed, he also was listening to his medical logical mind to watch out for any signs of regression.

"I'll drop them off at the hospital on the way to pick up the twins from Sylvia's house."

"Are we still on for tonight?"

"Yes." She replied

"See you around 7:00 p.m."

"Don't be late. We have tickets for the circus. The children are excited."

Joseph hung up the phone and wanted to jump for joy. He had a family.

Cʒ   Cʒ   Cʒ

Later that night, Margaret sat on her bed and stared at the two books in front of her, both by Catherine Ponder: *The Secret of Eternal Health* and *The Hidden Secrets of the Holy Bible.*

If what Fillmore and Ponder said was true that you can create your life with your mind by using the universal laws, she wasn't going to no loony house or the big house. She only had a short time to learn all she could about the laws, but first making sure they were from God. She read late into the night until Nurse Ever Carol came into her room.

"I'm sorry." She grabbed Ever Carol's hand.

"He loved you." Ever Carol smiled broadly at Margaret as tears formed in her eyes. "You were all Ben ever talked about from the first day he met you. He told everyone at the hospital that he was going to marry you."

"Thank you," Margaret whispered to her as Ever Carol hurried out of the room.

Chapter Fifty-Four

Before going to see Lindy, Joseph put the finishing touches on Margaret's medical report and hand carried it to both Dr. Walker and Dr. Higgs' offices. He was two days early.

His report never mentioned clairaudience, demons, or anything metaphysical. He wrote about her dysfunctional childhood, post-partum depression and grief of her husband and father that caused her temporary delusional behavior. He recommended outpatient therapy and small doses of medication when needed. His final line—she was ready to meet with the detectives.

Chapter Fifty-Five

Detective Pete Sullivan and his partner found Margaret in the small conference room. She was sitting next to Rev. Pennybacker and another gentleman that he figured was her lawyer. In his business, he could smell a criminal and a lawyer before he entered a room. As far as he was concerned both had the same smell-deception.

He'd been waiting for months to interview Margaret Pierce about the night she shot her husband. Her testimony had been delayed too long, much too long for police work. Labor Day weekend was not far away and he looked forward to some time off. The streets were mean and ugly in DC and the only way to stay sane in an insane city was to go south with the family.

When the detectives approached the group, Rev. Pennybacker stood up, closed the Bible he'd in his hands and tipped his hat to the detectives as he left the room.

"Mrs. Pierce, how are you?" Detective Sullivan smiled and the fat around his neck got larger.

He'd photos of Margaret, but they didn't do her justice. The woman was beautiful, regal and didn't look her age. *What could that husband of hers have been thinking?* He'd done his homework and found that the gossip in the church and city was that Pastor Pierce was screwing his secretary, Fanny. Margaret tried to shoot or kill him because of his infidelity. There were also rumors that Margaret was a basket case and only got worse after her father died.

"Fine," she murmured.

Kyle Berg, her attorney, stood up and the three men shook hands.

"I need to find out what happened the night your husband was shot."

"What do you want to know?"

"Tell me in your own words what happened. I'm going to record it."

Margaret sighed and took a deep breath.

"Take your time, Mrs. Pierce. No one is here to hurt you." Her newly appointed lawyer, who was representing her pro bono, looked up at the detectives.

Detective Sullivan's partner switched on the recorder.

"It was late and my husband, Pastor Pierce and Fanny had gone to the board meeting. I asked him if I could come, but he said, no. Later, I heard a voice and went down to my husband's office. I went in, and then I was back in my room and I heard the voice again and a man came charging into my room and you know what happened."

Detective Sullivan stopped the tape and rewound it. He played it again and made a few notes.

"Do you remember calling a locksmith and letting him in to open your husband's office?"

"Locksmith? What locksmith?" She looked puzzled.

"On the day of the shooting you called Warren & Hoyt to come to your house. Does that name jar your memory?"

"No, sir, I don't remember calling any locksmith. They must have mixed me up with someone else."

"I don't think so. You gave Mr. Johnston a large tip. He remembers you." The detective had found the receipt on her nightstand in her bedroom.

"I don't remember," she said, blinking several times. When he mentioned the large tip, her eyes flickered.

"Why did you need to get into your husband's office?

"I don't remember."

Why didn't you just ask your husband to let you in?"

"I don't remember."

"Do you remember hearing a voice?"

"Yes."

"When was the first time you heard the voice?"

"I heard it after Alan and Fanny had gone to the meeting."

"Where did you hear it?"

Margaret looked at the detectives, then her attorney. "I went downstairs."

"Did you see anyone?"

"No."

"Did you hear the voice again?"

"At that time, no."

"So, when did you hear the voice again?"

"When I returned to my room."

"Someone was in your room?"

"No."

"But you'd heard a voice."

"Yes."

"Was it a man or woman's voice?"

"Sounded like a man."

"What did it say?"

"They lied."

"Hold up, the voice told you they lied?" he asked slowly.

"Yes."

"Who lied?"

"My father and grandmother."

"I thought your family was deceased."

"They are."

Stopping here, the Detective stared at her. "Mrs. Pierce who is the voice and where was he?" His patience was wearing thinner than the lawyer's mustache.

"What church do you attend officer?"

"Hum, uh… I'm Catholic, ma'am."

"Then you tell me if the devil is a person and where does he live?"

"I'm not following you," he said, looking over at his partner who had put his hand over his mouth to suppress his laughter.

"It was the devil, and he can live in our minds"

"Mrs. Pierce did you mean to shoot your husband?" He decided to change his way of questioning because what she was saying didn't make sense or did it?

Margaret broke down in tears. "Alan. He's a good man, not much of a preacher, but a good man. Papa liked him and said he would make a perfect husband for me. He wasn't like my first husband, Ben, but he was good to me in the beginning."

"Did you intend to shoot your husband?" he insisted.

Margaret looked at the detective. "It was Papa's gun. It brought back memories. I remember when Papa first got it. I was young and he told me never to go near it. He kept it in a brown case. I forgot about it until I saw the case in Alan's office. I carried it upstairs with me. It reminded me of Papa. I miss Papa. I heard the voice and people running. I was so frightened and then they came charging in my bedroom and…."

"And what?"

"The devil said, get rid of them."

"Your husband and Fanny."

"Of course not, the letters."

"What letters?" He was thoroughly confused by then.

"The letters my mother sent my father, and they were stashed away in the brown case."

He held up his hand, interjecting. "Where are these letters now?"

Margaret reached into her jacket pocket and pulled out three thin small envelopes. Dr. Lopez had given them back to her. She held on to them tightly.

"Mrs. Pierce, I'll need to look at the letters."

Reluctantly, she gave them to him.

The detective scanned the letters quickly. "I'm going to have to keep them."

"No, those are mine. Give them back," she demanded.

"I like a moment with my client," her lawyer interrupted.

The two detectives stood in the hallway as the attorney pulled his chair closer to her.

"He has to keep the letters, because they are evidence once you bought them into your story. In fact, it strengthens your story. You have done well, so just let's end it here."

He waved to the detectives to return to the room.

"I think this is enough, detectives. As you can see my client is a bit distraught and any further questioning will only aggravate her more. She has willingly cooperated with you and given her side of the story, plus you now have in your possession the letters. My office needs a copy of everything detectives. We'll have her sign the statement when it's ready. This interview is over." The attorney stood up and escorted Margaret from the room.

At the elevator, Detective Sullivan's partner looked at him and said, "So what are you thinking?"

"Lots of loose pieces that are not fitting in."

"Yeah, and what else is new?"

"They're covering up something."

"What does the Captain want you to do?" he asked, glancing at a nurse who had walked by them. He let out a low whistle.

"Close the case out," Walker replied.

"Why don't you do it, man? With all the crime we have in the streets, we don't have time to get involved with this church thing. The Reverend is okay and the wife is getting help. You know this could turn ugly?"

"I'm writing up my report and turning it over to the D.A. It's not my call, buddy."

"Just remember one thing."

"What?" he asked as they pulled out of the parking lot.

"The Captain's mama when she was alive was a member of the Mt. Olive Baptist Church and he was baptized there."

"That's what's wrong with this city. It's not what you did, but who you know."

Chapter Fifty-Six

Rev. Pennybacker didn't share with Margaret just how bad the distress in the church had become among the congregation. The members were distraught and worried about the bad press the church was receiving. They were the laughing stock of the DC community. Grace Perry seemed to fuel the situation. The gossip mill was at its highest level.

Phones were hot at night and tongues wagged. What was Mt. Olive coming to? Sister Margaret was locked up in a mental ward and no one could see her except Rev. Pennybacker. Not even her own husband had gone to see her. The board members were being pressured by their wives to get rid of Fanny. Behind closed doors they called her 'that heifer'. She'd brought disgrace and shame upon the church family. Knocked up and they didn't even know if the father was Pastor Pierce or Rev. Pennybacker. She was glued to both men.

When Rev. Pennybacker found out that the congregants thought he was the father of Fanny's baby, he decided to take action.

Something had to be done.

CB CB CB

His chance came the Sunday morning he was scheduled to preach before the onset of the Homecoming preparations. Rev. Pennybacker's strong alto voice rang throughout the church as he stood at the pulpit holding his hands up to the congregation, putting his heart in the refrain of *Blessed Assurance*:

This is my story, this is my song,
Praising my Savior all the day long;

He looked out at the people and saw sheep, his and the Lord's. The Lord had come to him right after that first sermon he'd given when Pastor Pierce had taken sick. He was ready to leave Mt. Olive for greener pastures when the Lord spoke to him and said, "There were no greener pastures than the one he was attending. Trust me," said the Lord, "And follow my word."

He always waited for the Lord to tell him what to do.

The music finally stopped and all eyes were cast on him. They waited as he cleared his throat and sipped from a glass of water.

"We all have a story. What we must ask is whether our stories are praising and serving God all the day long or doing the bidding of the devil?"

"Yeah, preach, bring it," someone in the congregation hollered out.

"So, let's look at the story of three of the most famous people in the Bible, Abraham, Sarah, and Hagar." Rev. Pennybacker looked into the bewildered eyes of Pastor Pierce and Fanny sitting in the first pew.

"Hagar, an Egyptian princess or slave-girl, we don't really know, became a part of the household of Abraham and Sarah, of the faith of Jehovah. Part of the household, one of the family, worshipped with them, lived with them. She slept with Abraham and bore him a son." He could see Pastor Pierce's face change from peace to fear. But that didn't stop him.

"Now this action was not unbeknown to Sarah. It was custom. She gave her husband, Abraham, the slave girl to do what she couldn't do. Give him a child—a story. Was this a story of sin? Should Abraham have refused Sarah's offer in spite of the current custom? What was God's divine promise to Abraham? He would give him the Child of Promise. And Hagar should have not yielded to such an unholy alliance merely to gratify any ambition she may have had." He looked directly at Fanny who squirmed in her seat.

"It is a story full of tears and unbelief in God's good for us." He paused and looked around the church. "The folly of people can cause so much hurt that impact on generations to come. Hagar bore Ishmael and Sarah bore Isaac creating a story of jealousy, separatism, guilt and blame.

"Think about all the tension and stress in Abraham's household—cruelty, lack of love and compassion. If God can forgive sinners so can we. We can start this second, this moment and ask for forgiveness. We can rewrite the pages of our story."

Rev. Pennybacker walked back and forth on the pulpit, stopping to stare out at the crowd and let his glance linger on Pastor Pierce and Fanny sitting in the front pew. Pastor Pierce had refused to sit on the pulpit on the Sundays that he preached.

"You can make what's wrong right by asking for forgiveness." Rev. Pennybacker started waving his handkerchief and singing, *This is my story, this is my song, praising the Savior, all the day long.*

The choir and the congregation joined in.

"I want to ask anyone who needs to rewrite his or her story today to ask for God's forgiveness and grace. Ask God to show you how to write a new chapter in life, a chapter full of love and compassion. Come on up to the pulpit and let the deacons lay their hands on you. Come on brothers and sisters," Rev. Pennybacker sung the last words. "Come on up to God…no matter what your story is today. God loves you. Come on up and be saved."

Perfect submission, perfect delight. The choir sang in the background. Fanny stood up.

Angels descending from above, echoes of mercy, whispers of love

Pastor Pierce grabbed Fanny by the wrist and tried to pull her back into the seat, but she yanked herself free. Head in the air, tears running down her cheek, she came forward and took Rev. Pennybacker's hand. The deacons surrounded Fanny as the congregation sang along with the choir; Rev. Pennybacker prayed and asked God to forgive Fanny's sins.

No one noticed until everyone had calmed down and returned to their seats that Pastor Pierce was gone.

CB   CB   CB

The next day Reverend Pierce submitted his resignation to the Board of Trustees. He'd hoped that they would reject it, but they didn't. Many of the members told him he did the right thing so that the church could move on. He received a call from Dr. Lopez, saying Margaret was coming home. He packed his belongings and moved in with Fanny, who had quit as secretary of the church.

Chapter Fifty-Seven

Margaret was up early. She looked around her hospital room as if she was seeing it for the first time. Today, she hoped it was the last time.

Memories floated in and out of her consciousness of what had happened over the last several months. She was frightened but also excited about starting a new life. A new life weren't her words but those of Rev. Pennybacker's. He was the one coming to take her home. Alan was gone. Rev. Pennybacker told her everything about Alan and Fanny. She never told him about the night she saw the two making love. Some things she decided never needed to be voiced.

Her packed suitcase was next to the door. Ever Carol came to see her for the last time.

"You take care of yourself, Margaret."

"What church do you attend?"

"I go to New Hope Baptist."

"Visit Mt. Olive when you get a chance. Rev. Pennybacker is a fine preacher."

"From the looks of him, I'll say he's more than a fine Preacher. Is he married?"

"No," she blushed.

"Young, but a good catch. Age is nothing but a number."

"I'll remember that."

The morning flew by fast as she prepared to go home and gather her thoughts for her discharge appointment with Dr. Lopez. Today was special and she wanted it to start off right. She was going home to Mt. Olive Baptist Church.

On bent knees, she prayed.

ᘓ   ᘓ   ᘓ

Rev. Pennybacker was as excited as Margaret about her coming home. He was at the hospital early. They sat together in the Day Room waiting for her session with Dr. Lopez.

"Sister Margaret, the members can't wait for you to come home," he told her as he took her hand in his.

"I'm a little frightened about seeing everyone," she replied lowering her eyes but not removing her hand. She felt safe with him.

"You don't have to be. The members of the church loved your father and they love you. Give them time."

"All I ever wanted to do was preach God's words, like my father and his father before him. I guess I should have been a boy."

"I would be sorely disappointed if you were born a boy. I think the good Lord knew what he was doing when he made you a woman. And I say amen to that because you're quite a woman." He smiled at her.

Margaret smiled back.

"And you never know what the Lord has planned for you. So, why not take it one day at a time."

"You sound like Dr. Lopez."

"Well, most ministers have a little psychology in them and most doctors have a little religion in them."

Lopez found them laughing together as if they didn't have a care in the world.

ଔ   ଔ   ଔ

"Excited about going home?" Lopez asked her minutes later. "Lots of mixed feelings floating around in my mind."

"That's to be expected. Just go slowly returning to your old routine."

"Okay," Margaret said, not sharing with him her plans for a new life.

"Heard any voices lately telling you to do bad things?" His gaze was intense.

"No, I locked it up."

"Good. Don't ever let it out. My report is filed with the police department and your attorney. I haven't heard anything yet. Now, we wait…I'll see you as an outpatient weekly. Take your medication. We'll re-evaluate your need for it after you have been home for awhile. Agreed?" He came from around his desk and stood in front of her.

"Yes." She smiled back at him.

ଔ   ଔ   ଔ

Margaret felt like a bride when she arrived at her home and church. Several cars were parked in the driveway and on the lawn. She'd thought she would return to a big empty house, full of ghosts and bad memories. Instead there was a wonderful, happy, joyous feeling in the air.

Margaret stepped out of the car and looked at the well-kept lawn. It looked just the way she liked it.

Several of the church sisters came running from the house, hollering, "Sister Margaret's home."

They kissed and hugged her.

"We have been praying for Sister Margaret. Thank you, Lord."

Margaret couldn't hold back the tears as they led her inside the house to get settled. They had prepared food for her for the rest of the week.

"I've something to share with you," Rev. Pennybacker said once they were alone in Pastor Pierce's old office.

"The board has appointed me senior minister." He waited for her reaction.

She ran to him and hugged him. "I'm so happy for you. I know it was you who got us through this awful mess."

Margaret walked around the desk, thinking how she was going to turn the office into something else, but she wasn't quite sure what.

"I have an office in the church," he stated as if he knew what she was thinking. "It's best."

"I agree."

Later that night, staying in the house alone for the first time in her life, Margaret couldn't sleep. She walked through every room, running her hands over the recently polished furniture, checking the floor for dust, but everything was spotless. Her nerves were still rattled, not even prayer and a glass of warm milk calmed her down. After hesitating several times, she dialed his number.

"I know it's late, but I'm a little..."

"Say no more. I'll be there shortly," Rev. Pennybacker said, quickly hanging up the phone.

Chapter Fifty-Eight

Four weeks later Margaret stood outside the church's conference room ease- dropping on what the board members were saying about her. Rev. Pennybacker had told her to wait in the house while he presented to the board his recommendation to have her ordained. Not able to contain her anxiety, even with the medication, she quietly positioned herself outside of the door.

"I'll be speaking for the trustees and deacons," Trustee James Henderson stated. "Sister Margaret just got out of the psych ward of the hospital and you want to ordain her now?"

"Yes," Rev. Pennybacker answered.

"How do we know she still not crazy...I mean still ill?" He didn't like the look on Rev. Pennybacker's face.

"How do we know anything?"

"She shot Pastor Pierce and the town is still talking about all that mess," Dr. Henderson shuddered.

"No matter what you do people are going to talk. I only listen to God and God told me to ordain her now."

"She's a woman."

"And?" Rev, Pennybacker raised his eyebrow.

"You know in the New Testament the pastoral office is limited to men. The apostle Paul told Timothy: *I do not permit a woman to teach or to have authority over a man, but to be in silence.* 1 Timothy 2:12. It does not get any clearer than that."

"In a society that viewed women as property and inferior, Jesus elevated them and had women disciples. Now who do we follow Paul or Jesus?"

For a few seconds no one spoke.

"She hasn't gone to ministerial school for training."

"She had the best teacher, I'm sure you'll agree, her father Reverend Perlie Johnson. Ask her about any verse or passage in the Bible, she can quote it to you and give you an interpretation. How many here can do that? I see no one is raising his hand. She knows the working of a church better than anyone here. The church has been her life and God has called her to preach."

"Rev. Pennybacker you were recently hired as senior minister. We think it's pretty bold of you to force this ordination down our throats. Some of us will leave the church if you insist on carrying this ridiculous recommendation forward."

"May I speak, Reverend?" A voice from the back of the room spoke out.

"Let me bring you up front Deacon Coleman, so everyone can hear you better." Rev. Pennybacker hurried to the back of the room and pushed the deacon to the head of the table.

"I'm a founder of this church, with Sister Margaret's father. I've watched her grow as if she was my own daughter. It hasn't been an easy path for her, not having a mother to raise her, Rev. gone all the time after her grandmother died. She had to practically raise herself and even worse, she carried this church."

Margaret continued to stand at the outside of the door listening to Deacon Coleman.

"She took on the role of First Lady of this church, performing all those functions, taking care of all the church's needs and maintaining excellent financial records. Rev. always included her in the board meetings, even when she was a teenager. Taught her the Bible; she could read it before she could read her primer. Gentlemen, she's not only qualified, she's over qualified." He took a large breath.

"Let's vote," Rev. Pennybacker said, looking around the room.

Margaret walked briskly back to the house and went into the kitchen and made herself a cup of coffee. She didn't have to wait to hear the results of the vote. Those old fogies would never let her be a pastor. *I won't fall apart*, she told herself. There was still a way. Charles Fillmore's Unity Church allowed women to become ministers and preach. She'd been studying everything about their religion. They were Christians. She could get her ordination and preach the way she wanted, maybe becoming an Evangelist. Deep into her thoughts, the ringing of the phone brought her back to the present moment.

"Mrs. Pierce, this is attorney Kyle Berg?"

"Yes."

"Sorry to call you so late, but we got a call today from the D.A. office that they are moving forward to bringing charges of assault with a deadly weapon against you."

Margaret swallowed hard.

"I have to go to jail?"

"Not unless you're convicted. But the first step is a hearing for a judge to determine if there is enough evidence for a trial."

"When is this hearing going to take place?"

"Monday, September 10th at 10:00 a.m. I'll be in touch with you."

Margaret hung up the phone.

Rev. Pennybacker found her sitting at the kitchen table crying. He kneeled next to her and put his arm around her. "Why are you crying?"

"The lawyer just called me. The D.A. is bringing assault charges…against me… and there is going to be a hearing…." she said, speaking incoherently between sobs.

"Sh…don't cry. We can't have the soon to be newly ordained minister crying. She has to be strong enough to help others through their troubles by demonstrating inner strength. The board voted in favor of your ordination."

Margaret let out a holler that came from the depth of her soul.

Chapter Fifty-Nine

Dr. Joseph Lopez had become a steady part of her life and she was caught between Nick and him. Lindy didn't know what to do. Sitting in her bedroom, staring at the diamond ring that was still in the box, she heard a tapping on her door.

She got up and opened her bedroom door, thinking it was Michael. John was standing there with a mischievous look on his face. He walked past her and sat in one of the chairs next to the window.

Lindy, dressed in her nightclothes, sat opposite him in the other chair.

"Have you been having fun, kiddo?" He gave her a wink.

"John, don't you take anything seriously?"

"Why should I? My theme song is *row, row, row your boat gently down the stream, merrily, merrily, merrily, life is but a dream*," he sang the nursery rhyme. "You know, I helped the writer of that little piece come up with that."

At this point in their relationship, she didn't doubt him.

"And what can I help you with? You haven't been reaching out to me lately. Think you can handle it all by yourself, uh?"

A flood of thoughts flowed through Lindy's head. Things had gotten out of hand with Joseph. She didn't mean for it to go that far. He was such a wonderful man, but she couldn't get Nick out of her mind.

Another article had popped up in *Ebony* magazine with Nick and the same long-legged blond model standing very close together at a function in Italy. *So much for Russia*, she thought.

She didn't know if their presence was part of publicity stunts or if he was actually involved with her. Searching his face for hidden clues was useless, he was expressionless. Nevertheless, it didn't stop her from getting jealous and angry.

"I'm torn between Nick and Joseph?"

John chuckled. "I support the spiritual awakening of your soul. I'm not a modern day matchmaker. But I'll tell you this. Love is more than a tumble in the bed; it is the opening and expanding of your heart. When you know and feel that within yourself, you'll know the spirit of love in you and others. I say check out what's going on with you?"

She watched him dematerialized. It always fascinated her, even though she'd watched her spirit guide, Mary Magdalene, do it numerous times.

Lindy put the ring back into her jewelry drawer and pulled out a sheet of her personalized stationary from her nightstand drawer. Betty had given her the expensive stationary before going away.

"There's no excuse for you not to write me," Betty said to her.

"I'm the one who's supposed to be giving you a going away gift."

"You have already; I'm going to be the godmother of twins."

"Then hurry back to us."

Tears forming in her eyes, thinking about the task ahead of her, she knew in her heart that it had to be done in order for her to move forward with her life.

Lindy picked up her pen and began to write.

Dear Nick,
This is probably the most difficult thing that I've ever done. I won't go into the details of how and when, but Paul, my ex-husband, is the biological father of Gabriela and Raphael. We had the necessary test done for paternity. I've been remiss for not telling you sooner. Please forgive me. I'm sending the ring to your Paris address.
I need space at this time to focus on my life and what I want to do. I'll be in touch regarding visitation for Michael.
Lindy

Lindy read the letter several times before folding and sticking it into an envelope. Not wanting to sound angry, she deliberately left out about his philandering and non- acceptance of her and the twins' spiritual gifts. She would rather talk to him in person; but she didn't want him to come home, not yet anyway. She didn't want to lose Joseph, who offered her the comfort, support and love that she needed in her life now. He would be there for her and not off on another assignment with a long-legged model.

Sealing the envelop, she put it under the ring box to mail tomorrow. Dialing Joseph's number, she smiled.

Chapter Sixty

Margaret sat in her white robe on the right of Rev. Pennybacker, who wore a purple robe, on the temporary pulpit in the tent for homecoming. It was surreal to her; none of this could be true. It was the second Sunday in September and Homecoming. She was being ordained as a pastor and her court hearing was tomorrow and she might be going to jail. Her ordination had caused quite a stir in the church and the Baptist convention even though Mt. Olive was an independent church. A few of the deacons left the church and even some women.

"Some of the deacons and trustees are resigning. Are you sure about this?" She'd asked him just before her ordination.

"People are entitled to worship wherever they want to."

"I'll understand if you don't do it."

"I'm only following what God told me to do and not deacons and trustees, Rev. Margaret." He smiled at her.

She looked out at the congregation. The tent was packed with people. She recognized many of the faces. Deacon Coleman was seated with the deacons. He smiled at her and she nodded her head.

Margaret was excited to play a major part in the Homecoming services. For the first time in her life, she was nervous being in front of so many people. Rev. Pennybacker wanted her to do the opening prayer and read scripture. After her ordination, she would speak about God calling her to preach the word. With trembling hands, Margaret wiped away the perspiration that had formed on the top of her lip.

It was a beautiful summer day but hot and humid and the air conditioning units set around the tent were no match for Mother Nature. She was glad she wore a thin cotton dress under the robe and had cut her hair, for the first time in her life, off her neck.

The combined choirs from two visiting churches were singing as the people still poured into the tent. She looked out at the audience again and saw a woman, three children and man walking down the center aisle. Her heart skipped a beat. Lindy, holding the hands of a little girl and boy, was coming toward her and the older boy was walking along- side Dr. Joseph Lopez. He could have been his son. They looked like angels from Heaven dressed in all white.

They stopped half-way down the center aisle on the red streamer and looked at her. The music stopped as Margaret stood up and walked to the edge of the pulpit with Rev. Pennybacker following behind her. Everyone turned to see who or what they were staring at.

The two women stared at each other. A thousand unspoken words flew between them. Margaret turned and looked at Rev. Pennybacker who nodded his head and smiled. She stepped down off the pulpit. Lindy let go of the kids' hands and ran into the opened arms of her crying mother.

            ෪ ෪ ෪

Standing in the center of the deacons, Margaret remembered years ago when another set of deacons had surrounded her to pray the devil out of her after she'd cut off her hair. Now they laid their hands on her shoulders and head, giving their blessings and prayers. She'd waited all her life for this moment and it was overshadowed by what lay before her tomorrow.

In a daze, she stood at the lectern before the audience, glancing every now and then at her daughter telling her story, the same one Deacon Coleman had told the board.

Chapter Sixty-One

Rev. Pennybacker drove the car through early morning traffic and Margaret sat by his side staring right ahead. He grabbed her hand; it was cold, not from the air conditioner but fear. Her court hearing was at 10:00 a.m. in the courtroom 308.

"The whole time I was in the hospital I promised myself if I ever got out, I wouldn't take any of this—she nodded to outside of the car—for granted."

"DC is a beautiful place."

"May I put down the window for a few seconds?"

"Of course."

Margaret rolled down the window and sniffed the hot, humid air. It was September and the temperature was expected to be in the nineties. *Would today be the last day of my freedom?* she thought.

"Did you finish Fillmore's book?" she asked trying to take her mind off her predicament.

"I did, kept me up most of the night."

"The same happened to me. What do you think about the mind controlling your life?"

"I believe God controls our lives."

"Fillmore believed that people create their life experiences through their way of thinking and using positive statements can keep the mind focused on good outcomes. His wife cured herself of TB using affirmations."

"Are you trying to tell me that you have an affirmation?" He glanced at the clock on the dashboard. They had run into some traffic, but he'd allowed for the rush hour.

"I see myself walking out of the courtroom a free woman. I've been saying and writing it since I received the call about the hearing."

"Do you really believe that saying or writing a statement repeatedly affects the outcome of an event or situation?"

"I've nothing to lose. I'm testing the use of affirmation today."

"Trusting God is the most powerful thing you can do."

"God is omnipotent and affirmative statements strengthen our connection to God."

"Maybe you should consider preaching about this one Sunday."

"I plan to, if I'm not preaching in the jailhouse. But are our people ready for talk about mind control and affirmations? We already lost several members because of my ordination."

"I met this older heavy-set gentleman, reminded me of Santa Claus, a couple of weeks ago, when I was leaving the hospital after a visit with you. We started talking as I walked to the parking lot. Don't ask me how we got into religion, but I figured because he saw me carrying a Bible." He paused for a second.

Margaret smiled.

They had arrived at Superior Court on 5th and E Streets, and without any difficulty, he found a parking space, which he believed was the first blessing of the day from God.

Turing to face Margaret, he continued his story. They had plenty of time before entering the courthouse. "He told me that he'd recently talked to a woman who told him God had a plan for humanity; for all of his children to come together in oneness, love and compassion."

"Sounds like what Fillmore and Ponder are talking about in their books."

"I thought about what he told me and realized that we have a divine calling to make Mt. Olive a church of oneness, love and compassion." He took her hand in his. "I want a good woman by my side, teaching and preaching God's Word; helping me to open the hearts of our people to be a part of God's plan. Do you understand what I'm saying, Margaret?"

She nodded, looking out of the car window at the people hurrying into the courthouse wondering if they were in the same predicament as she was. "But first I have to see what's God's plan is for me." Reluctantly, she pulled down on the car handle and stepped out of the car.

ଔ ଔ ଔ

The lawyer who had met with Margaret and the detectives was replaced by one of the senior partners, attorney Larry Griffin. Impeccably dressed, medium height, thin, distinguished man was waiting for them outside of courtroom 308.

"Good morning, Mrs. Pierce," he said, shaking both her and Rev. Pennybacker's hand. "I'm Larry Griffin. We have talked several times on the phone and I've reviewed your case thoroughly. As I told you I don't think you have anything to worry about."

"God be willing, I'll leave out here a free woman."

"The judge is hearing another case and will be with us shortly. I suggest you go down to the cafeteria and get some coffee. I'll have someone come and get you when she's ready."

ଔ ଔ ଔ

The thought of waiting made Margaret more edgy than anything. They took the long escalator two levels down and entered the cafeteria. Grabbing on Rev. Pennybacker's sleeve, she froze in place. Alan and Fanny were sitting at one of the tables talking. She hadn't seen either one of them since the night of the event that had brought all of them to the courthouse today.

"It's alright."

"What are they doing here?"

He led her to a table on the opposite side of the room.

"The court requires that all witnesses be present. Just in case the judge has any questions. I'll get us some coffee. Do you want anything else?"

"My stomach is in knots, don't bring me anything."

She looked over at her ex-husband. He sat very close to Fanny, who was showing. Alan looked up and their eyes locked. He turned away. She was tempted to go to their table, but she wasn't quite sure what she would say when she felt a hand on her shoulder. Lindy smiled at her and reached down, and kissed her on the cheek, as did Dr. Lopez.

"You came." Margaret moved her purse out of the chair so Lindy could sit down next to her.

"To support you mother and you know Joseph has been subpoenaed by the court."

"Yes." She sighed.

"You're going to be fine," Lindy said, feeling the stress her mother was going through.

Margaret couldn't believe that months ago she was alone, now she was surrounded by family and friends. Her relationship with Lindy was sensitive, but they were trying. On Joseph's recommendation, after her ordination, they met alone for a couple of hours to talk. Lindy had told her about the Elder Healer, her mother Amanda, and the role she'd played in teaching her spiritual mind healing techniques and the healing of her adopted son Michael. The very thing that had separated them, religion, now brought them together. They had so much catching up to do.

Margaret wasn't sure about that, her fate now lay in the hands of a judge. She looked at Lindy and wanted to recant her parting words, which had passed between them that evening.

"I can't be the mother you want me to be." Noticing how Lindy's body tensed up, she added, "But we can be friends."

"That's a big start, Mother."

 C3 C3 C3

After a half hour, the lawyer summoned them to return to the courtroom. He was waiting for her again, outside the courtroom. With him on one side of her and Lindy holding on to her other arm, they led her into the courtroom. Every seat in the courtroom was taken by mostly Mt. Olive church members. As she walked down the center aisle, the chatter stopped as all eyes focused on her.

Out of the corner of her eye, Margaret saw the beefy detective sitting in the front row next to Sister Joyce. Grace Perry, wearing a grey suit with a white silk blouse, appeared out of nowhere and snapped a photo of her. Pushing past her, Margaret looked straight ahead at the judge's bench, trying to remain calm and upbeat. She was now a pastor and had to demonstrate faith for her church members.

She sat at the defendant's table with Lindy directly behind her. Her hands trembled as she took out a three-by-five note card from her brown snakeskin purse and read silently, "I'm free; no one can incarcerate my body or mind," as they waited for the judge.

Chapter Sixty-Two

Judge Ashley Honeywell, a small petit woman, with graying hair, worked out every morning and practiced yoga. She was a vegetarian and no-nonsense person. She sat in her office reviewing the case waiting to be heard. Her clerk had read the papers and brought her up to speed on all the essentials, but it was something about the case that intrigued her. Her instinct told her something was missing in both briefs by the prosecutor as well as the lawyer for the defendant. She wanted to know what.

The bailiff entered the courtroom from a side door and called the court to order as Judge Honeywell walked in from the same entrance. Everyone stood up until she sat down.

"Good afternoon ladies and gentlemen. I see we have a full house. So, we can get off to good start, I'd like to remind the audience that you're here as spectators and not participants. Do not disrupt my courtroom. I need the prosecutor and lawyer for the defendant to approach the bench."

She put her hands over the mike. "Why the crowd?" She looked from one lawyer to the other.

"Mrs. Pierce is now an assistant minister of Mt. Olive Baptist Church and her church members came to support her," Jerry Sterns, the prosecutor answered. A short balding man, who was overworked and underpaid, and always threatening to go into private sector, but was still a civil servant.

"Was her father Pator Perlie Johnson?"

"Yes," they both answered.

"She's also the one who tried to jump into his casket?"

They nodded their heads.

"Gentlemen, I don't want this to turn into a circus. Keep it straight forward and clean." She looked at them sternly.

Once the lawyers had returned to their tables, the judge looked at Margaret and said, "Mrs. Pierce, this is a preliminary or evidentiary hearing to determine whether there is enough evidence to require a trial. It is my duty to determine if there is probable cause that a crime has been committed. Do you understand these proceedings?"

Margaret looked from her lawyer to the judge. He nodded for her to answer.

"Yes, your Honor," she said softly.

"Then, Mr. Griffin, how does your client plea?"

"Not guilty, Your Honor. We're asking that the court rule this as an accidental shooting."

"Mr. Sterns please state the case for the prosecution," the judge instructed him.

"Your Honor, on May 5, 1982 at 5600 16th Street, NW, at approximately 9:00 a.m, Pastor Alan Pierce, senior minister of Mt. Olive Baptist Church, was returning from a church meeting in the church across from his residence, with the assistant minister, Rev. Lawrence Pennybacker, and the church secretary, Fanny Mae Bishop. Upon hearing his wife, Mrs. Margaret Johnson Pierce, yell out in duress, he ran up the steps to her bedroom, entered and she shot him intentionally, with an unregistered loaded firearm. The prosecution would like to present this weapon as exhibit number one."

Prosecutor Sterns walked toward the bench and Margaret's lawyer followed suit. Sterns presented the gun to the judge.

"It is the prosecution contention that Mrs. Pierce shot her husband out of a jealous rage. She'd recently discovered that he was having an affair with the church secretary, Fanny Mae Bishop. In her own words in her journal or notebook, Your Honor, she describes in details, her husband having sex with his secretary in his office. She watched them."

"I would have put that hussy out of my house," someone shouted out from the back of the courtroom.

"Order or I'll clear this room." Judge Honeywell looked around.

"Your Honor, I would like to present the notebook of Mrs. Pierce as evidence number two. May we approach the bench?"

Margaret grabbed the sleeve of her attorney as she watched her black and white book being handed over to the judge. "How did they get my notebook?"

"The prosecution subpoenaed your medical file and it was included in there. It was out of Dr. Lopez's hands."

The lawyers returned to the table and Mr. Sterns finished up his statement. "We believe there is motive and enough evidence for her to be bound over for trial, Your Honor." He sat down.

"Attorney Griffin," the judge said, looking at the defendant's table.

"Your Honor, my esteemed colleague has stated the facts correctly. Pastor Pierce, Rev. Pennybacker, and Fanny Mae Bishop did return to Pastor Pierce's residence on May 5, 1982, around 9:00 A.M., and heard Mrs. Pierce, his wife, screaming. Rev. Pennybacker ran to Mrs. Pierce's bedroom first, opened the door, and founded her holding an old gun, a relic and a letter in the left hand. She was screaming, 'They lied to me.' He asked her 'Who?' Before she could reply, Pastor Pierce, her husband, who had entered the room, lunged at her and the gun went off accidentally, slightly grazing Pastor Pierce's shoulder. Mrs. Pierce, due to her poor mental state, was admitted promptly to the psychiatric ward for treatment for the next four months until she was fit for this hearing." He paused and walked from around the table and stood in front of it.

"Did Mrs. Pierce know about the relationship between her husband and Ms. Fanny? Yes. However, they were no longer living together as husband and wife. Living under the same roof, but they had separate sleeping quarters, an arrangement between the two of them.

"The gun belonged to her father and was purchased before the DC hand gun control law and her father died the year the law was enforced. Margaret Johnson didn't willfully shoot her husband. She'd just discovered the gun that night in his office, not knowing it was loaded. She had no way of knowing that Pastor Pierce would come to her bedroom. Your Honor, she was distraught over finding letters disclosing the truth about her mother not abandoning her as a child, but was forced to leave not only the family home but also the country due to her different religious beliefs. She hollered out 'They lied,' referring to her father and grandmother, the people she loved and trusted. The shooting was accidental and had nothing to do with a love triangle. It's all in her notebook." Attorney Griffin took his seat behind the table.

"Why aren't these letters offered as evidence?"

"Your Honor, may we approach the bench?" Attorney Griffin asked.

The courtroom was quiet, as the two lawyers stood in front of the judge. The prosecutor handed her the letters still tied with the string and the journal.

Looking at the clock hanging over the door directly in front of her bench, Judge Honeywell finally said, "The letters will be entered as evidence, and it's 12:30 p.m., gentlemen; we'll take a two hour lunch recess and return at 2:30 p.m."

Sitting at her desk while eating a chef salad, Judge Honeywell opened Margaret's notebook and began to speed read. When she finished she carefully untied the string from around the letters and settled back in her black leather ergonomic chair to read them.

CB   CB   CB

Margaret didn't know if she could wait another two hours to find out her fate. The church members crowded around her as she was leaving the court room.

"We're praying for you, Rev. Margaret," one of the women whispered to her.

"I would have shot him, too, if he were my husband and had her up under my nose," another member voiced her opinion.

"We ain't going to leave you," one of the deacons patted her arm.

"God is good," Margaret said, looking at the group that surrounded her.

"All the time," they responded.

"We're going to take Sister Margaret to get something to eat and relax a bit. We'll meet back here like we planned," Rev. Pennybacker said to the church members.

Lindy, Dr. Lopez, Rev. Pennybacker and Margaret walked the few blocks in the blistering heat to China Town for lunch.

"How is it going?" Rev. Pennybacker asked her, holding on to her elbow as they crossed the streets.

Margaret was still too distraught to talk; Lindy recanted everything that had happened that morning. They kept the conversation light. Margaret, who could barely eat her lunch, let Rev. Pennybacker finish her shrimp fried rice and egg roll.

Glancing at his watch, he said, "It's time to go back, not that I don't enjoy the company."

"Will they haul me off to jail today?" Margaret asked, looking at all three of them.

"Of course not," Dr. Lopez answered.

"You don't sound very convincing." Margaret started taking off her rings. "Lindy you take all my personal items."

"Wait a moment. What happened to your affirmation? Trust God's plan. Don't give up yet." Rev. Pennybacker held her by the shoulders, looking directly in her teary eyes.

Walking back, she held onto his hand tightly. "Why now? Just when I've found happiness."

"Hold on a little longer. It will all be over soon."

She wanted to say, "You mean my life will be over." The lawyer had told her she could get up to five years or more, if it went to trial and she was found guilty.

ααα ααα ααα

The people were just entering the courtroom when they returned. As mother and daughter entered the courtroom, Grace Perry was waiting for them just inside the door.

"Isn't this a touching moment," she mocked.

"What do you want, Grace?" Margaret asked, looking closer at Grace's outfit to see if she recognized the designer.

"Your story."

"This is no time to be bothering my mother about a story. Stay away from us or I'll get a restraining order where you won't be able to come within arm's length of us," Lindy said, grabbing Margaret by the arm and moving forward.

"Witch," Grace mumbled under her breath, returning to her seat.

They waited another fifteen minutes before the judge entered the courtroom and was seated.

Margaret could feel herself shaking. She didn't know if she was going to make it. Death seemed like the only way out now.

"I've reached a decision. Would the defendant please stand."

Margaret stood next to her lawyer with her chin up.

"Mrs. Pierce, it is a serious matter to assault another individual with a firearm. However, I've reviewed the evidence and have determined that there is no motive and not enough evidence for this to bound over for trial."

Margaret was so nervous, she didn't grasp what the judge had just said. Her attorney grabbed and hugged her and the audience hollered out, "Halleluiah." Some say that they heard the judge say, "How do you put a voice on trial?"

"Order in this courtroom, order," Judge Honeywell shouted out. "I'll clear this room if I hear another sound before I finish. Now, Mrs. Pierce, I would like you to think about all that has occurred in the last several months of your life. You have been detained for months on a psych ward of a hospital. This, in itself, has been sufficient punishment. However, this court orders you to continue to see a psychiatrist of your choice for the next year or until he or she releases you. Court adjourned."

Margaret stood mesmerized. Rev. Pennybacker and Dr. Lopez rushed into the courtroom and made their way through the crowd to get to the two women who meant so much to each of them.

The four of them walked out the courthouse holding hands, with the church members following closely behind and Grace Perry snapping photos.

Margaret stopped and looked around at the buildings, the sky, and the people who stood there with her as if she never had seen them before.

Reaching into her pocket, she pulled out the three-by-five card and read the affirmation aloud, "I'm going home a free woman," and smiled at Rev. Pennybacker, the man she planned to walk side by side with.

Epilogue

Margaret and Lindy stood in the basement of the Church of Melchizedek with their heads bowed and holding hands. Dressed in white robes, similar to the one the Elder Healer had worn years before, they silently tuned in to the healing energy of Jesus.

A year had passed and the church had reopened. It didn't take long for the word to spread throughout the Metropolitan area that the Church of Melchizedek had reopened and was holding its special Friday night healing session. Only, these were different.

They were conducted by the three ministers on a rotating basis: Rev. Pennybacker, Rev. Margaret and Rev. Betty. They also rotated which church held the services. But the crowds came to witness the healings performed by the mother and daughter.

Deacon Coleman sat hunched over in his wheelchair waiting for them. The pains in his knees had become unbearable. He'd played a major role in each of their lives and now they were going to help him.

Rev. Margaret glanced quickly at the large audience as she ascended the pulpit with Lindy following closely behind her. The lights had dimmed, the organist played softly in the background as silence fell over the crowd.

Her gaze fell on the spot where her father had died. She caught her breath as old memories surfaced and a voice deep down inside her mind screamed, *Let me out.*

About the Author

J.J. Michael is a professional numerologist, blogger (http://jjmichaelblog.blogspot.com) and author whose novels include *Life is Never as It Seems, It's Not Over Yet* and the non-fiction book *Path to Truth: a Spiritual Guide to Higher Consciousness.* She resides in Washington, DC. Visit J.J. Michael at http://jjmichael.com.

LaVergne, TN USA
17 September 2010

9 780615 359014